SPECIAL MESSAGE TO READERS

THE ULVERSCROFT FOUNDATION
(registered UK charity number 264873)
was established in 1972 to provide funds for
research, diagnosis and treatment of eye diseases.
Examples of major projects funded by
the Ulverscroft Foundation are:-

- The Children's Eye Unit at Moorfields Eye Hospital, London
- The Ulverscroft Children's Eye Unit at Great Ormond Street Hospital for Sick Children
- Funding research into eye diseases and treatment at the Department of Ophthalmology, University of Leicester
- The Ulverscroft Vision Research Group, Institute of Child Health
- Twin operating theatres at the Western Ophthalmic Hospital, London
- The Chair of Ophthalmology at the Royal Australian College of Ophthalmologists

You can help further the work of the Foundation
by making a donation or leaving a legacy.
Every contribution is gratefully received. If you
would like to help support the Foundation or
require further information, please contact:

THE ULVERSCROFT FOUNDATION
The Green, Bradgate Road, Anstey
Leicester LE7 7FU, England
Tel: (0116) 236 4325

website: www.foundation.ulverscroft.com

After a childhood spent acting professionally and training at a theatre school, Laura Madeleine changed her mind and went to study English Literature at Newnham College, Cambridge. She now writes fiction, as well as recipes, and was formerly the resident cake baker for Domestic Sluttery. She lives in Bristol, but can often be found visiting her family in Devon, eating cheese and getting up to mischief with her sister, fantasy author Lucy Hounsom.

You can discover more about the author at www.lauramadeleine.com

Follow her on Twitter — @esthercrumpet

THE CONFECTIONER'S TALE

At the famous Patisserie Clermont in Paris, 1910, a chance encounter with the owner's daughter has given one young man a glimpse into a life he never knew existed: of sweet cream and melted chocolate, golden caramel and powdered sugar; of pastry light as air. But it is not just the art of confectionery that holds him captive, and soon a forbidden love affair begins . . . Almost eighty years later, an academic discovers a hidden photograph of her grandfather as a young man with two people she has never seen before. Scrawled on the back of the picture are two words: 'Forgive me'. Unable to resist the mystery, she begins to unravel the story of two star-crossed lovers and one irrevocable betrayal . . .

LAURA MADELEINE

THE CONFECTIONER'S TALE

Complete and Unabridged

CHARNWOOD
Leicester

First published in Great Britain in 2015 by
Black Swan
an imprint of Transworld Publishers
London

First Charnwood Edition
published 2016
by arrangement with
Transworld Publishers
Penguin Random House
London

ACC. No.

CLASS No.

B. N. B. No.

B.N.B. CLASS

BOOKSELLER
UC

PRICE
£20.99

DATE RECEIVED
12\10\16

RM

The moral right of the author has been asserted

Copyright © 2015 by Laura Hounsom
All rights reserved

This book is a work of fiction and, except in the case
of historical fact, any resemblance to actual persons
living or dead, is purely coincidental.

A catalogue record for this book is available
from the British Library.

ISBN 978–1–4448–2997–6

Published by
F. A. Thorpe (Publishing)
Anstey, Leicestershire

Set by Words & Graphics Ltd.
Anstey, Leicestershire
Printed and bound in Great Britain by
T. J. International Ltd., Padstow, Cornwall

This book is printed on acid-free paper

For my mother

For my mother

Prologue

Paris, 1910

The boy ran up the stairs of the metro, emerging into the quiet evening. It was earliest April, and cold enough still for his breath to mist in the air before him. For a moment, he listened to the bells of a church somewhere, striking ten o'clock. He looked about, almost furtive, before movement caught his attention. He grinned and leaned down the stairs, holding out a hand.

Slim fingers encased in dark kid gloves took his, and a young woman hurried up the last few steps to stand beside him.

'Les Halles?' she asked breathlessly, pushing an elegant hat back into place. 'What are we doing here? Everything will be closed at this hour.'

'Don't be so sure.' The boy rubbed his bare hands and held out an elbow. His jacket was thin and did nothing to keep him warm, but for once, he didn't care. 'I believe you will like this evening's trip, Mademoiselle.'

Face bright, the girl took his arm.

A fine mist was hanging above the streets, softening the light from the gas lamps, as if they shone through cotton. Winter's fingers held onto the night, but the cold was ebbing, and soon it would be spring.

They walked together as any respectable

couple might, sneaking looks at each other until neither was able to suppress a grin. Through the mist, a noise was growing, not one sound but many: a voice that was a hundred voices, a rattling, squelching, feathery, drumming din. The girl's eyes were wide as they rounded a corner and were confronted by a building with high glass and riveted arches that embraced the chaos and bounced it back all at once.

'You said you wanted to see the real Paris, Mademoiselle,' the boy murmured in her ear. 'Here it is.'

Despite the late hour, the market was seething with life, spilling onto the pavement in a riot of peelings, sawdust and straw. Horses and motorized carts stood alongside each other. Errand boys danced in their boots to stay warm. Braziers gave up the scent of charcoal and chestnuts.

'Can we go in?'

Beaming, the boy took her hand, and they stepped into the fray.

At first there were stares — the girl's fine clothes were out of place among the threadbare linen and much-darned cotton — but as they pushed forward, and the more crowded the space became, no one saw their clothes, no one cared. Here, the only language was commerce. It was spoken in a constant bellow, a market patois of sous and weights that made no sense to outside ears.

The girl pulled on his arm and pointed towards a vegetable stall. Wooden crates of pale new potatoes sat in their dirt, old wrinkled winter onions and garlic woven into loose plaits above them. A man with frostbitten fingers was tying up bunches of sorrel. The girl laughed as a pair of vegetable women tossed spring cabbages from the back of a cart into a large wicker basket. They were making a game of it, seeing how fast they could throw them, egged on by the traders all around. Their pinned-up hair was untidy, their cheeks red with exertion and mirth.

A crowd had gathered around the next stall. Here, the shouting was particularly fierce. A man was filling paper bags, handing them out to the buyers as fast as he could take their money. Dropping the boy's hand, the girl gave him a wild smile and pushed her way between the muscled shoulders. He tried to stop her, anxious about the jostling crowd, but a minute later she was back, her dress trampled at the hem. Triumphantly, she placed a small yellow globe into his hand.

'What is it?' he asked, as she began to take off her gloves.

'What, something you don't know, Monsieur Guide?' she teased. 'It is a blood orange, all the way from Italy.'

She showed him how to peel the fruit, and together they stood, near a brazier at the edge of the vast place, sucking at the ruby flesh and laughing at the juice that escaped. The girl's eyes shone, and abruptly, the boy felt a wave of sorrow. In the morning, she would be in her world once again, elegant and poised, perhaps eating these same oranges for her breakfast with silver utensils, one thin slice at a time.

She must have sensed the change in him. 'Please,' she whispered, stepping close, her breath citrus sweet upon his cheek, 'this time is for you and I, no one else. Tomorrow does not happen here.'

The firelight painted her pale skin, made the colour ebb from her blue eyes until he thought he might drown in them.

A burst of shouting made him jump back, and they flattened themselves to a wall as a screaming gaggle of chickens made their escape from a broken basket, dander and feathers flying. A woman was swearing, snatching at the fowl as they ran through her skirts.

They plunged deeper into the market, down a dark stairwell into the tunnels and underground passages below, lit by gas and fizzing electric bulbs. In a tiled hallway, the girl's foot skidded. The boy caught her as she fell, barely managing to keep his own balance on the wet ground. Fleetingly, she was in his arms, half-laughing, half-stunned, her hat over her eye, and it took all of his restraint to not hold her closer.

They edged their way around the slippery puddle. It was dripping from a fishmonger's barrow, laden with huge, silvery beasts, the stench of sea and river rising from the mess of guts on the floor.

'Are you hungry?' the boy asked, his eyes on a bucket where piles of rock creatures waited, sealed and silent.

'Ravenous,' the girl replied. 'Are we to eat oysters?'

Digging in his pocket for the meagre change

there, the boy handed over a couple of coins. The fishmonger pulled out six of the things, shucked them with a little knife, and wrapped them in newspaper.

Emerging into the cleaner air once more, they found a baker's cart, stacked high with dark loaves of bread. They bought one, and wove their way towards a bar, where spindly tables and chairs were crammed between the cold night and the heady market.

Squeezed into a corner, elbow to elbow, they drank cheap red wine and feasted on bread and oysters, straight from the paper. The food was glorious; it was as if the essence of the world had been captured and infused into this one meal, for this one hour, in this one square of Paris. The boy wondered why it had never tasted this good before. Watching the girl drain her glass, he realized he already knew the answer.

Tomorrow does not happen here, she had said. But he knew better. Tomorrow would come, and with it, the truth that neither of them wanted to acknowledge. Outside, the pensive bells of Saint-Eustache began to toll eleven.

Damn tomorrow, he thought, and reached for her hand.

1

Cambridge, March 1988

I burst through the gates of King's College just as the chapel bells mark the hour. I'm late, and of all the appointments I could be late for, this is the worst.

A group of anorak-wearing tourists are blocking the road. I weave through them, checking my watch. I had hoped to arrive in plenty of time, to find an inconspicuous seat at the back of the room, not to barge through the doors sweaty and dishevelled.

I take the courtyard at a run and a set of damp stone stairs two at a time. My reflection flashes past in a window: rain-soaked, ratty blond fringe dripping into my eyes. I push it back and hurry towards a pair of huge oak doors.

15th March, 11.00 a.m., reads a piece of paper tacked to the noticeboard outside: Unmasking a Legend: biographer Simon Hall on the late historian, author and critic J. G. Stevenson.

I quickly rearrange the scowl that has risen to my face into a grimace of apology at the woman minding the entrance. She sniffs disapprovingly but lets me pass. Bracing myself, I ease open the heavy door. The room is packed; students and academics alike are crammed into chairs, their breath fogging up the windows. Despite my efforts, the door creaks loudly on its hinges, and

6

the man on the podium falters, looking my way. I keep my head lowered and edge along the back row to a spare seat.

'As I was saying,' the speaker continues, 'we all know what happens when a well-known person dies: they get an obituary in The Times, a new commemorative volume of work and retrospectives in journals left, right and centre.'

Some of the younger members of the audience titter, eager to show their appreciation for the lecturer's off-hand manner.

I eye him carefully. Simon Hall, the current darling of the history scene. Whenever comment is needed, on the radio or in newspaper articles, there he is. He's not as young as his pictures suggest, I decide. True, his curly hair and open face make him look youthful, but there are creases at the corners of his eyes and the hint of a paunch developing. I slump down a little further in my seat and try to pay attention.

'There is nothing wrong with paying homage to a great,' he says, 'and no one can deny that J. G. Stevenson was a talented historian. But how much do we truly know about him? Who was the man behind the books?'

He pauses for effect, looks around the room.

'As a biographer, it is my job to answer these questions, and that means delving into a person's past, discovering the things they might have preferred to keep to themselves. And, ladies and gentlemen, what I have discovered is that J. G. Stevenson was no saint.'

He leans forward on the lectern, intent,

inviting every person there into his confidence.

'Recently, I was granted access to Stevenson's private correspondence, and there I found a letter. Written to him when he was a young man in Paris, it places him firmly at the centre of a scandal, one that he kept hidden even from his own family. I will discover the truth behind this mystery, and show you all the *real* J. G. Stevenson.'

When it is time for questions, I fidget and try to keep my arm wedged by my side, even though I'm simmering with anger. I listen to inane comments and sharp words, until finally, at the very end, I can't stop my hand from shooting into the air.

'I'm rather afraid we have no more time,' the academic in charge of the event tells me. 'Perhaps you could — '

'So, it's your intention to vilify a man just to be fashionable?' I challenge Hall. 'Or are you taking liberties with the dead, digging through private possessions in order to get more publicity?'

A hundred plastic chairs creak as people turn to look. I feel myself flush under their scrutiny, but keep my eyes fixed on Hall. He is smiling in a puzzled way as he peers through the crowd.

'A bold question, Miss . . . ?'

'Stevenson.'

A volley of whispers sweeps the audience. The academic on stage is leaning forward to whisper something in Hall's ear. I see the shape of my name on his lips and fight to keep my expression neutral. Hall, meanwhile, is surveying me with newfound interest.

'I understand your indignation, Miss Stevenson, but you can't deny your grandfather had his secrets.'

2

Bordeaux, September 1909

Six o'clock on the Rue Vauquelin. Voices rose from the streets, echoing within the walls of cramped, peeling workrooms to greet the end of the day. Guillaume du Frère tripped onto the road, staggering under the weight of a suitcase. The smell of home lingered around him, but dropped away as he broke into a run.

His boots skidded in a pile of rubbish. He grimaced, yet grinned in almost the same instant. The airless courtyards and overcrowded alleyways of Bordeaux were not his home any longer.

At the end of the Rue Francin the pavement was filled with traders, pouring boisterously from the Cattle Market. Gui pushed through them, through the stench of beasts and offal, towards the arched windows of the locomotive workshop. They were propped open to release metallic fumes.

He hauled himself up, sent his suitcase tumbling from the windowsill to land with a thud on the gritty floor. He scrambled down behind it.

'Evening, Jacques!' he gasped to an oil-stained man who was wrestling with a length of pipe.

'Bon voyage, lad! Better fly, that train's already whistled once!'

10

'Thanks!'

Gui clutched his luggage to his chest and burst through an open gate onto the track. Ahead stood the tiled platform and beyond that, the grand glass roof of the Gare St Jean, trapping the light and insects like a gas lamp. Stragglers lingered to wave off the departing train. A small boy was perched on his father's shoulders, staring at the plume of steam that had already started to trail backwards.

Gui threw himself into a sprint. A whistle sounded behind him, the guardsman's indignant shout, but he surged on, legs pistoning up and down, worn boots pounding the track.

'Gui!' a voice cried. His friend Nicolas was beaming over the back railing of the train. 'More haste, more haste!'

Gui's throat burned with exertion as he drew close; almost enough to grasp Nicolas's outstretched hand.

'Come on, Gui, they'll never let us be railwaymen if we can't even catch a train!'

With a strangled laugh and a final burst of effort he pitched the suitcase at his friend, leaped for the railing and hauled himself aboard.

Oblivious to his final dash, the train rattled on, gathering speed as the track curved and the station receded into the distance. Still red from laughing, Nicolas refolded his long legs, fished a crumpled cigarette from his pocket. Collapsed against the wall, Gui pulled off his cap to wipe sweat from his brow.

His scalp prickled. Ruefully, he ran a hand over it. His hair had grown long over the summer, had turned from brown to gold during the hot days working the river dock. He would rather have kept it so, but his mother had insisted that he would catch lice in the capital, and had shorn it all off.

Nicolas said it made him look like a convict. *His* blond mop had escaped undipped. Gui thumped his friend with a grin and crammed the cap back on his head.

'Hadn't we better go inside?' he called over the noise of the wheels on the track.

'No,' his friend replied, 'too crowded in there. We'll get stuck next to an old matron who'll lecture us all the way to Paris. Better stay out here.'

'What if they come around for tickets? Won't they throw us off?'

Nicolas snorted. 'Course not. We'll just show our letters and say we're colleagues. We're railwaymen now, Gui. Never have to pay a fare again so long as we live!'

The train passed through the fringes of the city. The last buildings of Bordeaux dropped away, replaced by long grasses that hissed along the banks of the river. Light flashed in planes across the water. The train's shadow was black upon the surface, intricately detailed. Gui saw the texture of the glass in the windows, grit and baked-on flies, silhouettes of passengers within. Fascinated, he raised a hand to see if a shadow figure would do the same, but the reflection snaked away, engulfed by vegetation.

It grew late. Hills rose up on both sides, casting a chill shade. It would take all night to reach Paris. Beside him, Nicolas woke from a doze and stretched for his duffel bag. Gui heard the rustle of paper and wrapped an arm around his stomach.

His mother had made him up a parcel of food, but he had left it behind when she wasn't looking. He hadn't been able to bear the thought of her going hungry. Even if he had the money, the train's dining car would never serve him, dressed as he was in shirtsleeves and a grubby necktie. His glance over at Nicolas was rewarded with a smirk.

His friend was unwrapping something from several layers of newspaper. Gui caught a scrap of warm, yeasty scent. Half a small loaf landed in his lap. It still retained a trace of the oven's heat. He tore off a piece and stuffed it into his mouth, trying to thank Nicolas between chews.

'Don't mention it,' said Nicolas airily, scraping at the soft inside with his teeth. 'I knew you'd forget to bring anything.'

Gui swallowed the last mouthful with regret. Nicolas brushed the crumbs from his chest.

'What I wouldn't give for a cup of coffee,' he said and sighed.

Smiling, Gui tucked his chin into the collar of his shirt. Even the resourceful Nicolas would struggle to produce hot coffee from a duffel bag. He closed his eyes, and felt himself slip into a doze, until his thoughts merged in time with the clacking of the wheels on the track, which did not seem so loud any more.

Nicolas's wish was granted later that evening, when lamps were lit in the train's corridors and the ticket inspector made it to the end of the last carriage. The sight of two sunburned stowaways produced an official scowl, but it only took them a minute to explain. Soon after, the man returned with a jug of coffee from the dining car, laced with brandy. Whilst they drank he removed his hat and leaned over the back railing to nurse one of Nicolas's battered cigarettes.

'Every piece of track,' he said, clearing his throat, 'every piece between here and Orléans, is a piece I helped to lay. Hard work it was, outside in all weathers, sometimes only moving an inch at a time. But it's a fine job for young men. Good solid work, make you strong for life.'

His big, rough-skinned face hovered in shadow as the track — *his* track — flashed by beneath.

'If you're lucky,' he flicked cigarette ash into the darkness and replaced his hat, 'you can go on to work the locomotives. Then you'll end up like me. Decent pay, a uniform, nice watch. If you work hard and make yourselves known to those what matter, you'll do well indeed.'

The inspector wished them luck and took his leave. Gui wrapped his hands around the cooling tin mug as night pressed closer to the train and thought about the ticket man's words. He could not imagine his own skinny frame made large by work, couldn't see himself in a stiff uniform, carrying a watch in his pocket. But in Paris, he told himself, anything was possible.

He must have slept then, for when he woke the space they were passing through was black — country or town, he couldn't tell. Hulking

14

shapes that might have been trees or rocks or huge stationary beings loomed in the night. He was cold. An arm's length away Nicolas was snoring, wrapped in a hairy green blanket.

Gui smiled, fumbling in his suitcase to drag out his own. Above him were stars, wheeling to the corners of his vision. He let his head fall back against the metal railing, and slept.

3

March 1988

My anger has subsided into a hollow nausea as I trudge across town towards my supervision. Hall's words about my grandfather repeat themselves over and again, yet all I can see is an old man, pausing in his dictation to smile at me across the room, at my fingers, busily punching the letters of a typewriter.

It has been almost two years since he died, but too often I catch a glimpse of his photograph in a book, or hear a recording of his quick voice crackling back at me on the radio. Sometimes it seems that his ghost is everywhere.

I have very little left of him. His house was finally sold a few months back, and there was nothing I could do but watch. Ever since I can remember, before my parents' divorce even, that rambling, run-down place had been a haven; a home. My father didn't care about any of that. He sold it without even bothering to tell me.

I found out just in time. I shut myself in grandfather's study while the house-clearance men tramped through the rest of the building, stripping it of my memories and throwing them into a pile on the lawn. The study had remained untouched, right down to the final article we had been working on, a half-written sheet in the typewriter, covered with dust.

I took what I could, gathered up a lifetime of papers, diaries and notebooks, fifty years' worth of correspondence. I sealed them into coffin-like boxes, and took them home where I thought they would be safe.

Lost in thought, I walk through the college gates and into one of the buildings. I wish I could talk to Grandpa now, tell him about Hall, ask him what it all means.

On autopilot, I climb the stairs. My first knock on the door goes unanswered, so I try the handle, but it is locked. I stare at the name painted above it, scrabble for my Filofax.

Prof. Whyke, 15th March, 12 p.m.

I check my watch. Ten past. I'm not that late. He can't have given up and gone away. Is he running late, like me? Halfway down the stairs is a deep, stone windowsill. I wedge myself into it to go through some notes while I wait. My plimsolls are sodden with rain and grit. I brush at them half-heartedly, feeling like a mess.

My notes are similarly untidy. Vague timelines, blocks of third-hand quotation, isolated paragraphs. Grandpa would have laughed, made me pull it apart and explain each section to him, piece by piece, until it made sense. I'm gripped by the old, familiar fear: that I'm letting him down.

I never intended to go into academia. I was halfway through a Masters when Grandpa died; we'd had plans to start writing a book together after my degree, a social history of the *belle époque*, but then he was gone, and everything was so uncertain. Applying for a Ph.D. at his old

17

university in order to carry on the research seemed like the obvious choice.

The first year passed in a frenzy of work, of endless research and long hours in the library, distracting myself from his absence. Now, no matter how hard I try to convince myself otherwise, I know that I'm only here because of him.

Church bells jolt me from my thoughts, marking the half-hour. I rip a page from my jotter to leave a note.

'Can I help?'

Professor Whyke is standing at the bottom of the stairs, a muffin in his hand. There are chocolate crumbs down the front of his shirt. After a few seconds, his expression brightens with recognition.

'Ah, Petra. Miss *Belle Époque*. Yes, we had an appointment. Come in.'

I crumple the half-written note and follow him up. He bustles about the door, balancing the muffin in one hand and fumbling for the key with the other.

'Did I get the time wrong?' I ask, settling into one of the scratchy chairs by his coffee table. 'I thought we said twelve, on the fifteenth.'

'Honestly, I was expecting you last week. Fifteen hundred hours on the twelfth. No matter, I'm clear for lunch so we can fit it in now. Tea?'

I nod, consider requesting no sugar, decide against it. The tea will arrive with two lumps no matter what I say.

'So,' he begins, flipping through a ledger.

'How far did you get during the holiday? You were looking at Paris, and at pre-war correspondence. Did you read Fuller's letters?'

I fumble through my notes, explain a few possible leads. Whyke listens and suggests some further reading, but I can tell he's not engaged. When the hour is almost over, I force myself to mention what is really on my mind.

'I found something else that could be interesting. I'm afraid it's a bit off target, though.'

'Let's hear it.'

My heart begins skipping. I hadn't realized how nervous this would make me.

'I discovered a café, a *salon*, in Paris. It seems to have been hugely successful before the First World War, but then sank without a trace.'

'What's the name?'

'*Clermont*. Have you come across it?'

Whyke purses his lips at me.

'Sounds vaguely familiar. Did you find a reference in the letters?'

The heat is rising to my cheeks as I pull a plastic folder from my bag.

'My grandfather's house was sold in the holidays. I cleared his study, sorted through all of the papers he had stashed away. I . . . found a photograph of him, taken in Paris, when he was young. I'd never seen it before, but it has a date on the back, and the word 'Clermont'.'

Whyke looks confused, until I hand over the old photo. A few moments later he taps one of the sepia faces.

'J. G. Stevenson. I always forget that you're

following in his footsteps.'

I say nothing. We both know that my place at the university has more to do with my grandfather's legacy than anyone will admit.

'Stevenson had a connection to it then, this *Clermont* place?' Whyke says, flipping the card over. 'Do you know what he was doing there?'

I shake my head, struggle for the right words. 'I knew that Grandpa wrote about Paris, but I never knew he actually lived there. He told me about his university days, the war, but never this.'

'Well, it certainly would be interesting to find out, but that's the new biographer's job, I suppose. What's his name, Hill?'

'Hall,' I correct, trying to suppress a scowl as Simon Hall's face elbows its way into my thoughts. 'I thought maybe *I* could look into the idea, work it into my research?'

Whyke makes a doubtful noise and gives the photo back. He hooks his hands behind fraying brown hair.

'You know as well as I do what people will say if you spend too much time studying your own grandfather.' He hunts around for a working pen. 'Look into it, if you want, but try not to get sidetracked. Shall we meet same time, next week?'

The stairs are cold after the warm clutter of Whyke's room. I pause by the windowsill, listening. The hallway is empty. I pull out the photograph again. It's a portrait of a group, printed on cheap card that has yellowed and split at the edges.

My grandfather lounges to one side, as if only

20

a moment ago he had flung himself into the seat, a stick-thin figure with a shock of pale hair. His nose is long and straight, not crooked like I remember. The picture must have been taken before he broke it.

Beside him are two people. One is a young man, not much more than a boy. He has an angular, handsome face, dark curly hair that threatens to escape its pomade. The second is a young woman, her lips and lace collar in focus, her face half-turned.

It is an unusual photograph for its time, candid and unarranged. I flip the card over. The word 'Clermont', is scrawled in ink, next to a date and a place, in what I know to be my grandfather's handwriting: *Paris, 1910*.

Gently, I slip the photograph back into the folder. Perhaps I should have told Whyke about my confrontation with Hall, explained about this letter he has supposedly found, and the scandal. Yet there, at the back of my mind, is the fear I can't quite vocalize: that the biographer is right. That my grandfather kept secrets, even from me.

I close my eyes, but I see it again, the place where I found the photograph. It was hidden at the bottom of a trunk, folded within an envelope that was labelled with only two words: *Forgive me*.

4

September – December 1909

The steam train groaned and clicked into place, like a huge creature settling its bones. Hands swarmed to its doors, wheels hurtled away stacked high with pallets and boxes, unloaded by the men and women who carried the day on their backs.

Gui jumped onto the tiles of the platform and craned his neck: above, the huge glass roof arched outwards, a sky held together by bolts. It too seemed alive, great grey girders furred with a skin of pigeons. On every side the walls sounded back the disorientating language of a new city, full of noise and swinging elbows and glistening faces.

Nicolas was at his back, poking him into the fray. Gui tried to focus on setting each foot in front of the other, though he was shunted and jostled, almost knocked down by a pair of raucous young men, their faces sharp, sacks balanced high on their shoulders. A porter roared a curse as a crate slipped from his grasp and smashed into the platform. Gui veered to avoid him only to collide with a woman with green stained fingers, picking through boxes of freshly cut flowers.

Nicolas's face surfaced for an instant between the shoulders of the crowd, mouth open in a wordless shout. Gui staggered and was swept in the opposite direction. He could barely keep hold of his suitcase as he was pushed towards the opposite platform. An army of newspaper boys were shoving past him, yelling from beneath their bundles. He backed away hurriedly, breath coming short, searching for a way out. Then a space appeared, alongside an open compartment. Without a second thought, he dashed forward.

Too late he saw the pale glove grip the door, the tightly buttoned boot appear beneath rustling skirts and petticoats, descending towards the platform. He tried to stop but only managed to trip, crashing into the figure. The next thing he knew he was falling, the sound of a gasp following him as he sprawled across the tiles.

For a heartbeat, the entire world was winded. His lungs sat empty as he gazed up at the woman who had caught herself upon the side of the carriage, her ankle twisted beneath her. A dark hat slanted across her face, but beneath its brim he saw blue eyes, wide with shock. They stared at each other, stunned, their faces separated only by an arm's length. Then the air rushed into his chest and he coughed, opened his mouth to speak.

'Mademoiselle!' someone cried from within the train, and bodies were materializing all around, voices angry and fingers pointing his way. He scrambled to his feet, too bewildered to apologize, and ran back into the mêlée.

The burning in his cheeks had subsided by the time he found Nicolas. He dragged his friend to the exit, looking over his shoulder all the while.

'I told you to stick close,' Nicolas scolded. 'What happened?'

Gui rubbed at his back. It was beginning to ache from the fall. He'd been too busy thinking about the girl to notice it before.

'Nothing,' he mumbled, 'bumped into some rich folk.'

Nicolas pushed back his cap ruefully and extracted a wad of papers.

'You got to watch yourself here,' he said briskly. 'Come on, or we'll miss registration.'

★ ★ ★

The instant the clerk stamped his papers, Gui's life became a blur. He had no time to dwell on what had happened at the station, no time to think of anything at all among the haze of newness and rules and bellowed instruction. Then one day, just as abruptly, it all became routine.

The weeks fell away. They burned great holes in time as he learned to stoke the furnace in the ironworks, as he practised how to weld and hammer, to share the load of a sleeper on his shoulder. Muscle slung its way down his arms; his face grew wind-toughened from long hours on the tracks under the autumn's fading sun.

Every so often he found himself alone, outside the makeshift dormitory where those who were not from the city fell onto pallet beds at night. The place smelled of gas lamps and unwashed bodies; he listened to the flip of cards on wood,

24

the worn, wavering note of an accordion. Away from that close, stuffy company, he sometimes found himself thinking of a different Paris. A city where people wore silk and furs and had never picked up a hammer in their lives; where people like the young woman from the station lived. As he imagined it, the cold October air whispered to him of possibility.

Nicolas's shout would pull him back, to damp clothes and musty bedding. The ticket inspector from their first journey was right, it was a hard life, harder than either of them had imagined, but Gui didn't hate the work. Neither did he like it. He was too busy concentrating on landing hammer blows evenly, on squinting away a headache in the glare of the furnace. He did not even think about his home until many weeks later, when he wrote his mother's name and street upon an envelope.

'A whole month's pay,' said Nicolas, gazing lovingly into his pocket. 'Look at it, Gui. I've never had this much money in my life!'

Gui stared down at his own wages, then resignedly tipped half of it into the envelope for his mother. She would struggle to get by without him.

The sleeping quarters were ringing with payday activity, a holiday feeling in the air. The rail workers crowded around a tiny square of mirror, to clean their ears and comb their beards. Creases were being pulled out of long-stored jackets, neckties folded to hide their worn edges.

Nicolas produced a bottle of cheap cologne,

which smelled like gin and dead flowers. Unperturbed, he used it to smooth down his hair. Smiling, Gui declined the bottle and fought his way in front of the mirror. For a few seconds he stared. His eyes were the same as ever — like a muddy pond, his mother had always teased — but his face was leaner, browned by the wind and the sun. He raised a hand to his chin and saw his fingernails, blackened despite a trimming. He had begun to change.

He would have lingered, but Nicolas was waiting, his eyebrows raised in an expression that meant a special kind of trouble. An answering grin rose to Gui's face. The two friends took to the streets, along with some of the other workers, snorting and shouldering each other in the cold air. They were a pack, all clean, pink faces and excitement, and the night spread before them, dark and bright as an animal's eye.

'*Attendez!* Wait!' someone yelled.

Gui joined the chorus as they broke into a run across the Place Valhubert, racing for the omnibus that was pulling away from the centre. He leaped for the back step and swung up the twisting staircase with the others. They collapsed onto benches, laughing and panting, to the other passengers' disapproval.

Face hot, Gui accepted a hip flask and took a long swig. The liquid burned its way down his gullet as he leaned over the wooden side of the vehicle. The air chilled his skin, crisp in his lungs as the pavement swept by below. Advertisements and signs clacked against the side of the omnibus, staccato with the horses' hooves. They broke free of the Left Bank onto the Pont d'Austerlitz and Paris rose before them, light and glass, stone and shadow.

Gui felt himself laughing wildly. He had truly arrived.

5

March 1988

The photograph leaves me restless, unable to focus. I find myself drawn time and again to the sepia faces on the card, propped up on my desk. I have been missing my grandfather more than ever during the past few days; have longed to hear his dry, quick voice on the other end of the phone.

I search the faded inks of the image as if they will give up some clue. Grandpa Jim would have been younger than me in 1910, I realize. Sprawled nonchalantly in the chair, he would have been barely more than twenty-one. Raw in the world, sucking hungrily at everything Paris had to offer. What had he done, that he would live to regret, beneath the bright lights and in youthful folly?

Forgive me.

If not for those two words I could have dismissed Hall's claims about my grandfather, I could have assumed that he was fabricating a scandal, just to sell copies of his book. But now, I feel a terrible uncertainty, a pang of hurt. I thought I knew everything about Grandpa Jim; why had he never told me about Paris?

I try to search for the word, 'Clermont', in the library but find nothing useful. There is no one else I can ask. My grandmother is long dead. I

28

doubt that my mother would know, and I'm not on speaking terms with my father, not since he sold the house.

On Friday night I trudge through Cambridge's dark and rainy streets, in search of a friendly face. My hair is plastered to my cheeks by the time I ring a bell, carrier bag in hand. A waft of perfume engulfs me as the door is thrown open, and I smile in relief. Cass hugs me with one arm and ushers me inside with the other.

'For you,' I tell her, handing over the bag. 'I think I need your help with something.'

Cass grins as she pulls out a bottle of wine and a large bar of chocolate. 'If you're trying to bribe me, it's working.'

It is cosy in her tiny kitchen, the rain pattering gently on the windows, and I feel at ease for the first time in weeks. Cass potters around, turning on the record player, while I find a couple of glasses.

Cass is one of my few close friends at university. She's two years older than me and, technically, could be my supervisor, although the idea of that makes us laugh too much to consider it seriously.

'Finally.' She sighs, flinging herself into a chair and pushing a stack of papers aside. 'I thought the weekend would never come.'

She pours the wine, filling the glasses to the brim. Cass is based at the History of Art department, and everything about her is generous: masses of frizzy black hair, infectious smile, always ready with a cheerful word or a sympathetic nudge.

'So,' she takes a sip, 'what's this thing you need help with? You were vague on the phone.'

I tell her about the photograph, about Simon Hall and his so-called scandal. She collapses into giggles when I describe what happened at his talk.

'Can you imagine what he would say if he found this?' I'm flushing with laughter and embarrassment as I hand her the photograph. 'He'd see it as evidence of my grandfather's secret, sordid past.'

'I have to admit, I kind of agree with him.'

'Cass!'

'Sorry!' She smiles ruefully. 'I know it might be hard for you to consider, but 'Forgive me'? Come on, Petra, he must have done *something*.'

'Well, whatever it was, I need to know,' I insist, reluctant to concede that she's right. 'Hall mentioned a letter that was written to Grandpa; he said it was proof of this scandal. What if it's just a misunderstanding? If I can find out, then I can stop him before it goes any further.'

'Stop Hall?' Cass asks. 'I think you'll be fighting a losing battle, he *is* the official biographer, and he sounds pretty determined.'

'He's grave robbing,' I take another gulp of wine, 'and he could cause some serious damage to Grandpa Jim's reputation.'

Cass holds up her hands in surrender. 'All right, all right. So, you think this photo has something to do with it?'

'I'm not sure. Hall said something about Paris in his talk, and that Grandpa was a young man when . . . whatever it was happened.'

30

Cass nods vaguely, squinting down at the faces. 'Not much to go on. When did you say this was taken?'

'Nineteen ten, if we go by the date on the back.'

She is silent for a long while, turning the picture this way and that.

'Every famous café or *salon* in Paris was painted at some point,' she says slowly, 'usually by a loner, scratching away with charcoal like the next Toulouse-Lautrec. I'll bet that if this Clermont place was even vaguely well known, somebody drew or painted it.'

'What do you mean? How does that help?'

She grins. 'Get your coat.'

Ten minutes later, we're plodding through leaf mulch, cheeks burning with high spirits as we take a short cut along the black, muddy riverbank. Cass stops outside the darkened windows of the History of Art faculty. I cool my cheeks with the back of my hands; a couple of large glasses of wine are having their effect on me.

'It is nine o'clock at night,' I remind Cass, a little too loudly. 'It'll be closed.'

'Don't be so sure.' She is running her finger down a list of brass buttons next to the entrance, each with a name beside it. 'Let's see if he's here.'

'Who?'

In the depths of the building a bell buzzes fiercely. A long minute of silence passes. Cass is just about to ring again, when the intercom crackles into life.

'Who's there?' The voice does not sound impressed.

'Evan? It's Cass, Cassandra Wakeman. Would you mind terribly if we came up to check something? Just for a minute?'

'Do you know what time it is?'

'Please, Evan? We won't be long.'

The sigh that follows sounds pained.

'Wait there.'

'Who is he?' I ask, as Cass bounces on her heels in expectation. A light flickers on a few floors above.

'Librarian, he's a good sort.'

Finally, Evan unlocks the door, peering out with interest. He's overweight, balding, but has a lively face behind huge spectacles, and an obvious soft spot for my friend.

'Evan, this is Petra.' Cass flashes her most charming smile. 'She's got a mystery on her hands and is in need of some expert advice.'

'Couldn't this have waited until Monday morning?' He is trying hard to remain peeved, but a smile threatens the corner of his mouth.

'You know how slow the faculty is with visitor cards. Ten minutes?'

Evan's office is in the main library, on the second floor. A desk lamp illuminates a tiny room, crammed with papers, cards, boxes of periodicals and, of course, books. The smell of take-away chips lingers. A bottle of whisky stands half-empty next to a glass. Evan catches me looking.

'The sole perk of working more hours than I'm paid for.' He smiles. 'Are you going to tell

32

me what you're after?'

Cass nudges me. Briefly, I explain her theory and what we're hoping to find. Evan takes his time looking at the photograph.

'I hate to break it to you,' he says kindly, 'but this might be a bit of a wild-goose chase. Do you have anything else to go on, except for this name and a date?'

A blush creeps down my neck as I shake my head.

'Sorry, I wish I knew more.'

'Not to worry,' he claps his hands, 'there's no harm in checking the archives. I'll be back in a minute.'

When he returns, his arms are full of heavy ring binders, each stuffed with what look like magazines.

'The archive card *does* have an entry for that date, and 'Clermont',' he pants, face bright, 'but it's vague. Apparently, the reference is in one of these.'

Cass groans, hefting a few of the folders out of his arms.

'These are exhibition catalogues,' she explains, pushing one at me. 'They list everything that's been exhibited in certain galleries, year by year. We'll have to go through the lot to find out.'

I tell them that I don't want to take up their time, but they both wave away my protests. A warm hush descends upon the room, broken only by turning pages. I look at Evan, frowning over his second folder. Cass, equally absorbed, is leaning against the radiator.

'Thanks, both of you,' I tell them, touched.

Cass only winks. 'You know I love secrets.'

My eyes are starting to blur from page after page of tiny writing when Evan yells.

'Here!'

We crowd around the desk, squeezing into the tight space.

'It's from an independent gallery in London,' he tells us, checking the front page. 'I don't think they're very well funded, but they focus on exactly the period you're interested in. Look, near the bottom.'

It is a reference to a portrait, oil on canvas, c.1910. The artist is Piet Ahlers, the title: *Mademoiselles at Pâtisserie Clermont.*

'Evan, you're a genius!' Cass gushes.

My heart is thrumming, even as I notice the title of the catalogue.

'This is old, it's dated nineteen eighty-three.'

'It's the only one I have.' Evan shrugs apologetically. 'I can't say now for certain, but five years ago, that painting was on display.'

34

6

December 1909

Montmartre was another world; the streets rose and twisted, screaming with advertisements for absinthe, cabarets, dancers. Some bars promised heaven, while others offered all the temptations of hell. Motor cars and carriages stood waiting for their masters, the men in white silk scarves come to experience the filth and thrill of the underworld. Gui's group were turned away from the larger establishments, their worn clothes unwelcome beneath the lights.

They stumbled deeper into the rabbit warren, to other bars, tatty and pungent with sweat and tobacco, warmed by gaslight and the breath of the crowd.

Here, the girls were not haughty or prim but wild. They flung their arms and twisted their torsos, dancing to the music of accordions and guitars, their hair coming loose as they spun about the floor. A plump brunette took a shine to Nicolas and placed herself on his knee, near emptying his wallet in the process. For the rest of the night he acted as though the rough gin and soda in his glass was champagne.

Time began to move strangely. Gui's head swam with the cheap perfume, the bodies and liquor. Then, somehow, he found himself inside a room, sprawled out on a pile of cushions. It was dark, the noise of the bar subdued by thick curtains. Smoke drifted about his head. A girl with eyes like shadows knelt beside him, offered him a pipe. Gui took it, shook some coins into her hand.

He had smoked tobacco before, but this pipe was different. It filled his head and burned his lungs with a bitter scent. He dragged upon it for longer and longer, and his limbs turned to lead as he sank into a deep, black oblivion.

Then he was outside, a motor car roaring past. Startled, he tripped and landed heavily in the gutter, biting his lip. Blood flooded his mouth. He spat out what he could onto the pavement. His face throbbed, but at least the pain brought some clarity to his mind. He blotted the rest of the blood away with his sleeve.

He looked around, and found himself hopelessly lost. At home, he had always been able to sense the river, curving flat and wide at the edge of town, grey as the skin of a fish, but not here. He was cold, shivering uncontrollably. How long had he been outside? He wrapped the thin jacket tighter around his chest, but it did little to keep away the chill.

Nausea rolled over him and he retched — not for the first time, he suspected. There was a sour taste in his mouth, mingling with the blood from his lip. He searched his pockets for a handkerchief, but they had been emptied, down to the last centime. The city had lured him with its bright smile, shaken him of his money and fled, closing the light and laughter up inside itself like a clam.

From further up the street came the sound of footsteps. Out of the fog staggered a pair of young men, their evening dress dishevelled. Gui croaked a greeting, relieved to see fellow humans in the darkness.

The bottom of a cane whistled past his face.

'Son of a bitch,' one of the men slurred, eyes unfocused. His fine shirtfront was stained with vomit.

Gui let them go, and was faced with yet another empty street. He was afraid and exhausted. Perhaps he should find a doorway to sleep in; he had nothing left to rob, after all. Ahead was a narrow alleyway that twisted in the middle and offered some shelter. One hand on the wall, he ventured forward.

A huge wooden cart was blocking the way. It was stacked high with crates, milk churns, sacks and packages, precariously balanced. There were sounds, muffled by the fog, the thump of feet, a pair of horses shifting their hooves.

A woman's voice was giving orders. 'Take the flour to the pantry, Yves. Could we have it the right way up this time? Papa was furious. Marc, no, we'll carry the cream in last, it is cold enough out here for now.'

Gui hunched closer. Golden light was spilling from the doorway, warm, carrying the scent of sugar. It made the fog glow, and through it, he could make out a pair of black leather boots standing on a step, the edge of a skirt. He inched forward.

'Who's there?' the woman called.

He tried to turn away, not fast enough. Before

he could run, a man materialized behind him, cuffed him around the head. A strong grip clamped down on the back of his jacket, and he had no choice but to obey as he was pulled towards the building.

The fog gave up a woman's face. She stepped down from the doorway, blue eyes suspicious. She was slim, wrapped head to toe in furs, her cheeks flushed pink with the cold. She stopped, an arm's length away. Gui couldn't help but notice that they were of a height, to a fraction of an inch.

Déjà vu. Abruptly, he was back at the station, winded upon the platform, a face gazing down at him in shock. It couldn't be the same girl, and yet, he remembered those eyes . . . Horrified, he ducked his head to his chest, praying that she wouldn't recognize him.

'Caught him creeping around back there, Mam'selle.' The large deliveryman shook him like a puppy. 'Probably waiting till we were all out of the way so he could have a go. Fetch a good price at the market, these goods.'

'I wasn't!' Gui protested, straining away from the crushing grip on his neck. 'I work for the railway, I got lost on the way home. We were in . . . ' He groped for details of the evening. 'In a bar, on the hill, and I lost everyone.'

'He likely means up in Pigalle, Mam'selle.'

'I know where he means, Luc.' The girl's accent was impeccable. She was still staring at him.

'Let me see his eyes,' she demanded.

The grip on his collar tightened as he was

38

pushed forward. He was intensely aware of every muscle in his face as the girl grasped his chin, her gloved fingers brushing his injured lip. Gui met her gaze.

Everything stopped: his breathing, the throbbing in his head and lip. He caught the girl's scent, spring flowers and sweat and soap. The light from the doorway clung to the fine down of her cheek. For an instant, her eyes widened. Then time rushed to catch up, and she stepped away abruptly.

'Opium, I wouldn't doubt,' she murmured, rubbing her gloved fingers as if they burned. 'I believe he's telling the truth. By the look of him he's fresh from some backwater. Where is it then?' she asked indifferently, though she avoided his gaze, her cheeks redder than before. 'Brittany? Limousin?'

'Bordeaux,' he whispered. The pain had returned when she'd stepped away, leaving him cold.

She pursed her lips at him for a second.

'Do you know where this is?' she asked. He shook his head. 'We are in the Opéra district. Go to the end of the alley, take the first left, then the first right. Follow your nose and you will find the river soon enough.'

He took a couple of steps, but the ground tilted beneath him, his eyes clouded with black snow. A wall, blessedly solid, slid against his back.

The mademoiselle sighed. Her breath was a cloud in the air.

'Let him sit there until he can walk.'

Sick and ashamed, Gui held his head in his hands and fought back the urge to vomit. The business of unloading went on around him, thumps and creaks, the girl's quiet directions and the crisp hush of pages being turned in a ledger.

He must have dozed, for when he opened his eyes, the cart was empty. The deliverymen were leaning against the side, talking softly, their hands wrapped around steaming bowls. The darkness of the streets felt less oppressive; Gui sensed early morning, rather than late night. The young woman stepped from the door.

'Would you like some chocolate?' she asked.

He stared blankly. She rolled her eyes, motioned to one of the deliverymen, who came forward, thrust a white china bowl at him. It was hot and burned his chilled hands, but he took it. The girl remained on the step, her own bowl clasped between kid gloves.

'You should drink,' she said, 'it will help to clear your head.'

He rotated the bowl. A rich steam rose and he took a sip. Sweetness flooded his tongue, followed by cream, sugar, spices, chocolate finer than anything he had ever tasted, dark and bitter and delicious. Greedily, he raised the bowl again.

A faint smile lifted the corner of the young woman's lips.

Gui remembered to wipe his mouth.

'I . . . ' He coughed to clear his throat. 'This is wonderful. Thank you.'

She shrugged. 'I am not supposed to serve the best chocolate to tradesmen, but they work hard.

I think they deserve it.'

She nodded at one of the men, who returned the greeting respectfully. The delivery workers were keeping a safe distance. No wonder, thought Gui, eyeing the young woman warily. He put down the bowl, picked it up again, uncertain how to behave. She did not seem to notice.

'So, now that you have found your voice again, you can tell me of your adventure,' she said calmly. 'You were in Pigalle?'

'Yes. It was our first night out so we went to see the city,' he answered between sips. 'Don't remember much about it, though, except for the lights. Have you ever been?'

'I beg your pardon?'

'Have you ever been to Pigalle?'

Her eyebrows shot up in surprise. The expression betrayed her stern manner. She was no older than eighteen, he realized.

'I should think not!' she laughed, and he felt himself smiling along with her. 'You should be careful, boys such as you can lose their wits, smoking opium there.'

'I . . . ' He paused. The deliverymen were watching the conversation with interest. 'I didn't know what it was . . . Mademoiselle.'

The word was clumsy in his mouth. He watched the smile drop from her face as she drew back into herself once again.

'These men are going across the city.' Her voice was perfectly flat. 'They can take you as far as the Place de la République. I am sure you can find your way across the river from there.'

Briskly, she shook her skirts, held out a hand

towards him. He staggered to his feet, clasping her gloved fingers in thanks. Her face flushed red.

'Might I have the bowl back?' she asked awkwardly.

He snatched his arm away, cursing himself.

'I'm Gui,' he blurted, almost dropping the china as he placed it in her hands. He could hear the deliverymen trying to cover their laughter. 'Guillaume du Frère.'

'Indeed. I am Mademoiselle Clermont.'

'Thank you, Mademoiselle.' He hesitated, ashamed of his behaviour. 'I'm afraid I can't pay for the chocolate. My money was stolen. But if I can ever be of any assistance . . . '

Mademoiselle Clermont opened her mouth as if to speak, but said nothing. Gui made his escape towards the cart. Her voice followed him as he climbed up.

'We are expecting a large delivery next Saturday,' she called quickly. 'I believe we could use more staff. If you wish to assist, and do not mind lifting and carrying, you may come along. Luc there will tell you the details.'

Before he could respond she hurried away through the door. A key scraped in the lock. He caught a glimpse of writing, engraved onto a brass plaque, before the cart lurched away: *Deliveries: Pâtisserie Clermont.*

7

March 1988

My grandfather poured the hot chocolate from a pan into a round china bowl.

He had found me crying, sitting where my mum had left me with a pile of toys, before racing off for yet another meeting with the solicitors. I knew she'd come back silent and angry, knew that my dad wouldn't be coming to collect me like he had promised.

Grandpa Jim had scooted me through to the kitchen, lifted me onto the worktop while he bustled and hummed, pouring milk and chopping something into a pan. He had told me to blow my nose on his handkerchief, the one with his initials sewn in the corner.

A strange, rich scent rose from the hob. I sniffed hard, through the hiccups, and asked him what it was.

'*Chocolat chaud.*' He had smiled. 'Proper hot chocolate, the way they make it in Paris . . . '

The train jolts, shaking me out of a doze. Blinking, I refocus on my handwriting, the words 'Mademoiselles at Pâtisserie Clermont' scrawled across a page in my notebook.

I scrub at my eyes, feeling strange. The memory of being in my grandfather's kitchen was so vivid, but those words . . . *the way they make it in Paris*. Had he truly said that, or was my mind playing tricks on me?

Before I fell asleep I had been thinking about the last time I saw Grandpa Jim alive. He had become frail by then, no longer the energetic, wiry old man I'd known as a child. I'd been staying with him for a few days. He'd said it was because he needed help with a particular piece of work, but in hindsight, he must have felt that something was wrong.

I had spent the day in the cool, dark house, watching the countryside beyond the windows of his study. It was peaceful there, smelled of camphor and paper and old soot from the unswept chimney. Grandpa read in his chair while I typed up some university work on his old Smith-Corona, his head drooping into a doze now and then.

In the evening we had sat in the kitchen with the door open to the night. He'd shared some of his best old whisky and we'd played rummy. I should have noticed how weak he was, but I think he was trying his hardest to hide it from me.

Then he was gone, and all that was left was his literary estate, obituaries with the same decade-old photograph that graced the dust jackets of all his books. Grandpa Jim — the sad, funny man with the same grey eyes as me — had slipped away, and in his place he left 'J. G. Stevenson'.

When the train arrives at King's Cross, I try to shake off my pensive mood. Hopefully, I will find something conclusive at the gallery; something to help me understand Grandpa Jim's secrecy, to

44

show Hall that there is nothing to be seen, nothing to be dug up from my grandfather's past.

I brave the crowded tube and head towards North London. By the time I reach Belsize Park, it's after two.

The weather is skittish; rain showers and weak sunlight. I pull out my *A to Z* and struggle to find the right page as a breeze grabs at the paper. I hunch into my jacket and walk. Ten minutes later I almost miss the road and have to backtrack. On a grimy Victorian building I see a notice, taped to the glass-paned door: *Lewis-Medford Gallery*.

I venture in. At the top of a flight of stairs is a reception area. Thick rugs carpet the floor; pamphlets are piled lazily on a desk. Through a pair of double doors I can see paintings, stretching along a gallery.

'It's fifty pence entrance!' a voice shrills at me.

A middle-aged woman swathed in cardigans has emerged from an alcove and is staring at me, half-eaten biscuit in hand. I smile at her, count out a few coins.

'I telephoned earlier, about the Ahlers painting?'

Her expression brightens as she drops the money into the till.

'Yes, you found us, then. I'm so sorry I don't know more, it's my brother who's in charge here really, I'm just covering. The Saturday girl's gone off sick. You'll want to have a look round then, here . . . '

She scrabbles through the papers and comes

up with a photocopied sheet bearing details of the exhibition. Thanking her, I escape into the gallery. It is a silent place, the sunlight dimmed by blinds. There are little nests of dust in the corners. Many of the paintings have tarnished frames, and the unmistakable scent of objects long untouched.

Through the first hallway, then the adjacent one, I peer at anything that might resemble a café scene. I eventually find Ahlers down a flight of stairs in the lower gallery.

It's darker here, and musty. I pull my denim jacket tighter, moving along the line of frames. They are all Paris scenes: Notre Dame, the Canal St Martin. I don't see any 'Mademoiselles' on my first pass, so I check more carefully, reading each label. After a third examination, my heart sinks.

'Looking for the missing Ahlers?' someone asks.

A small man in an oilskin cape has emerged from a side door marked 'Private'. It must lead to the outside, because he brings the smell of rain with him.

'Yes,' I stutter, searching my bag for the details. 'I'm looking for a café scene, *Mademoiselles at Pâtisserie Clermont.*'

Unclipping his cape, the man produces a handkerchief and wipes the rain from his face.

'Gone, I'm afraid, miss.'

It takes a second for his words to sink in, and even then, I hope that I've misheard.

'Pardon?'

'Gone. Sold, about five years ago. Surprised

me, too, no one ever expressed much of an interest before.'

'Do you know where it is now? Is it in another gallery, or — '

'I'm sorry.' He stops me. 'It was a private sale, the details are confidential.'

'Yes, of course,' I falter, staring at the piece of paper in my notebook. It was stupid to have pinned my hopes on one picture. The curator is asking me if I'm all right. I swallow with difficulty, pushing down my disappointment.

'Yes, thank you anyway.'

'Young lady?' His voice stops me in my tracks. He is smiling. 'If it's important, I do have a facsimile.'

Back in the reception, he pulls cardboard tubes from a long cupboard. It is warmer here, the smell of coffee pervading the air. The curator and his sister are friendly, ask about my research. I tell them about the thesis I am writing, about my interest in the *belle époque*. I can't quite bring myself to mention Grandpa Jim.

'I was a historian once,' the curator says brightly, squinting at labels. 'Studied Classics. Didn't stay on, though. Ran off to art school halfway through. Here we are.'

He struggles to extract the roll of paper, using a couple of mugs as paperweights. A black-and-white copy of a painting is stretched out on the desk. It shows a fairly ordinary tableau, a pair of hazily painted women reclining in café chairs, cups or glasses at their fingertips.

One of the women catches my attention. She is at the front of the table, the painter's main subject, her head turned as if she has noticed something just beyond the frame. My neck prickles. It is the woman from my grandfather's photograph.

'Who is she?' I murmur.

The curator has pushed his glasses onto his forehead and is surveying the picture with something like tenderness.

'A young lady, enjoying afternoon tea with her friend, I suppose.'

I look for a long time. There's an arresting quality about the girl and I study her face, captured more fully in paint than in a blurred photograph. Her skin is pale, save for some shading high on her cheeks to suggest a flush. Her hair is painted as a dark sweep above a high-necked gown. She looks taut, as though she is about to spring to her feet.

'I don't suppose you know anything about this place, Pâtisserie Clermont?' I ask, straightening up.

'Afraid not,' the curator says. 'I've always assumed it was just a café, named after the owners.'

I stare in astonishment. The idea that 'Clermont' might be a person hadn't even occurred to me. It's such an obvious suggestion I could kick myself.

'Hope it's been of some help,' the curator continues, re-rolling the copy. 'The work isn't a masterpiece. Ahlers was a rather average painter, but I miss the mademoiselle and her friend. I think they were just starting to like me.'

'Why did you sell it? If you don't mind me asking?'

48

'To be honest, we needed the money. You've seen the state of this place for yourself. Besides, the buyer was quite intent on possessing it.'

I desperately want to ask him more about the painting — who bought it and why — but I know he'll only tell me it's confidential. I thank him, and shoulder my bag.

He stops me as I turn to leave.

'Would I be right,' he murmurs, 'in assuming that your interest in this painting is more than simply academic?'

I feel the heat rise to my cheeks.

'How did you know?'

He smiles kindly. 'Call it a hunch.'

At the door, I find him reaching for my hand. He shakes it warmly, wishing me luck. It isn't until I reach the street that I open the scrap of paper he pushed secretly into my fingers:

Mademoiselles at Pâtisserie Clermont,
Ahlers, 1910
SOLD: 01/08/1983
Monsieur G. du Frère, Bordeaux 33000

8

December 1909

Pâtisserie Clermont. The words plagued Gui. They were strangely familiar, like an old school hymn, half-forgotten.

'You're a fool if you're going to go,' Nicolas told him bluntly as they sat in the canteen, slurping bowls of onion soup with the other men. 'I've heard stories like this: rich girl lures poor young man into the house for devious purposes. It won't end well.'

Gui laughed along with his friend, but in truth, he was uneasy. Why had Mademoiselle Clermont asked him back? Had she recognized him from the station? He could not fathom it, and relived their conversation in his head, only to remember time and again how she'd flushed when he had taken her hand. By the time Saturday night rolled around, he was a mess of relief and excitement.

It was strange to slip out of the silent dormitory, to walk the frozen streets sober and fully dressed. There was not another soul to be seen, all the way to the river. The cart was waiting in the Place de la République. The horses stood patiently beneath the gas lamps, their nostrils steaming. A figure was huddled in the driver's seat. When Gui approached, the man checked his watch and motioned to the back.

Two other men stood there; they grasped his outstretched arms and hauled him onto a narrow ledge.

Soon they were rattling through the streets towards Opéra. Gui examined the other workers, clinging to the tie-ropes. One was a boy around his age who looked like a taller version of Luc, the driver. He had the same square jaw and wide shoulders. The other man was older and sinewy. His greying blond hair poked out from beneath a battered hat. He caught Gui's eye and grinned, breath fogging the air.

'Had a wager going on whether you would show or not,' he said.

Gui shifted his footing on the step.

'Why wouldn't I?'

'Why would you, is more the question. Hoping to get in good with herself?'

'Enough, Yves.' Luc's voice rumbled back to them from the driving seat.

'Does she,' Gui began eagerly, 'I mean, Mademoiselle Clermont, does she run the pâtisserie?'

Yves snorted with laughter. He began to speak only for Luc to interrupt.

'Doesn't run anything of account.' His voice was taciturn. 'It's her father's business.'

'He allows her to work there?' Gui could not help but ask. 'Receive deliveries at night?'

'He does. Whether he likes it or not is none of our business. As long as there's someone to take the goods, we get our money. It's nothing to me who does it.'

His words were followed by silence, save for

the sound of the horses' hooves slipping on the frozen cobbles.

'The old night manager there was a drunken sot,' Yves whispered, rolling the gossip around his mouth. 'Don't think Monsieur rightly noticed, but the girl did. One day she appears, cool as you please, holding the order book. Reckon she pestered her father until he gave in. Monsieur hates to be disturbed in his work, see.'

Luc made a noise like a laugh. They all craned to look at the large man. His eyes were fixed ahead into the darkness, but he was smiling.

'Known Mam'selle Clermont since she was a child. Mother died when she was barely a week old. Little thing used to hang around the kitchens like a lost kitten till they got her a governess. Even then, she'd run back again. Just wanted her papa, but he'd no time for her. He blames himself for her accident, though.'

'Accident?' Gui asked.

Clearing his throat, Luc urged the horses into a faster trot.

'Like I said, nothing to me who does the job, and Mam'selle Clermont is as good a clerk as any.'

The lane was dark and quiet as they shuddered to a stop. Gui peered around. An old man with a handcart stood waiting, smoke curling from a cigarette jammed between his lips. The only other sounds were the jingle of reins and the creak of leather as they dislodged their chilled fingers from the tie-ropes.

Luc hammered on the door, already shifting a

crate to prop it open. Yves flexed his hands, smirking at Gui.

'Hope you've got a head on your shoulders, boy.'

The door flew open before Luc could land another knock. The Clermont girl was there, as before. In her gloved hands she held a huge ledger.

'Good evening, gentlemen,' she said briskly. 'The kitchen is on night shift, so you shall have to have your wits about you.'

Luc nodded, stepped back into the cold.

'You heard Mam'selle Clermont, let's get this unloaded. Marc, Yves, crates in the hallway until they can be unpacked. You,' he jerked his chin at Gui, 'help uncle over there.'

Everything happened at once. Ropes whipped past Gui's face as he scrambled down to the stones. A sack sailed over his head to land in Luc's arms. He fought through the activity towards the old man with the handcart. Amongst the bustle, he hadn't moved an inch.

'*Bonsoir!*' Gui said breathlessly.

There was no response. Waiting for an answer, he blew on his hands and stamped his feet in what he hoped was a friendly way. The old man ignored him and puffed harder on his cigarette.

'What are you doing, lad?' bellowed Yves from the other side of a crate. 'Stop doing a jig and move the wretched goods!'

Gui began to untie the load. His numb fingers slipped and half of it tumbled to the pavement. He bit back a curse; the wooden boxes were stamped 'Fragile'. Stacking a few in his arms, he

53

headed for the doorway. Unloading was well underway, piles of goods growing mountainous in the hall.

'What shall I do with these?' he shouted, hoping someone would hear.

'What are they?' Luc was red-faced under an enormous sack.

'They say 'Fragile' on the side.'

'Mam'selle?' Luc asked.

The girl was turning up the lamps so that the small space resembled a fire-lit cave.

'Is there an old man with a handcart?' she asked, without looking around.

'Yes.'

'He will be from Goebel then; they make our moulds. The boxes need to be stored at the back of the kitchen, in the cabinet. Follow Marc there, he'll show you.'

The younger deliveryman had staggered up the steps, a metal dairy churn in his arms.

'Cream,' he grunted. 'Need a hand to set it down.'

Gui shifted his grip on the boxes. He felt clumsy and slow-witted as Mademoiselle Clermont stepped past him with half a glance; *she* seemed wholly at home in the chaos.

He followed Marc down the corridor towards a pair of double doors. Hoisting the churn in his arms, the other boy kicked them open. Noise blasted Gui. For a long moment, he stood, stunned by what he saw.

It was another world, one of brightness and steam. Huge electric globes hung overhead, suspended on gold wires, illuminating every corner of the room. The light they gave bounced from the shining wall tiles, from the patterned wooden floor, from the row upon row of hanging copper pots. He had never been anywhere so clean. Men in pristine white uniforms lined a dozen marble-topped counters, some in tight groups, others working alone.

A cloud of white swirled high into the air on his left, as a chef measured out sugar as fine as powder. It drifted towards Gui and he breathed in deeply, tasting it in his lungs.

There were a thousand noises: spoons clattering, liquid being poured in glugs, a deep, unctuous bubbling from the stove. Heat blasted him in a roar as someone opened an oven. It carried the glorious smell of fresh baking.

Gui's mouth was watering as he tripped forward, trying to look at everything at once. Mahogany shelves lined the counters, stacked with glass bottles and jars, like something from a fairy tale. There were whole, plump roses steeping in honey; purple-stained sugar, thick with lavender, tiny jars of crimson threads, cherries and peaches suspended in syrup as if they had fallen there from the trees.

The luxurious scents wrapped around him. *Butter*, his nose relayed, *cream, nuts, brandy, chocolate* . . .

He was so preoccupied that he collided with one of the busy chefs. The man's angry shove brought him to his senses. He blinked up. Marc was waiting for him at the side of the room. Impatiently, he jerked his chin towards a door with a heavy bolt, and Gui hurried over to elbow it across. A waft of cool air billowed out.

'They're a highly strung lot, the chefs.' The other boy dropped the churn with a grateful sigh. 'Keep out of their way and you'll be fine.'

But Gui did not want to keep out of the way. He found himself gawping like a child, as he stacked box after box of rattling metal into the cabinet at the end of the kitchen. Every time he walked its length there was something new to be seen.

On a vast hob, he saw a pot of *chocolat chaud*, like the girl had given him the week before. At one of the counters, a single chef was cutting intricate patterns from a sheet of something white and fine and powdery, another was pouring out batter in a smooth golden ribbon. He laughed with delight when he saw a man burn a pot of custard with a hot iron, so that it set, as hard and brittle as ice. He almost reached out a finger towards a bowl piled high with thick, sweet cream.

Stacking the last box of moulds, he left the kitchen with regret. He lingered in the empty hallway, peering through the crack in the door, transfixed.

'Hands empty already?'

Mademoiselle Clermont stood behind him, the heavy ledger balanced on one hip.

'I was, I mean . . . ' He scrabbled for words as heat flared up his neck. He wanted to tell her that the kitchen was miraculous; that he wished he could watch the chefs for ever, but she would laugh at him, think him ignorant.

'I used to stand at the door like that when I

was small,' she told him quietly, a smile playing across her lips.

Luc appeared at the end of the corridor then. Two sacks weighed down his shoulders. Close behind were Yves and Marc, each in a similar state. Gui hurried forward to catch one of the sacks as it slipped.

'Mam'selle,' Luc puffed, 'where do you want the sugar?'

'Two-thirds in the pantry, the rest at the end of the workstations, please.'

Her smile was still in place when she glanced up at Gui from her rows of numbers as he passed.

The pace in the kitchen had increased. A tall, blond chef was roaring orders; apprentices skidded back and forth, fetching pans or ingredients. The more accomplished workers hunched over individual creations, perspiration beading their foreheads as they stacked pastry as thin as tissue, grasped squares of gold leaf with tools that belonged in a doll's house.

A thin man with greying brown hair now stood alone at the front of the kitchen. Gui had not noticed him before. Trays and bowls surrounded him; the kitchen's labours laid out like a feast, picked apart. The man wore a white jacket like the other chefs, but his was tailored to fit, embroidered at the collar with gold thread. He was holding something tiny to the light, as small as his smallest fingernail, blue as a duck egg.

'Who is responsible for the dragées?'

His voice was quiet, yet it silenced the clamour. Even Luc stopped what he was doing.

Only the gentle bubbling of the stove remained. A team from one of the workstations raised their hands, one chef in particular. He was short and plump, black hair slicked down under his cap.

'Monsieur Melio. If you please?' the older man invited.

The chef approached the front, holding a bowl full of the tiny objects. Wordlessly, the man took the dish from his hands, and tipped its contents into a sack of refuse. The plump chef stared down into the empty bowl, then hurried back to his bench, face burning with humiliation.

Gui glanced round for some clue as to what was happening, but Luc showed no sign of moving, even though they had long completed their task. Gui opened his mouth to ask, but felt Mademoiselle Clermont's restraining hand on his cuff.

'Wait,' she whispered.

The activity in the kitchen had come to a standstill; all gazes were turned expectantly towards the man at the front.

'It has been said,' he began, addressing the whole room, 'that architecture is the noblest of the arts. Every day, we see structures ascending from the street into the sky. We step onto the majestic boulevards, we witness this old city turn her new face towards us.'

The man had a powerful presence. Gui could feel his attention being dragged across the kitchen.

'Thus,' the chef continued, 'if architecture is the noblest of the arts, then I say that pastry *must* be the highest form of architecture, the purest and most delicate. How are we to achieve this if we are presented with building blocks unequal to the task? Who can tell me what steps must be taken to ensure a dragée presents a seamless covering?'

The noise of a discussion filled the kitchen. Gui loosed a pent-up breath.

'Should be safe to venture out now,' Luc said. 'What do you say, Mam'selle?'

'I should think so.' She smiled.

They strode through the kitchen once again. From the outer door, Yves and Marc appeared, arms loaded with packets. They were obviously accustomed to such episodes.

'What was that about?' Gui murmured as they walked, glancing back at the chef over his shoulder.

'My father believes in discipline,' Mademoiselle Clermont said quietly. 'His kitchen is known to be the best in Paris; he has a reputation to uphold. Besides, poor work can cause accidents.'

Gui looked at her out of the corner of his eye, hoping that she would continue, but she hurried away. He had no time to talk, in any case. The work kept him busy.

He thought about Monsieur Clermont's words as he emptied crates and passed the contents to Yves. He had never considered pastry to be anything other than a luxury, something for the plump, rich people who drove their carriages around the parks, but Clermont had described it as an art form, a trade. It too must have its foundations then, its bricks and mortar. Gui was so absorbed in contemplation that the bottom of the final crate came as something of a shock.

'No need to look so surprised, young man,' Luc announced cheerfully. 'We're done for the night.'

Gui blinked his eyes to clear them. The sky outside was lightening with dawn, the air of a clear December morning brushing his face from the door. Mademoiselle Clermont was watching him as she signed a piece of paper and handed it over to Luc. There came a build-up of noise from the kitchens. Chefs and apprentices burst into the corridor, steaming cups of coffee and wedges of bread in hand. They talked boisterously, laughing, released from the pressure of a long night's work.

'They must be finished,' said Mademoiselle Clermont, peering around.

'Finished?' croaked Gui. His throat was dry with fatigue.

'I will show you, if you like. Would anyone else care to see? Marc?'

'Nothing that interests me I'm afraid, Mam'selle.'

'We shall take a peek through the scullery window,' she told him archly and headed towards a different door.

With a smirk, Marc nudged Gui forward. The door led to a narrow galley space, lined with deep enamel sinks. It was warm and dark and filled with steam. Freshly washed pans dripped from racks upon the walls. A second door with a tiny circular window connected to the kitchens.

'I would take you closer,' said Mademoiselle Clermont as she stepped to avoid the puddles, 'but the sugar is drying. Father will not allow anyone near until it has properly set. There.' She sighed happily, her breath fogging the window. 'It's *twice* as magnificent as last year.'

Gui shifted uncomfortably, unsure how to move. The space was cramped, and squeezing in next to the girl did not seem entirely proper. As if sensing his embarrassment, Mademoiselle Clermont shifted to one side, beckoned him closer.

He hesitated. The whole evening had been like a dream, a glorious, golden world that he would have to forget when he returned to the rail workers' dormitory, to the furnaces and the damp, barren tracks. Yet he was desperate to see what had kept the kitchen so busy all night.

Before he could think better of it, he stepped to join Mademoiselle Clermont. She raised an arm to give him room, and he caught her scent again, spring flowers, clean linen. He forced himself to concentrate and peered through the glass at the kitchen's creation.

It was a cathedral, the one that stood upon the hill of Montmartre, slender and towering. The windows were filigree rings, delicate as the halo of an icon, glass stained with brilliant blues and reds, but it was sugar, all sugar. Marzipan arched upward in domes; tiny green and blue almonds took the place of stonework and gargoyles carved from sugar paste perched upon the towers, topped with gold leaf.

Slowly, his awareness returned to the cramped

scullery room. He felt Mademoiselle Clermont sigh.

'The festive season is just glorious,' she said.

Gui looked at her. Her face was alight with admiration, her fine dress trailing in the puddles, her lace cuffs stained with ink. Beyond her shone the sugar cathedral. The cost of it could have fed a family like his in Bordeaux for a year. Abruptly, he turned away.

The other men were waiting in the cart outside the door. He almost ran to join them, wanting to be away from that place, from the emotion that was weighing on his chest.

'Guillaume!' Mademoiselle Clermont was smiling, hanging from the doorway as the cart began to trundle away. 'Would you like to come back next week?'

9

April 1988

I'm sitting at my desk, watching the sky change colour through the rain. A page of my thesis is wedged into the typewriter, abandoned mid-sentence. The pale evening light falls upon my grandfather's photograph, propped up next to the scrap of paper handed to me by the curator at the gallery.

During the past week I have tried my best to ignore it, but every time I sit down to write, it prickles at the back of my mind, like a burr that can't be shifted or ignored. I have been bluffing my way through supervisions and tutorials; have barely done any work. If Whyke has noticed, he hasn't mentioned it.

I gnaw at one of my nails, already bitten down to the quick. What would Hall be doing, if he'd found the photograph instead of me? And how did he discover anything? I thought that I had taken all of Grandpa's correspondence when the house was sold. It is at my mum's house, neatly stacked in boxes, waiting for me to sort through it properly.

Unless . . . a horrible thought creeps upon me. Quickly, I pick up the phone and dial a number from memory.

'2763?'

'Hi, Mum.'

'Petra! How are you? Everything OK?'

My mother sounds preoccupied, as though she has been laughing and I've interrupted the joke.

'Yeah, fine,' I say. 'I was thinking of coming home tonight. Will you be in?'

'Of course! Can you afford the fare?'

The question makes me grimace. My funding for the year is running out, and it has to last me another two months. I ignore the question; tell her that I'll be there for dinner.

I shove some things into a bag, feeling guilty for not mentioning the real reason behind my visit. Maybe I should have asked her about the papers straight out, whether anyone else has been to look at them, but then, she would have wanted to know why. I'm not sure that's a conversation I'm ready to have.

A minute later I'm rattling through the streets on my bike, trying to convince myself that I've got it wrong, that everything will be as I left it. Thankfully, it has stopped raining and the evening feels fresh and clear. As I pedal, some of the fug begins to drain from my head.

I'm still worrying over 'what ifs' when I reach London and change stations. The tube is thick with the smell of cigarettes and hairspray; people heading for big nights out in the capital. At Charing Cross I buy my mum a bunch of flowers, and sit with them balanced across my lap as the train slides out towards the suburbs. Eventually, the sign for Staplehurst creeps into view through the grubby window.

My mother's house is a short walk from the station, and as soon as the lights appear around the corner I feel a welcome rush of calm. I let myself into the garden and stand on the back doorstep, trying awkwardly to remove my shoes. Claws skitter and then Wilf, her dog, appears, tongue lolling, tail thumping the door and wall. He'd jump, but he's too old and arthritic, so he contents himself with hopping and leaning against my legs. I bury my head in his ears.

My mother emerges from the hallway, cheeks reddened. I give her the flowers and can't help but laugh as she engulfs me in a hug. For the next few minutes I'm inundated with news from the past month. She has been on the phone to my dad recently, she tells me. He's going to call later, from America where he's covering a story. I answer non-committally; he is the last person I want to speak to.

'Gin and tonic?' Mum asks, already getting down the glasses. 'I was about to make Simon one when you arrived, but I suppose he'll want to be off in a minute.'

I remember the phone call earlier, Mum laughing with someone as she answered.

'Who's Simon?'

'Simon Hall. He's writing Jim's biography. Your father told him about those papers you took from the study, and said that he could take a look. Simon's been sifting through them for a few weeks now. You'd know this if you called more often.'

The hint of reproach is unmistakable. I grit my teeth, trying to stay calm, even though she's just confirmed the very thing I was afraid of.

'Anyway, Simon says they're an absolute

treasure trove,' continues my mum, oblivious to my rage. 'It's a good job you cleared them out, isn't it?'

'Yes, well, *I* need to look through them now.'

'What for?' She tops up the glasses with tonic water. 'Come and meet Simon. He's really very friendly.'

Of course, she doesn't know about Hall's talk at the university. I'm simmering with anger as she gives me the drinks, but there's nothing I can do except shuffle behind her through the house. Sure enough, Hall is sat in the dining room, at one end of the long table, my grandfather's papers spilled out before him.

He smiles as we walk in. Today, he is wearing a colourful tank top and a tightly buttoned shirt.

'Simon,' my mum says, 'this is Petra. She's home for a night from university.'

Hall is grinning as I juggle the glasses in order to shake his hand. It is clammy from holding a pen.

'I believe we spoke briefly a few weeks ago,' he says, 'at my talk. I would have introduced myself then, but you were in rather a hurry to leave.'

'I had a tutorial,' I shoot back. My mum laughs, hurrying off to the kitchen to fetch some nibbles.

I put the drink down in front of him and look at the papers. I want nothing more than to snatch them up and hide them away. Hall takes a sip and smacks his lips in appreciation.

'I understand it's you I have to thank for saving these from your grandfather's house.' He reclines in his chair. 'I could never have hoped for such an extensive personal collection. It's proving fascinating.'

'What are you hoping to find? Dirt?' I can feel my face burning.

'My readers certainly aren't interested in plain facts,' he is still smiling, 'there are already plenty of those about your grandfather.'

'You can't — '

'Petra,' he interrupts, looking up at me with a degree of compassion that I almost believe, 'I realize that this must be difficult for you, but I'm only expanding upon things that are already there. The formative experiences of your grandfather's life, good and bad.'

'You mean this so-called scandal you've found?'

'Nothing 'so-called' about it. If you were listening in my talk you would've heard me say that I have proof.' He taps a pile of papers before him. 'Thanks to you.'

I stare at him. I've had an idea, although I suspect it might be a very stupid one.

'You're talking about Pâtisserie Clermont,' I say slowly.

Hall's face tightens.

'Pâtisserie Clermont?' He is trying to keep the interest out of his voice, but I can tell he's bluffing. 'What's that?'

'Just a place I saw in a photograph once.' I take a sip of my drink.

Hall is on his feet. 'A photograph? Where? I haven't seen one.'

I shrug, relishing his confusion.

'Can't remember.'

It is Hall's turn to be angry. He knows that I'm lying, and leans across the table towards me, features twisting. My mother appears in the doorway with a bowl of crackers and he pulls back sharply. Fuming, he shrugs himself into a blazer and collects his notebooks.

'Thank you so much, Mrs Stevenson,' he gushes to my mother. 'I must get out of your hair now. Petra, I'm sure we'll speak again.'

Then he is gone, and all that is left is the buzzing of nerves in my head. I desperately want to look through the papers on the table, but my mum is steering me into the kitchen. I realize that I am ravenous, and soon, a plate of sausages and buttery mashed potato eclipses all other worries. My mum has opened a bottle of red wine and the kitchen is warm and cosy.

I almost forget about Hall and the photograph and my grandfather as I sit, sleepy and full in front of the television. The phone rings before midnight; it is my dad. My mum tries to hand me the phone, but I just shake my head, escape upstairs. I hear her sigh as I walk away. I know she thinks I'm being stubborn, but I still can't bring myself to speak to him.

We were never friendly after the divorce, and weren't even that close before. He's a journalist, and was always away from home, but it all got worse when he started working for the tabloids. I didn't really understand at the time. I only knew that Grandpa disapproved, that my mum was unhappy and that my dad was around less and less.

Then came the fights, the divorce proceedings

68

and the long afternoons at Grandpa Jim's, when he would pour me hot chocolate, read to me and make me feel safe. Mum told me recently that my dad was jealous of how close I grew to Grandpa Jim, but that isn't enough to make me forgive him.

My old room is exactly as I left it. I breathe in the smell of home, falling into the worn cotton sheets.

I must have gone to sleep like that, because I'm still fully dressed when a scratching at the door wakes me. Blearily, I check my watch. Two a.m. Wilf stands outside, tail wagging furtively. He isn't supposed to come upstairs, but we turn a blind eye. Thirsty, I plod down to the kitchen for a glass of water. Wilf follows and settles into his bed. I kneel on the floor for a while, smoothing his ears and the white hairs on his muzzle until he's too sleepy to follow me.

Passing the dining room I catch sight of the papers and creep in to investigate. Hall has been arranging them into a ring binder: that act alone is enough to make me angry all over again. I peer down in the darkness. The folder lies open where he left it. The spine has been marked *Paris*. Inside, there are plastic wallets filled with loose sheets, what look like letters written in faded blue and black ink.

I scan through the top pages. Strangely, they are all in my grandpa's own handwriting. They repeat the same sentences again and again, but in different orders, topped with different dates. I flick past. A few sheets later I find another letter, in writing I don't recognize, elegant and heavy.

69

Halfway down the page, a word that could be 'Clermont' leaps out at me.

I try to decipher the old-fashioned script, but my eyes are itching with tiredness. Carefully, I remove the letter and slide it into my own notebook for safekeeping.

Upstairs, the duvet is warm. By the time my head touches the pillow, I am ten years old again, and roll untroubled into sleep.

10

December 1909

Dear Maman,
I cannot speak too much of it now, but I have found extra employment outside of the railway which I think may be of great benefit. I am sorry that I cannot return home for Christmas . . .

Gui paused, the pencil hovering. He missed his mother, but in truth, he would not be sad to miss Christmas. He would send her as much money as he could spare, and she would go to her relatives with a few extra coins in her purse and stories of her son, hard at work in the city. He hoped it would be enough.

He had been back to the pâtisserie four times. There was always something new to see, or smell, new sounds like the hiss of scalding cream or the crack of brittle sugar. And, of course, there was Mademoiselle Clermont. The last time he had been there, the kitchen was quieter, only a few chefs proving dough at the workstations, her father nowhere to be seen. She had made them all hot chocolate again, and had stood with him on the step to drink it.

He had not known how to behave, what to feel, but he had made her laugh, remembering aloud the state he had been in when they first met. Her smile, as much as the hot chocolate, had left his body tingling with warmth.

Yet the long nights were taking their toll. He was often tired in the daytime, and made mistakes in the forge, which did not go unnoticed. His wages were docked, and the handful of centimes he received from Luc were not enough to cover the difference, leaving him short.

'Come with me to St Malo,' said Nicolas, as he prepared to leave for Christmas. 'My aunt's a miserable old trout, but at least you'll be fed.'

It was a tempting offer. The dormitory would be empty for the two days of holiday and Gui barely had enough money for one meal, let alone a companionable drink. He walked Nicolas to the main platform, along with several other young men. They were merry, freed from their work for a rare day of enjoyment.

He let the others board the train, perching where they found space, among the freight or in the corridors. He stood alone on the platform, despite Nicolas's protests. Eventually, his friend gave up and waved goodbye, as the running boards slid away and the train streamed out of sight.

Alone in the city. He could not explain, even to himself, why he had stayed behind. He felt as though he had been split in two; that there was another Guillaume du Frère who had boarded the train and was even now sharing liquorice and idle talk with his friend.

This Guillaume walked aimlessly. His steps took him away from the station buildings towards the river. It was not beautiful here, it was the gut of the fish rather than the rainbow scale or shimmering eye.

The drizzle that had been threatening all day increased its pace, as if it too hurried breathless towards home. In a matter of seconds he was soaked through, but it did not slow him down. Rather, he saw himself as part of the landscape, cold as the stones of the embankment. A motor car rumbled past, tyres flinging up grit. A man and woman shrieked as they dodged out of the road and tripped into the nearest café.

Music and laughter gushed from the doorway as they elbowed their way inside. Faces were red and merry away from the unforgiving winter winds. Breath fogged the windows, made the place radiant. Gui could have been one of them, used his few coins to buy a drink and a place at the bar, but he did not. Instead, he stepped onto the Quai de la Tournelle. Rain melted the grey afternoon darker still, and Notre Dame floated across the river like a scribble of chalk. He trudged a few feet further, until a shape rose from the gloom like an upturned boat.

A bouquinist was packing up, oil cape raised against the driving weather. He was the last of the booksellers on the stretch. He struggled with rheumatism-gnarled fingers to stack the volumes into the wooden chest. It was slow work. Forcing his own numb hands to cooperate, Gui bent to help him, grasped an armful of books and placed them in the trunk. Perhaps in summer, the man would have growled from behind his pipe and told him to leave off, but the rain was getting heavier and the cheap ink would soon run.

Then he saw it. A drawing like Clermont's cathedral, but smaller, dissected into sketches like a puzzle. Words upon a page: *sugar, paste, almonds* . . . The book's cover was missing, but even so, it would be more than he could afford. Before he knew what he was doing, the book had found its way beneath his jacket. He thrust the final handful of papers at the old man and turned away, heart thundering in his throat. A noise behind him could have been a shout, but the wind was too loud to hear clearly. He risked a glance over his shoulder: the man was staring after him, but was soon lost to the weather.

Gui broke into a run, arms wrapped tight around his wet coat and the precious object beneath. In the hammering rain he felt elated. His steps became leaps, over puddles and onto the pavement, where he bowed absurdly to a carriage horse that stood in the gutter. By the time he reached the station quarter, the shops were closing.

His coins bought him a bottle of red wine, poured hurriedly from a vat. He had no money left for food, but the wine would help him forget that. He stood to one side as a woman elbowed past, arms and baskets weighed down with groceries. A drainpipe belched its load over the pair of them and the woman gasped, grappling for her hat. One of her packages slipped unnoticed into the mud.

The thought of an empty belly was enough to send Gui stooping for it like lightning. He hurried away before she realized what had happened, fingers releasing the sodden wax paper to find a slab of cheese. He told himself that feeling guilty wouldn't fill his stomach, and shoved it into his pocket, whistling a Christmas hymn as he squelched back to the empty dormitory.

By the time night fell he was huddled by the coal stove, wrapped in a blanket. His clothes hung dripping onto the wooden floor. Wind and rain rattled the roof, but he was cosy. The book lay open before him, waiting to be explored. A loose sheet shoved hastily into the middle contained the title page. He smoothed the worn paper with careful fingers, entranced by the letters. They were grand, ornate even, surrounded by curls and illustrations.

He had never owned a book, beyond his catechism for school. This one was by a Monsieur Carême, who described first-hand the creation of wonders: palaces, temples, even ruined castles, all constructed from sugar. *An architect*, Gui realized with a jolt. There were many words he did not know, but read them over and again until he almost understood.

Monsieur Carême was his companion that Christmas night. He turned the pages deep into the early hours, his head filled with images of construction and confection, explained by the voice of a master at his craft.

Early the next morning, he awoke to the hush of rain upon the roof. For long minutes he lay still, taking in the rare, melancholy luxury of waking alone. Somewhere, it was Christmas morning. His mother would be trudging the muddy track of a country town to visit their relatives without him. He rolled over in his cocoon of blankets. The book was on the floor, pages splayed. He must have fallen asleep reading it; he stroked a page lightly in apology and turned to where he had left off.

Eventually, church bells began to chime nearby and Gui's surroundings clarified themselves: cold, damp dormitory, an empty bottle, a rind of cheese. Monsieur Carême's lessons were not for the likes of him, yet he could not help but smile as he tucked the book carefully beneath the hard pillow.

He drank water, ice-cold from the pitcher, to quell the hollow in his stomach. He would have to venture out to scrounge a meal. Sometimes, the churches gave out food on Christmas Day. He should feel ashamed, he knew, begging for alms, but since no one knew him here, he did not see the harm.

Most of his clothes were still too wet to wear. He scrabbled into his trousers, wincing as the clammy fabric caught about his legs. His spare shirt was threadbare, but dry, so he pulled it over his head.

In another boy's trunk he found a waistcoat, worn red velvet, and in another, a scarlet neckerchief. Their owners would surely not begrudge their use on a holiday. He combed at his short hair with his fingers, and stood in front of the mirror to survey the outcome.

He had grown thinner, he noticed with frustration, no doubt due to the long nights of work. He slapped some colour into his cheeks and pushed his cap to a jaunty angle worthy of Nicolas. With his wind-tanned face, his tawny hair growing back and the bright red scarf, he looked more gypsy than good Christian, but that did not stop him from stepping out into the Christmas morning.

In the cold, he retraced the previous day's route. He did not pause when he reached the quay but ventured onto the bridge. His steps led him to the back of Notre Dame, where great buttresses propped up the bulk of the chapel. The rain had slowed to a fine drizzle, chilling his skin and sending him hurrying into the cathedral. A service was taking place and worshippers filled the pews, radiating their heat. Candles blazed — hundreds of them — and the light was so golden that it was hard to believe in the grey weather outside.

He slipped into a back pew. Here, the people were like him, with chapped fingers and patched clothes, never quite warm enough. The rich took their places nearer to the front, in their velvet and fur.

Gui sat quietly and listened. He had never paid much attention to his prayers as a child, but the presence of others was comforting; murmuring in unison with them made him feel less alone.

Soon, the service drew to a close and he found himself in a crush of people eager to leave, to return to their hearths and Christmas toasts. He stepped into the aisle only to be shoved aside by a wealthy man in leather gloves. He swore and turned angrily to confront the man, only to come face to face with familiar blue eyes.

Gui dropped his gaze and stepped back, shame flooding his stomach. Mademoiselle Clermont was staring at him. An older woman took her arm and hurried her away. Gui kept his head lowered until they were gone, then inched his way along with the rest.

Outside, the congregation evaporated onto the streets. An enormous fir tree stood solitary in the square, its little tin ornaments clinking in the rain. He stood under its branches to look up. Water dripped through the thick needles, and he closed his eyes, breathing in the scent of greenery.

'Guillaume?'

Mademoiselle Clermont was standing a few feet away, blinking at him through the rain.

'What are you doing here?' he asked without thinking.

She hurried under the shelter of the branches and raised her face veil.

'I should ask you the same.' She gazed at the sheet of water on the stones. 'I assumed you would have gone home for Christmas. Bordeaux, did you say?'

He jammed his hands in his pockets, for warmth, he told himself.

'Yes, Bordeaux.' He paused. 'It is a long way.'

'What of your family? Won't they miss you?'

'There's only my mother now. I sent her my wages. It will mean that she's comfortable, I hope.'

The rain continued to fall on the square, reaching them in fat droplets that smelled improbably of deep forest.

'I am sorry,' he said awkwardly after a while, 'about earlier in the church.'

'No, I am to blame.' She sighed, voice fading. 'I forget . . . '

Her skin was pale, almost translucent against the heavy fabric of her high collar. It reminded him of tempered glass. Impulsively, he wanted to take her hand, to run with her from the rain into a crowded bar, see her laugh again. He would order a jug of wine and they would sit close together, watching the passers-by, growing warmer as they drank.

'Would you . . . ?' he began.

Her eyes were fixed ahead; he followed her gaze. A carriage stood at the edge of the pavement. A man was lingering on the step, waiting for her to board.

'I must go,' she stammered, 'but I hate the thought of you having a gloomy Christmas. Please, take this.'

From a tiny bag on her wrist she produced a coin. It shone against the suede of her glove and told Gui how she saw him: poor and dirty, with ill-fitting clothes, coal dust ingrained beneath his fingernails. To his anger and shame he felt hot tears gathering in his eyes as she placed the coin in his hand.

He stared at it, knowing that she was doing the same. He knew he should thank her, tried to say the words, but could not. Then he was running, out into the freezing downpour, back towards the grey side of the river, where coins were scarce and where a woman like Mademoiselle Clermont would never care to venture.

11

April 1988

I board the train feeling glum. I've come away from my visit home empty-handed, or as near as. Mum caught me, when I was halfway through packing up Grandpa's papers. I tried to explain about Hall, about the photograph, but she told me that I was being ridiculous, that they weren't mine to take.

Technically she's right; they're part of Grandpa Jim's estate, of which my dad is the executor. Grandpa never got round to changing his Will before he died, and so my father has full control, even though they barely spoke. Apparently, he has given Hall permission to read and use whatever he wants. I argued with my mum about it, but in the end I could see she was getting upset, so I backed down, had no choice but to leave them where they were on the table.

Of course, she didn't know about the letter that was already in my notebook. I pull it out, excitement overcoming my guilt, and start to read:

Jim,
I was sorry to miss you last week in Paris.
I was in town for all too short a time, and
my business did not permit me to linger.

I did, however, have the good fortune to acquire a copy of The Word, and your article, before departing the city of light for the dull landschaft.

What a scandal! You must have had your nose to the ground, or were you lurking in the corner, scribbling away under cover of rum baba? I cannot believe you did not witness the event first-hand, so vivid were your descriptions, especially of the illustrious M. Clermont and his sorry apprentice: 'shaking the young Bordelais the way one would a pup'. Marvellous.

I need not tell you that you will go far, dear boy, for I know you harbour ambitions above and beyond the penny sheets. If ever you need introductions in London, do not hesitate to use my name. I will take the liberty of making a few enquiries among the literati; your observations on the social quagmire that is Paris would make for fascinating reading in a more robust form than the dailies.

I shall be sure to notify you by telegram when I am expected to return to France, so as not to miss another meeting, although thanks to your most thorough coverage I hear that P. Clermont is closing its doors. I shall have to find another place to indulge my sweet tooth! Rest in peace, Clermont's!

Until then, I am yours, &c,
L. Allincourt

I nearly spit the coke that I'm drinking all over the letter and have to apologize to the man sitting next to me as I recover from a coughing fit. Eyes streaming, I peer at the name again. L. Allincourt.

Lionel Allincourt was arrested in 1915 for high treason. He had been passing information to Germany for years, a huge blow for the Foreign Office, where he held an influential position. It's something every history student reads about. He killed himself in prison, or was killed, before a trial could take place. I search for the date on the letter: June 1910. Less than five years earlier.

I start to feel a bit sick. An original letter, from L. Allincourt, and I've been toting it around in my bag with the rest of my notes. The coke roils uncomfortably in my stomach. Hall will definitely notice that it's missing.

Caught between horror and exhilaration I stand in the middle of Charing Cross, staring at it. Grandpa Jim knew Allincourt — knew him well, from the sound of the letter. My grandfather must have moved amongst high society then, in Paris, one way or another. The scandal certainly seems to have taken place amongst the upper classes; it *must* be the same one that Hall is investigating. No wonder he couldn't resist.

An odd chill prickles the back of my neck. It's clear that whatever happened, it happened at Pâtisserie Clermont. The photograph of the girl comes instantly to mind, the painting, and the thing that scares me most, my grandfather's handwritten plea: *Forgive me.*

By the time I unlock the door to my room, a plan has formed. All I need to do is find a copy of the newspaper mentioned in Allincourt's letter, *The Word*, and read the article for myself. In my preoccupation, I almost miss a note, scrawled on the pad that hangs next to my door.

Hi P, it says in a messy, spiky hand. *Came round this morning but you're not in. Sorry haven't caught up for a bit — lab's been crazy. Pub tonight? Al x*

The pub is quiet on a Sunday evening. I lurk in an alcove near the open fire, flick through the newspaper someone has left on the table. It isn't long before I push it aside in disgust. My dad's name glares at me from the by-line of an article about a famous actress's drug addiction.

A gust of cold air ushers Alex in. I wave him over, pointing to a second pint next to my own. He grins back, unwinding a scarf as he heads across the sticky carpet. It's a tradition of ours to hide out in one of the locals, rather than braving the chaos of the college bar.

Cass teases me mercilessly about Alex, no matter how many times I tell her that we're just friends. We met when his housemate dated one of mine for a while. I think they were trying to set us up. Nothing ever happened, but I can't help but smile whenever I see him, with his permanently untidy brown hair and his terrible taste in T-shirts. He's in the second year of a Physics Ph.D. Neither of us have a clue what the other one is saying when we complain about our research, but we always end up laughing.

'Got you a lager,' I say as he sits down. 'If you're quick, it might still be cold.'

'Thanks.' He sinks into the chair with a mock groan and takes a sip. 'And where have you been? I came by but you were out. On a Sunday! I was going to buy you a bun.'

I make a face. 'Sorry, I was visiting my mum.'

'Thesis progress on a scale of one to dismal?' he asks, eyeing me shrewdly.

I run my hand through my hair. I haven't brushed it today and must look a state, but with Alex, it doesn't matter.

'Dismal. You?'

'Scientific breakthroughs take time,' he says airily. 'Why is yours so bad?'

I start to explain about Hall, about my grandfather, why I've been neglecting my work. He listens patiently, and I find myself telling him everything: the girl, the painting, the letter, and then, hesitantly, about Grandpa Jim asking for forgiveness.

He taps his chin when I'm done, mulling over my words. I'd forgotten what a good listener he is.

'This whole scandal, it has to be something to do with her then,' he says, 'the girl.'

'I think so too, but there's nothing to prove it.'

'Except for those words, 'forgive me'.' I wait for him to continue, but instead he stares intently at a beer mat, shoving it around the table. When he next speaks his voice is uncharacteristically serious. 'Do you think your grandfather was, you know . . . ?'

'What?'

'Do you think he was, maybe, in love with her?'

Alex is flushing pink, right to the tips of his ears.

'No,' I say, too quickly. 'Something like that, he would've told me. We talked about how he met my grandma often enough.'

'It's not exactly the kind of thing he would confess to his granddaughter, P. Perhaps there were things he didn't want you to know.'

'Why does everyone think that?' I try to swallow back the lump that has risen in my throat. 'If that's true, then it means he lied to me . . . '

'I'm not saying that he lied.' Alex's voice is soft. His hand hovers at the edge of the table, as if he doesn't know what to do with it. 'Even if he did keep things from you, maybe he did it out of love . . . '

I take a large gulp of my drink.

'Well, anyway,' I try for a smile, 'I have to find out before Hall.'

'Is this really about Hall?' Alex is looking me in the eye.

'Of course.' Quickly, I finish my drink, and reach for my bag. 'Look, I've got to go — '

Alex grabs my hand. I stop, astonished. His cheeks couldn't get any redder.

'Let me know,' he says, 'if there's anything I can do to help?'

I nod, and squeeze his hand in return. Alex

lets go and reaches for his pint, nearly knocking it over in the process. Suppressing a laugh, I relax, and drop my bag to the floor.

'Next round's on me,' he says and grins.

12

January 1910

Gui did not go back to the pâtisserie the next Saturday, nor the one after that. He told himself that it was for the best. Besides, work on the tracks had resumed quickly after Christmas and was harder than ever. Every morning, a layer of snow coated the yard, turning first to slush, then to dense, pitted ice.

Their washing water froze in its bowl and had to be broken with the handle of a razor. Gui's hands seized up around tools, screaming back into life when he took his turn working the furnace. Chilblains made the tips of his fingers swell and itch.

Some nights, he found himself reaching beneath his pillow, silently drawing Monsieur Carême out into the dark dormitory. In the weak moonlight, he turned the pages, and the voice of that architect filled his head once more. Before his eyes, the sketches and diagrams came to life. Sugar work spooled out like silk thread, crystallized into soaring towers and spires.

He imagined the ghosts of impossible scents, trapped and infused, just as he'd seen in the kitchens of the pâtisserie. Monsieur Carême summoned the essences of the world to his fingertips. Roses and violets from summer gardens, sun-drenched Sicilian lemons squeezed of their juice and mingled with juniper from the frozen north. Saffron threads and gold leaf from the Indies waited to be turned into something magical. And contained deep within all of this was a smile that flooded him with warmth, a pair of blue eyes, and the scent of chocolate . . .

A guttural snore from one of the men would break the spell and he would remember that he was cold, that the air around him was stale and damp, that Monsieur Carême would have sneered, had he been there in person.

So he hid the book at the bottom of his trunk and tried not to think about it, or about Mademoiselle Clermont every time the sky showed a patch of chill blue.

Instead, he threw himself into the life of a railwayman. He worked harder than any of the others; at night he fell onto his pallet bed and straight into a dreamless sleep. His arms grew stronger, his hands rougher, until he could put up a decent fight even to Léon, the largest man in the dormitory. Nicolas, for one, was delighted to hear that he had put a stop to his weekly sojourns across the river.

'Dangerous, is what it was,' his friend told him, as they planed down railway sleepers. 'When you stayed for Christmas, I thought I'd come back to find you drowned in the Seine, a love letter to your bourgeois princess tied to your jacket.'

'Who said anything about love letters?' Gui protested.

'You did, the way you'd try to comb your hair flat every Saturday without anyone noticing.'

88

'I did not!'

'As you like.' Nicolas winked. 'I'm just glad you've come to your senses. Men like us have no business with sugar plums.'

Gui laughed then and felt better, as he always did with Nicolas. His friend was right. The longer he stayed away from the pâtisserie, the more foolish it seemed. It was a child's fantasy, no place for him. He put it to the back of his mind, and tried to keep it there.

Perhaps he would have succeeded; perhaps he would have gone on to work the tracks, watched the years sweep across Paris from between two iron rails and never spoken the name 'Clermont' again, had it not been for the rain. The rain changed everything.

It came first as snow, then as sleet, and finally as a deluge that knew no end. Gui grew accustomed to the feeling of being damp, but nothing prepared him for the morning when he awoke to find his boots floating away. The water in the dormitory was ankle-deep and rising.

'Shit,' said Nicolas over and over, staring at the churning brown river that had once been the yard. They could not stay. Men hurriedly wrapped photographs and letters in oilcloth, hid them deep in their clothes. Just in time, Gui remembered Monsieur Carême at the bottom of his trunk. The water had seeped through and wrinkled the pages, but he swaddled the book tightly in a handkerchief, shoved it into the crack where the roof met the wall and where it might be safe.

The sewers had burst and the Gare d'Austerlitz

was in chaos. Tracks were filling up into canals, water lapping at the platforms like an incoming tide. There were shouts and shrieks as people slipped, struggling to drag handcarts out of the flood.

A stationmaster recognized them as belonging to the railway and set them to work bailing out the tracks. Gui spent an unpleasant hour soaked to the waist, passing buckets hand to hand, but it made little impact. When they were shivering too much to continue, they hauled each other out and squelched up the stairs to the mezzanine, where a coffee vendor and roast-chestnut seller had set up business.

Gui inched as close to one of the burning braziers as he could, until steam began to rise from his clothes. The stationmaster handed him a mug of treacle-thick coffee laced with brandy. He gulped it gratefully. A man he knew to be the owner of the tabac booth was sharing rumours from other parts of the city, trying to stay dry by busily stuffing his clothes with yesterday's newspapers.

'Never seen anything like it,' he announced as he crammed a copy of L'Aurore down the front of his shirt. 'Looks like Venice out there, or a giant boating lake. I was born in this city and I wouldn't know it to look at. Salpêtrière's turned into a swimming bath and the Opéra district looks grim. Hear it crept up on them in the night from below. Stores, cellars, all underwater, and now the streets — '

'What did you say, about Opéra?' asked Gui, grabbing the vendor's arm. The man ignored him, shaking him off.

Gui did not wait to hear any more. He pulled his sodden jacket tight about himself and set off down the steps, skidding in pools of mud. He heard his name being called but didn't stop.

Outside, the water was shin-high, full of silt and debris. He waded along the embankment, stumbling on submerged objects. The water rose even as it sluiced into the river; the Seine hadn't yet broached its banks but licked at them, like a great tongue thrashing.

The bridge had been barricaded with sandbags and old pallets. A hastily assembled task force stood guard, staring miserably into the rising river. Before he could cross, someone grabbed his arm.

'What are you doing?' panted Nicolas furiously. 'Didn't you hear me calling?'

'I have to get past,' Gui said, pulling free. 'I have to go and help.'

'It's that place, isn't it? Don't go, Gui, they'll deserve what they get. Let them know what it's like to feel cold and scared for once.'

'You heard them back there, Nicolas, the whole district's in trouble! I can help.'

'You think they'll want you to stay,' he said incredulously, seizing Gui's waterlogged sleeve again. 'That's it, isn't it? You think if you act the hero they'll forgive you for being poor and keep you around.'

'You don't know them,' Gui protested. 'I have friends there.'

'What, that girl?' Nicolas shook him. 'Talk sense, Gui, she's one of them, she'll use you and throw you back here when she's done.'

Gui tore himself away and dashed for the barricade. This time, Nicolas didn't follow.

On the right bank, the flooding was worse. Water bubbled from the ground in a noxious spew, widening through the streets until it was knee deep. The city was deserted. Those who did venture forth were drenched and desperate, carrying sandbags and bundles of planks. Roads that were ordinarily packed with carriages and motor cars were empty. In a street lined with shops, looters had taken advantage of the chaos; almost every window had been smashed. Gui waded past the destruction.

The way was endless. In one alley he encountered a woman and a child, clinging to a set of metal stairs. Their basement home was underwater. Soon afterward, he met a small team of volunteers in a boat and directed them back, hoping that the woman would still be there.

By the time he neared the Boulevard des Italiens, the shivering in his muscles had become a deep, constant shudder. The walk had taken hours. His trousers were sodden, the water in the streets sometimes reaching his thigh. He was exhausted from wading, tripping and wading again, but he pushed on. Nicolas's words plagued him at first, but soon he found that it was easier to forget reasons and just keep moving. A few streets away from the pâtisserie he heard a commotion, sounds of a struggle: breaking wood, a woman's scream. He quickened his pace as best he could.

Ahead was a walkway, hastily constructed

between buildings like a bridge. A figure in black, a girl, was half in the water where the planks had collapsed. Around her were three men. Two grappled with her arms, a third ripped something from her hand.

'Hey!' Gui yelled, ploughing forward. 'Let her go!'

He launched himself at one of the assailants, grasping a handful of threadbare shirt. The thief writhed free like a cat to wallow after his companions into the shadows. The fading light showed their faces: they were boys, thin and hungry, none of them more than fourteen.

The woman clung to the planks, spluttering out the filthy water.

'Guillaume,' coughed Mademoiselle Clermont. He could not explain how, but he had known it would be her.

'What happened here? Are you all right?' he asked, trying to help her onto the walkway.

'We are flooded.' She scrabbled for purchase on the sodden wood. 'The whole ground floor, the kitchens. If the water rises any higher the damage will be dreadful. I came out to find the task force, but then I fell and they — '

She yelped in pain as he tried to lift her from the water, and clutched at his shoulders.

'The boards collapsed,' she said, teeth clenched. 'I believe my leg is stuck, but I cannot feel, everything is numb.'

He glanced down into the murky liquid, boiling up from the sewers.

'Can you wiggle it free?'

She tried and shook her head. He could see

the panic in her eyes, already bright with tears. Gently he took her hands from his shoulders and placed them on the walkway before her.

'Don't let go of this plank,' he said. 'I'll have to go under.'

The cold air was nothing compared to the freezing water that closed around his scalp. Clumsily, he groped out for her legs. At any other time his heart would have raced as he brushed her calf through the floating petticoat, but all he wanted to do was get her free.

He reached towards her ankle and found leather. Her boot was wedged tightly between two broken planks. His numb fingers felt like sausages as he tried to loosen the laces. It took a second breath of air and a third before they finally gave. Her foot squirmed free like a fish between his hands.

On the surface, he coughed muck from his nose and mouth.

'Do you think you can walk at all?' he croaked.

She leaned on her foot experimentally and her face flashed white with pain. He attempted to lift her, but they both nearly collapsed. Her waterlogged clothes almost trebled her weight.

'You will have to take off your coat,' he said over the increasing rain. 'It's too heavy.'

Without hesitation she struggled out of the long garment. Gui winced to see the costly velvet and lace brocade bundled up and muddy on the walkway. Her hat, too, was ruined; she threw it aside, wrapped her shawl quickly about her head and neck. There was something strange about the way she did it, almost furtive, but he was too tired to wonder.

The weeks of hard work paid off, for although his muscles leaped under her weight, they held firm. More than once his numb fingers began to slip and he tightened his grasp. If it hurt her, she did not complain.

By the time they reached the back door of the pâtisserie he could feel her shaking violently. Unable to let go, he kicked at the door and shouted, hoping there was someone to hear.

Light poured upon him, reflected blindingly on the water. Astonished faces met his. Someone pulled Mademoiselle Clermont away; his hands held on, stiffened into claws around her.

Monsieur Clermont was barging through the onlookers towards his daughter. Gui tried to stand, to gasp out some explanation, but his head was roaring, his knees buckling. Dry floorboards rose up to meet his cheek like a blessing.

13

The next morning my temples are pounding with a headache. I had one drink too many in the pub with Alex. When I finally got home, I couldn't sleep. Instead, I stared at the photograph of my grandfather. I searched for the person I knew in the young man of the picture, wondering if he had already made the decision that would haunt him so.

I walk across college, wincing in the bright spring sunlight. All around me are undergraduates, feverishly preparing for their finals in a few weeks' time.

In the porters' lodge I collect my mail. I've been ignoring it, and over the last few days my pigeonhole has filled up with paper. I stand by the bin, ripping up junk and photocopied flyers. I almost miss a thin letter hidden among the others. Wearily, I shake it open.

Miss Stevenson,
It has come to the faculty's attention that
you may not be progressing satisfactorily
with your thesis. In order to ensure that
your work does not fail when presented
to the review board later this term, your
teaching has been transferred to me.
You may continue to meet with Professor

*Whyke once a fortnight, if you wish, but I
will now conduct the majority of your
supervisions, effective immediately.
I expect your current draft to be in my
pigeonhole by the end of the day.*
Dr Elizabeth Kaufmann

I stare at the letter in horror. Has Whyke
reported me? He's been as distracted as ever in
our supervisions. Dr Kaufmann, on the other
hand, is a terrifying prospect. She is a tyrant for
detail and will not like my thesis one bit, even if
I do manage to pull a draft together.

At my desk I arrange and rearrange the pages,
trying to make sense of them. The Pâtisserie
Clermont evidence is scattered across my
workspace. Frustrated, I gather it all up. I am
about to shove the bundle into a drawer when a
phrase catches my eye. It is in the Allincourt
letter: *shaking the young Bordelais the way one
would a pup.*

For a second, I sit motionless. Then I'm racing
for the stairs, the letter clutched in my hand,
thesis already forgotten. I dash through college
and across the road towards the History faculty.
It is lunchtime, and I push impatiently through
cyclists and groups of students pouring from
lecture theatres.

I had thought that the only way to discover
what had happened in Paris would be to track
down grandfather's article, written over seventy
years before, but I was wrong. There is
something else, something that no one — not
even Hall — could have discovered without first

knowing about the painting.

I race up the stairs into the reference section, ignoring the librarian's glare, and snatch up the first dictionary I find. I flick through its onionskin pages to the letter 'B'.

Bordelais: of or pertaining to Bordeaux, in France, an inhabitant of the city of Bordeaux, or the surrounding area . . .

I stuff the dictionary back on the shelf. The note from the gallery comes instantly to mind, the name of the man who bought the painting and his address: *Monsieur G. du Frère, Bordeaux.*

It's a long shot, but there is no harm in looking. My heart is thumping as I reach one of the reference terminals. I wait impatiently for it to warm up. The screen flickers into life. I punch in a keyword search on 'du Frère' and 'Bordeaux'. The green cursor falters before flashing up a single entry:

Lefevre, Stephen C.,
Poste Restante: *The Dead Letters of Europe /*
by Stephen C. Lefevre
London. — 2nd ed. — Paris: Kingsley Press, 1972.
Index: p.89:
Bordeaux: J.S. to G. du Frère

14

January 1910

He dreamed that he was carrying Mademoiselle Clermont through the streets. The water he waded through was no longer icy, but hot and fragrant. The girl in his arms was incredibly light; he glanced down only for a sudden deluge to soak him from above.

He opened his eyes, spluttering out bitter, scented liquid. He was warm, blissfully warm, sitting in a metal tub with water up to his chest. He was also completely naked.

A hand appeared holding a bronze jug. Once again, hot water was poured over Gui's head. This time he held his breath under the stream until he was able to slick the hair back off his face and open his eyes. A stranger in black trousers and a pristine white shirt was wiping his hands on a cloth. He raised an eyebrow when he saw Gui looking and indicated the end of the tub with his chin. A dish had been balanced there, containing a sponge, a cloth and a round bar of soap.

'You can wash yourself, now that you're awake,' the stranger said brusquely. 'It took me half an hour to scrub away the top layer. Not an experience I relished.'

Face colouring, Gui picked up the soap. It had the same woody, spicy smell as the water and was soft, rather than the coarse, stinging blocks he was used to. He rubbed it tentatively over the sponge.

'I should start with the nails first, if I were you,' the other man sniffed, folding the hand towel. 'Unless you require a pick and hammer to clean them.'

For the first time, Gui peered around. He was in a kitchen, small but spotlessly clean. There were carved wood cabinets and a floor tiled in a complicated pattern. The tub had been set in front of a huge black stove.

On the floor was a newspaper-wrapped bundle. Gui recognized the corner of his jacket and lurched upright, slopping bathwater.

'What happened?' he demanded. 'Where's Mademoiselle Clermont?'

'Easy does it,' the stranger drawled, mopping at the puddle. 'The doctor has seen her, and says there's no real harm done. A hot bath and rest and she will be right as rain in a week or two.'

Gui sank back into the water, shaken. The stranger smirked slightly, but took pity on his confusion.

'You caused quite the stir, turning up at the tradesman's entrance like that,' he said, 'with Mademoiselle in your arms like a sack of potatoes. Naturally we all wondered what had happened, but you were insensible, so Monsieur ordered you to be generally cleansed and vivified. Which honour fell to me.'

'Who are you?' Gui's head had started to spin.

'Monsieur Clermont's valet.' The man raised an eyebrow. 'Do you intend to hold court in the

100

bath all night, like Marat?'

'Like who?'

'Never mind.' He sighed. 'Unless you get down to it, that water will turn cold, and apparently you *must* be kept warm. Doctor's orders. He saw to you briefly, said that you were frozen through, but looked tough enough. A meal and a hot bath were prescribed, although perhaps that was only an excuse to combat your extreme lack of hygiene . . . '

Gui's glare was wasted. His muscles felt as useless as string as he soaped the sponge and began washing. His efforts were accompanied by a commentary from Clermont's valet.

'My God, you do have a neck. I thought you had started a market garden in your collar. Try not to rub your head so hard, though, you'll frighten the lice.'

'I do not have lice!' Gui burst finally, throwing down the sponge in the cooling bath, which, admittedly, had taken on a grey hue. 'And I'd like to see you get clean with a bucket of frozen water after eight hours at a furnace.'

'A furnace?' The valet produced what looked like a tiny scrubbing brush. 'I see. Here, this will help.'

'What is it?' Gui baulked.

'This is a nail brush, and from the state of yours, it does not surprise me that its existence has hitherto been a mystery.'

The man started to scrub at Gui's nails with great zeal, but his tone softened.

'The railway, is it? You look young for such hard work.'

'I'm not so young.' Gui winced at the coarse bristles. 'I'll be nineteen in spring.'

'A ripe age. That must be why all of your clothes fit so badly. Speaking of which, I have been instructed to find you some.'

'My own are on the floor there.'

'I have not spent the past hour cleaning you for my work to be ruined by those sodden rags,' the man said sternly. 'They will be laundered, or burned if they are beyond salvation. I shall find some old spares of mine, unless you would enjoy wandering around the Clermonts' apartment in a bath sheet?'

The man bustled off, leaving Gui to haul himself regretfully out of the tub. It would be a long time before he had the chance to bathe in such luxury again. The bath towel was huge and warm and went on for ever. Safely wrapped, he paced the tiles as far as the door, but didn't dare to open it.

Here in the kitchen he was safe. He had the chance to be cleaner and better fed than he had been in months, and intended to make the most of it. Even though his legs shook with fatigue, he peered into every drawer and cupboard, dizzy with hunger. Finding nothing, he seated himself by the stove. The coppers threw back his reflection, pink and tousle-haired.

Waiting for the valet's return, he drifted into a doze. His eyes were so heavy that he barely noticed the noise of the door. Dressing seemed like a strenuous activity best avoided for as long as possible. It was only when the silence lengthened that he opened his eyes.

102

Monsieur Clermont stood there, one hand on the wall. He was dressed in a dark waistcoat and trousers, tailored perfectly to his slim frame. The sleeves of his fine shirt were carefully folded back and pinned.

They surveyed each other in silence. Gui's heart thudded to his throat.

'Who are you?' the older man demanded eventually.

Gui struggled to his feet, his mouth dry.

'My name's Guillaume, sir. Guillaume du Frère.'

Clermont's eyes remained fixed. They were the same blue as his daughter's, but narrower, deep lines stretching from the corners. They examined him, coldly.

'How is it that you come to be here?' he asked. 'My daughter tells me that you have worked in my pâtisserie, but I do not recall ever seeing you.'

Gui hitched the bath sheet a little higher.

'I helped with the deliveries, at Christmas, sir,' he stammered. 'Mademoiselle Clermont offered me the work.'

Clermont's face tightened.

'I see. But helping with deliveries is not your major occupation?'

'No, monsieur, I work for the railway.'

'Since you work for the railway,' he said, 'which I know for a fact is located on the Left Bank, how did you come to be here tonight?'

Gui swallowed. He could hear the anger, the suspicion, in Clermont's voice, barely contained. 'I heard from the news vendor at Austerlitz that

103

this district was going to be hit bad,' he tried to explain, 'water coming up from the tunnels and that. I remembered the kitchen here is below street level. I wanted to be of use . . . '

'Do not lie to me,' Clermont sneered. 'What did you do to my daughter?'

Gui's temper flared.

'I've done nothing, other than try to help,' he said angrily. 'I know two places in this city, my work and your pâtisserie. I couldn't help there, so I thought to lend a hand here. I would be sorry that I ever came, were it not for that fact that I was able to keep Mam'selle Clermont from harm . . . '

To his surprise, the older man held up his hand, rubbing at his eyes with the other.

'Very well, boy.' He sighed, studied Gui again. 'If I have been discourteous, blame a father's natural concern. A daughter is a precious thing, and Mademoiselle gave me cause for alarm. I suppose you should rest here tonight. Patrice will see that you have everything you need.'

The valet had entered silently from another door, a pile of neatly folded clothes in his arms.

'Put him in the guest bedroom, Patrice,' Clermont continued.

'Of course,' agreed the valet. 'Although may I make a suggestion, sir? The doctor recommended constant warmth. Seeing as the guest bedroom has not been aired, a bed set up by the stove might be better suited?'

'I leave him in your hands. I will speak to you in the morning, du Frère.'

Gui watched the door swing closed behind

104

Monsieur Clermont. He was already dreading the idea of another interview.

'Well, that was an impassioned speech you gave.' The valet was shaking out the clothes. 'With rhetoric like that, you should be on the stage. 'I would be sorry that I ever came!' Stirring.'

Gui took the clothes with a mocking smile. He unfolded clean underwear, much too large but serviceable, a pair of thick, brown trousers, a cream shirt with a small darn on the cuff, a matching brown waistcoat, a pair of slippers.

'There is a tie also,' Patrice told him. 'But at this stage in the proceedings, it would be gilding the lily.'

'Why should I not stay in the guest bedroom?' challenged Gui, hopping into the trousers. 'Are you afraid I'll steal the fittings?'

The valet gave a snort of laughter. 'Not at all. The guest bedroom was — how should I put this? — decorated by Monsieur's sister. I merely supposed that given today's excitements you would prefer something simpler.'

Gui had to admit that the valet was right. The thought of spending the night alone in a vast and expensive bedroom terrified him.

'Thank you,' he told the man, who was tying an apron over his elegant black suit.

'It is my job, young man, but in this case, also my pleasure. Now, I have been instructed to see you are fed. Monsieur has already taken supper, but I shall forage in the larder for another repast. No doubt the cook will berate me in the morning.'

The man disappeared into a small closet, whilst Gui lowered his aching limbs into a chair at the table.

'I suggest some of this broth that Cook made for Mademoiselle,' came Patrice's muffled voice. 'A little Toulouse sausage, some cheese perhaps . . .'

Gui wolfed down whatever was put in front of him, hunger a gnawing pit in his stomach. Fresh bread and butter, a savoury broth made from chicken, then sausage and a slab of cheese, cake made with pears, milk to drink. It was the best food he had ever tasted and he stuffed himself to capacity, knowing that he would not see a feast like this again for a very long time. Eventually tiredness forced him to slow, although he wished he could go on eating for ever.

Patrice, meanwhile, bustled about the kitchen, emptying the bath and stowing away the tub. Now he wrestled with the legs of a truckle bed. While he wasn't looking, Gui snatched up the leftover food, wrapped it in a napkin and hid it in the jacket, to take back for Nicolas. Then he stood to help, his stomach like an inflated balloon. Patrice kept up his constant stream of humorous insults, but despite the jibes, Gui realized that he liked the valet.

Later, he lay sleepily between crisp sheets. The kitchen lamps had been dimmed to a soft glow. It must have been late, but Patrice had promised to keep him company. He sat, smoking foreign tobacco in his shirtsleeves.

'Why did you return to the pâtisserie today?'

Gui stirred at the sound of the valet's voice.

The older man looked down at him, the question in his eyes.

'For Mademoiselle,' Gui told him, too exhausted to lie. 'I came for Mademoiselle Clermont.'

He did not see the valet's face turn serious, surveying the ash that hung from the end of his cigarette, nor hear his mumbled response, many minutes later.

'As I feared.'

15

April 1988

The book lies open in my lap. I've read the relevant page a hundred times already, but I turn to it again.

Sending a letter was an unreliable business in early twentieth-century France: especially when a recipient did not want to be found. Hopeful correspondents were often left to the mercy of the regional system, under the wider Post and Telegraph Office. Lacking a correct address, the best a letter writer could do was to address their message POSTE RESTANTE to the nearest town office and hope that the receiver might one day turn up to look for it.

An excellent surviving example exists in the form of twenty such letters, delivered to the central office of La Poste in Bordeaux between mid 1910 and 1914. The sender in each case gave only the initials, 'J.S.' on the reverse of the envelope. The post office ledger indicated that the intended recipient, a Monsieur G. du Frère, collected the first of these missives, yet never returned for any that followed.

The letters cease after 1914, no doubt due to the continent-wide devastation wrought by the Great War. Being one of the best surviving examples of pre-war poste-restante correspondence, the majority of the collection is held in storage at The Musée de La Poste, Paris, except for one letter, which is in the hands of an archivist. Due to laws surrounding secrecy of correspondence, the seals on the envelopes have never yet been broken. As such, we are unlikely ever to know the story behind this remarkable collection.

I close the book with a sigh. The elation that came with the discovery in the library has long faded. Now, to add to the mysterious photograph, I have a story of undelivered mail. Linked to 'du Frère', the initials 'J.S.' can't be a coincidence; they must refer to my grandfather. But even if they do, what does it prove? I know less than when I started.

Cass and I are on our way down to London. She's going to a new exhibition, while I pay a visit to the newspaper archive, to see if they have a copy of my grandfather's article. I shouldn't be here. I should be in my room working, but the desire to read the article — the hope that it will be the missing piece — is just too strong to ignore.

The day is warm as we emerge into King's Cross. Cass wishes me luck, arranges to meet me at the library in a few hours' time. I plunge onto the tube to head north. It's quiet in Colindale, a lazy Saturday afternoon, but by the time I approach the stark, brick library I'm buzzing with excitement.

I enquire at the front desk about finding a copy of *The Word*. The librarian checks her records; as I hoped, they have it archived. She tells me that since the publication was short lived, the entire back catalogue is available on one roll of microfilm, along with a few other English-language newspapers. I begin to fill in a request slip, but she frowns down at the clipboard in front of her.

'Seems it's already out,' she says briskly, 'accessed about an hour ago. Do you want to go and find whoever has it, see if you can take over afterwards?'

I follow her directions to a room at the back of the building, apprehension growing in my stomach. Who else — apart from me — could possibly be interested in one obscure newspaper article? Sure enough, a figure is hunched in front of a monitor, dressed in a familiar pullover. I swear and turn away. Too late.

'Petra!' Hall's voice reaches out into the hallway.

Reluctantly, I retrace my steps. He has risen from his chair, blinking after the brightness of the viewer. I cross my arms, ready to stand my ground, though part of me twists uncomfortably at the memory of taking the Allincourt letter from his folder in the middle of the night.

'What?' I demand.

'Petra, we've . . . got off to a bad start.' He smiles weakly. 'I behaved appallingly last time we met. I'm sorry.'

I don't move. He takes this as permission to continue.

'I'll admit, I hadn't realized how close you were to Stevenson, but your mother filled me in, about the problems with your dad, and the divorce . . . ' He trails off, perhaps sensing it isn't the wisest topic. 'Look, I don't want to cause upset,' he finishes, rubbing his temples, 'or to make either of our lives difficult. How about we try to stay out of each other's way from now on? Make this as painless as possible.'

I'm not sure what game he's playing, with this sudden change of tone. I shrug non-committally, hoping that will satisfy him.

'Fine.'

'Good.' He smiles shrewdly. 'Now, I suspect you're here to look at *The Word*?'

I can't help the blood rushing to my cheeks. 'You know I am.'

'Well, I'm finished with it,' he says, scooping up his papers and notebooks. 'How about we make a deal? You take a look now, and when you're finished, we have a chat about the Allincourt letter. Would you be willing to let me take a copy? Then we can leave each other be.'

Suspicion threatens to hold me back, but the article is right in front of me: once I've read it, I'll know what my grandpa did. I'll know whether Hall has a real case. *What if he does?* a small voice hisses in a corner of my mind, but I ignore it, dump my bag on a chair. Hall is still fiddling with his papers as I settle down in front of the monitor.

'I can see why you don't get along with your father, if it's any consolation,' he says abruptly.

I turn in surprise. He looks up from his

111

packing and grimaces.

'I've offended you again — '

'No,' I agree, though my voice is cautious. 'We're not the best of friends. It's no secret.'

Hall pauses.

'What happened? If you don't mind me asking.' His face is crumpled with concern as he perches upon the desk. 'Between them? Your dad and Stevenson?'

I stare at him, trying to see through his act, but he seems sincere. I guess there's no harm in setting him straight.

'Dad's career, more than anything,' I tell him bluntly. 'Grandpa hated the tabloids. He said they ruined people's lives, picking up their weaknesses and mistakes and parading them about for the world to jeer at. He used to say that no one had the right to do that.'

Hall has the decency to look awkward. He mutters something about leaving me to it, says he'll meet me in the entrance hall in ten minutes, when I've finished reading.

Relieved to be rid of him, I scoot forward on the seat and begin to crank the handle. The article is no longer on the screen. I search back through the microfilm for the correct date. The pages scroll past my eyes, tiny print leaving patterns on my retina. When I still haven't found it after a minute or two, I reach for my bag, for the reference number on the request form that I shoved in there.

My hand closes upon nothing. It's gone, and so is Hall.

16

January 1910

'But why does he want to see me?' Gui whispered, his stomach churning as Patrice pushed him along the corridor.

'Ours is not to guess why, young man. You have been summoned, that is all. Try not to hunch, it will stretch the jacket.'

A door opened onto a grand room, half panelled with dark wood and lined with books. Gui had never seen so many in his life. It was warm, a fire crackling in the grate. Monsieur Clermont was sitting at a small table, next to a stranger. He beckoned Gui over to a chair.

Gui obeyed, the carpet deep and soft beneath his shoes. He looked around for Patrice, but the valet had disappeared.

'Du Frère,' said Clermont, 'this' is Monsieur Edouard Burnett, an old friend of this family. Edouard, this is the young man I told you of, Guillaume du Frère.'

The second man said nothing, but offered his hand. He had a neat, black beard and a face marred by pockmarks. Beads of rain clung to his oiled hair, the only thing that hinted at the biblical conditions outside. Gui gripped the proffered hand, alarmed at its softness. His own fingers were rough with calluses along the joints, scored with burns from the furnaces.

'Monsieur Burnett and I have something of import to discuss with you, du Frère. Will you take a cup of coffee?'

Gui blinked in confusion. Patrice had reappeared, a tray balanced on his arm. He stared at the silver pot, the delicate china, and tried to recall what few manners he had learned from his mother.

'Thank you,' he managed, as Monsieur Clermont poured for him. 'You have been very generous.'

'You did not think me so last night,' the older man pointed out. 'In fact, you were most indignant. Sugar?'

'I . . . I did not . . . ' Gui stuttered.

'I am jesting, du Frère.'

Clermont poured for himself and settled back. Burnett was not joining them.

'Now,' he said, 'I want you to tell me about yourself. Where are you from? That accent is not of the Île-de-France.'

'Bordeaux,' Gui answered. The coffee was hot and burned his lip. He tried to keep his eyes from watering. There was a silence. He had the feeling that Clermont and Burnett were holding a private conversation in their heads.

Unsure what to do, Gui took another sip of coffee.

'Does your family have a trade?' Clermont pressed.

'No, sir. My mother works in a factory.'

'But your father?'

'He's dead.'

'I see,' the older man said slowly. 'What did he work at, before?'

114

'Labouring. He died the same year I was born. My grandfather raised me, mostly. He was a plasterer.'

'A noble profession.'

'As noble as yours,', he rejoined, before he could stop himself.

There was a silence, as though he had dropped a handful of mud onto the polished table. Both men were staring at him.

The door squeaked, breaking the stillness. They all three looked up. Mademoiselle Clermont stood in the doorway. She was dressed in a patterned, satin robe and was leaning on a crutch. Evidently, she hadn't expected them to be there, for her hand flew to her neck and then she was gone, the door juddering behind her.

At the table, Monsieur Clermont sighed.

'My daughter. I am afraid she has grown into a rather wilful young woman.'

'She has been spoiled.'

The unfamiliar voice belonged to Burnett. Gui glanced over, shocked that the man would speak so openly.

'You have been blessed with three boys, Edouard. Sons are infinitely less trouble than a daughter.' Clermont shifted his bulk in the delicate chair. 'Monsieur Burnett is not only a friend, du Frère. He is my business partner, and in charge of my legal affairs. Do you understand what that means?'

Gui nodded slowly, although he did not, entirely.

'Reputation is everything in this city,' Clermont continued. 'The rich are meticulous about

115

where they place their custom. My establishment cannot be touched by scandal. Monsieur Burnett is right; my daughter has been over-indulged. Now she has behaved in a way that might serve to ruin her prospects. I will be blunt. Do you intend to tell anyone of what transpired yesterday?'

'No, I . . . I'd have no one to tell.'

'Do not play us for fools, boy,' Burnett said, though he remained perfectly motionless. Gui felt as though he were being watched by a spider. 'How much will it cost to ensure you do not gossip about what happened? Come now, your sort always know the value of these things.'

Gui could only gape in anger. He surged to his feet, although for what purpose he did not know. Burnett only watched him with disdain.

'Is that what you think of me?' Gui spluttered. 'That I came here looking for *money*?'

'Well, what do you want?' Monsieur Clermont asked coolly. Both men remained unruffled by his outburst. It made him feel like a child throwing a tantrum. 'I remain mystified as to your motives, du Frère,' Clermont continued. 'If I believed you had come here to take advantage of my daughter, you would be sitting behind bars right now. In which case, I can only assume that you are looking to turn this situation to your advantage — '

'I don't want your money,' Gui interrupted, his heart beginning to race. 'That isn't why I came.'

'Yes, we established that . . . ' Clermont said with mock patience.

'I want a job.' The words tumbled out of Gui before he could prepare himself. 'A job,' he forced himself to repeat, 'here, in the pâtisserie. I don't care what the work is and I swear, I'll never breathe a word to anyone about what happened yesterday if you agree.'

He tried to hold his chin straight, but couldn't bring himself to look either man in the face. He could feel their astonishment, and for one, dreadful moment he thought that they would start laughing. Finally, Clermont spoke.

'A job,' he said slowly, the hint of a smile twitching his lip. 'I must admit I am surprised, if not wholly shocked. The request may not be quite so absurd as it sounds.'

'If I may — ' Burnett protested with a sneer.

'I must interrupt you, Edouard,' said Clermont. 'I know what you will say, that the boy has no experience, little schooling. However, these are modern times. They seem to suit the bold and the young.'

Eyes were turned upon him again.

'This will ensure your permanent discretion?' Clermont asked seriously.

'Yes,' Gui swore. 'I promise.'

'Very well, du Frère. I cannot guarantee that you will succeed in my kitchen, but you shall have your chance.'

He rose gracefully, shook Gui's hand once, firmly, before returning to his seat.

'Monsieur Burnett shall be in touch.'

He knew a dismissal when he heard it. The next thing he knew he was standing alone, outside of the dark doors, in a daze.

'A chance,' he whispered, too shaken up for joy. 'I have a chance . . .'

'Indeed you do.' Patrice had appeared from nowhere to take his elbow. 'And now, young du Frère, I'm afraid it is time for you to leave.'

'Did you hear that?' Gui asked, as he was ushered back to the kitchen, in order to change into his own clothes. They had been laundered, but in comparison to the borrowed suit of Patrice's, they looked like rags. He was too elated to care. 'I'm to be a chef.'

'An *apprentice* chef,' Patrice corrected, folding the garments that Gui had shed, 'and of course I heard. It is my job to hear.'

At the front door, the valet pressed a package into his arms. It contained the suit that he had loaned to Gui, neatly wrapped in brown paper. 'I will not miss it,' he said firmly over Gui's attempts at thanks, 'and I believe you shall need it.'

He caught Gui's shoulder as he left, his face strangely serious.

'Du Frère,' he murmured, 'be careful.'

Outside the floodwaters had begun to subside. It was deep enough still for a small boat, like the one that rocked gently near the doors to the apartments above the pâtisserie, a chauffeur squatting in the prow. It no doubt belonged to Monsieur Burnett. Holding the packet of borrowed clothes carefully under his arm, Gui stepped into the water. His entire skin shuddered as the world of hot baths and good food and fine coffee drained away into the cold.

He heard voices from the front of the building.

' . . . your actions would not be my own,' Burnett was saying.

'My actions are frequently unlike those of other men,' answered Clermont.

'As you like, it is your decision.'

'I am obliged, Edouard. What were your impressions?'

'Of the boy? I would not tolerate him in my business, but I suppose he seems honest enough. Although you should be wary; his kind can be cunning, if not intelligent.'

Gui inched forward. *Eavesdroppers never hear well of themselves*, his grandfather had always said.

'If taking him on will ensure that there is no gossip about Jeanne, then I shall keep to my side of the bargain.'

Jeanne, Gui felt an odd surge of happiness at the discovery. *Her name is Jeanne.*

'Let us hope that is the case.' Wood creaked as Burnett climbed into his boat. 'Even so, you should take steps to correct your daughter's waywardness,' he told Clermont, 'before it is too late.'

Gui listened to the boat as it wallowed down the street, aware that on the other side of the wall, Monsieur Clermont was doing the same.

17

April 1988

By the time I run into the entrance hall, it is empty. At the front desk, the librarian eyes me sternly. A concerned gentleman handed my bag in a few minutes ago, she says, after finding it unattended. She chides me for being careless, and tells me how lucky I am that my money has not been stolen.

I fight back tears of frustration. I don't need to look to know what has been taken, but I do anyway. The folder with all of my evidence is gone: the letter, the photograph, my notes. The library book is still there, but that gives little comfort.

Cass finds me not long afterwards, sitting outside on the steps. She realizes that something is wrong the second she sees my face.

'It was Hall,' I tell her, still trembling with rage.

'What? What happened?'

'Hall, the biographer, he was here.' I stare hopelessly into the bag. 'We talked for a while — I thought we'd sorted things out — but then I turned around for a minute, and he took it, the letter, the photograph, everything.'

'He can't do that,' she says incredulously. 'They're yours, it's stealing — '

'It's all part of Grandpa Jim's estate.' The

words are bitter in my mouth. 'None of it's mine.'

'Even so, can't you call him out? Insist that he gives back the papers? They're still your family's property.'

I shake my head. 'Either of my parents could contradict me, Dad especially. He'll just tell Hall to keep whatever he wants for as long as he wants.'

Cass sighs in understanding. We sit in silence for a while.

'At least you know some of the facts now?' Cass tries.

'It's not enough,' I tell her flatly. 'Now I can't challenge Hall, even if I wanted to. I have no proof.'

Cass looks over at me searchingly. She's a good friend, and doesn't say anything, but I can see the question that is running through her mind, the same one that Alex asked: *Is this really about Hall?*

For a long time we sit on the stone steps, warmed by the sun. Finally, I summon up the courage to voice a thought that has been plaguing me for weeks now.

'I don't think that photograph was forgotten.'

In the wake of the words I watch the traffic, the pigeons crowding along the grey pavement.

'It was hidden, not lost. The edges were all worn. I think he must have looked at it again and again over the years.'

Cass considers my words.

'Perhaps it reminded him of better times?'

'No.' I screw my eyes closed. 'I've been such

an idiot. I didn't want to know, but it all makes sense.'

I look across at her, swallowing hard.

'Cass, I think Hall's right. I think my grandpa did something wrong when he was young, something awful, and he regretted it for the rest of his life.'

18

February 1910

Two days later the envelope arrived, bearing his name in fine, curled writing. He weighed the letter in his hand, relishing the feeling. He rarely received correspondence, and never as fine as this.

His fingers left dirty smudges on the thick paper, though he tried his best to wipe them. Only after examining every detail of the front did he turn it over. A foil seal, embossed with 'Burnett & Sons' protected the contents. He broke it and pulled out the page. It was a typewritten letter of employment; his name leaped out at him here and there, amongst the official-looking words.

Gui winced when the foreman threw down the letter after half a glance. 'You best be leaving then,' the big man grunted, extracting a key from his pocket. 'No sense making trouble among the others.'

He thumped a moneybox on top of the letter, adding rust stains to the pristine lines of ink. 'Pay to date,' he said tersely, 'no severance for breaking your contract.'

Gui tried to smile as he took the pay packet. The foreman did not.

'I hope you know what you're doing, lad.'

In the dormitory, Gui changed into the suit

borrowed from Patrice. Fortunately, it was lunch time and the place was empty save for him and Nicolas, who stood smoking in the doorway.

'Where are you going to sleep?' his friend asked awkwardly.

'I'm not sure,' Gui said as he shoved his old clothes into the suitcase. 'I hope they will have arranged something.'

'They won't.'

'You don't know that.'

Nicolas only looked down and flicked ash onto the floor.

Things had not been the same since the flood. The night Gui had spent in the Clermonts' apartment had changed him. The work, the quarters, it all looked dirty and old to him now; like a memory already. The grime beneath his nails had begun to disgust him. He picked it away as best he could with a penknife.

It was too cold to wash, but he hunted about for a rag to wipe his neck, before any dirt stained the shirt collar. A flash of cloth near the roof caught his eye and he pulled at it. An object tumbled free. It was the book. Monsieur Carême had survived the weather, old and mildewed and dog-eared though he was. Nicolas watched as Gui smoothed the volume and stowed it reverently in his jacket pocket.

Before the threshold Gui stopped. His friend, his oldest friend, had finished the cigarette and stood, fingers twitching in a dance, squinting out into the grey noon light.

'So long, Nicolas. Tell the others for me.'

'They won't understand.' His friend sighed,

and summoned a twist of a smile. Gui gripped his shoulder, pulled him into a tight hug. Nicolas returned it before stepping back, clearing his throat.

'See you then, Gui.'

Gui's eyes stung. He blinked them clear. 'Luck, Nicolas.'

An omnibus was waiting in the Place d'Italie. Thinking of the pay in his pocket, Gui allowed himself the luxury of buying a ticket almost to the door of the pâtisserie.

'Coming or going?' the ticket inspector asked, nudging the suitcase at Gui's feet.

'Going. New job over the river.'

'Best of luck with it, sir.'

It was a typical February day, cold and drear with a heavy sky. The floodwater had receded, leaving behind flotsam in the strangest of places, like the aftermath of a night of revelry.

The Boulevard des Italiens was busy, full of men and women bundled against the cold. Motor cars honked, weaving between horses that stood impassive in the gutters. A black and white dog rushed between hooves, barking at the trees where pigeons squatted, like old feathered fruit in the branches.

Opposite was Pâtisserie Clermont. Gui stared, for he had never seen it by day. Great arched windows let out a golden light, sparkling upon the glass and beckoning him closer. Beyond, he caught glimpses of gilt and marble, of a grand counter that hugged the edge of the room, the produce of the miraculous kitchen displayed within, like jewellery. Hefting his suitcase a little higher, Gui pushed open the front door.

Warmth swirled around him; engulfing him in the smell of fresh baking, chocolate and coffee. Tall, fronded plants arched gracefully, straight from a tropical garden. Chatter, clinking and laughter filled the room. Women sat straight-backed in their chairs, men — all starch and shine — smoked lazily.

'Can I help you?'

One of the waiters was eyeing him with disdain. In the dormitory, Patrice's old suit had made him feel like a gentleman, but here his cracked boots and peeling suitcase gave him away.

'I'm here to see Monsieur Clermont,' he said clearly.

'Do you have an appointment with him?' the waiter asked.

'No, he has offered me a job — '

'Monsieur Clermont is busy. You will have to return another day.'

He was being ushered towards the door. Another waiter watched them steadily whilst pouring coffee.

'You don't understand,' Gui tried again. 'He is expecting me.'

'I don't think so.'

The waiter forced him forward. They were almost at the door when he saw her.

'Mademoiselle!' he cried.

She was sitting several tables away, in the company of another woman and a man. At his shout they stared, began to whisper to each other. The waiter increased his efforts to thrust

126

Gui onto the street. He grabbed the doorframe. 'Mademoiselle!'

'It is all right, Ricard,' she called, rising hurriedly to her feet. 'I know him.'

She apologized to her friend and to the man, who looked up from a sketchpad curiously. Several other tables had also turned to look. Mademoiselle Clermont crossed the few feet between them, limping slightly. Instinctively, Gui held out a hand to steady her, but the waiter batted him away.

'Monsieur du Frère, good afternoon,' she began coolly. 'Ricard, you may leave us now.'

Another table signalled for attention. The waiter looked torn. He threw Gui a filthy look, but finally bustled away. Mademoiselle Clermont transferred her hand to his arm for support. A pale lace dress rose to the top of her throat. She wore cream satin gloves. As soon as the waiter was gone, she turned her face away from her friends, and gave him her rare smile.

'Guillaume, what are you doing here?' she whispered.

'Your father offered me employment, last week,' Gui told her. 'I received a letter this morning, and am here to take up the position.'

Mademoiselle Clermont looked astonished.

'I did not know,' she said. 'How . . . ? But never mind. I am so glad you are here. I had not thought to see you again, and had no address to reach you by.'

'What for?' The thought of Mademoiselle Clermont writing to him was too much to comprehend.

'To say thank you, of course! So I shall say it now: thank you, Monsieur du Frère. You have my gratitude.'

Gui made the mistake of looking into her eyes. Abruptly, he found it rather difficult to breathe.

'It was nothing,' he murmured.

She returned his gaze. Their silence lengthened for a beat too long, sending him scrabbling in his pocket.

'Here, this is the letter I received this morning.'

She shook it open with her free hand. A frown wrinkled her forehead.

'But this is from Monsieur Burnett . . . '

Mademoiselle Clermont's friend called over discreetly, indicating the man with the sketchpad who had half-risen to his feet. She nodded at them.

'Come with me,' she told Gui. 'I will take you to the office. Leave your case. Ricard will put it in the cloakroom.'

'I can find it on my own,' he protested, 'you are busy, I don't want to interrupt — '

Mademoiselle waved her hand dismissively.

'Do not concern yourself. My friend Lili arranged for us to pose for a portrait by her friend Monsieur Ahlers. But he has spent more time eating than drawing, so far. They will not miss me for a few minutes.'

Obediently, Gui set down his case near a waiters' station. He wondered briefly if he would ever see it again. Before they set off, he cast a look over at the artist Mademoiselle had referred to. He was brushing pastry crumbs from his

128

board. A figure had been sketched on the white surface, only a few lines, but he could tell it was Mademoiselle Clermont.

Unexpectedly, Gui felt a surge of jealousy for the man who was able to sit respectably in Mademoiselle's company, where he could not.

They moved towards the back of the café. Gui couldn't help but notice that they traversed the outside edge of the room unobtrusively, rather than taking a path straight through the middle, but still, many pairs of eyes followed them.

'The people here are such horrible gossips,' Mademoiselle Clermont whispered, viewing the room with mild disgust. 'It may be wise to use the tradesman's entrance in future, Guillaume.'

Her voice was kind, but still he felt the barb that lurked within her words. Swallowing, he changed the subject.

'Your ankle, does it still hurt?'

To his surprise, she broke into a smile.

'It will mend. Luckily, it is not the same one I twisted previously, when I fell at the station.' She shot him a side-long glance and he felt his face turn crimson. He braced himself for the accusation, but it did not come.

Warmth emanated from her gloved hand into the crook of his arm. They passed another table and Mademoiselle nodded in greeting to its occupants.

'Might I ask,' she continued quietly, 'what was the nature of the agreement you made with my father and Monsieur Burnett? When I saw you in the study with them, I worried that they might have assumed the worst.' A blush crept up her cheeks, but she held her head straight.

'They offered me employment here.' Gui thought it best not to mention the conditions. 'A reward, I think, for making sure you did not come to harm. Your father has not mentioned it at all?'

'We are not on speaking terms.' Her face was tight.

'Is he angry with you?'

'Yes, and I with him.'

'You did get yourself into trouble,' Gui ventured, 'going out alone in the flood like that.'

'Yes, I did. But I only wanted to help. Father does not seem to realize that.'

'I'm sure he was simply scared for you.'

Even as he said it, Gui remembered Clermont's words to Burnett, about a daughter being more trouble than many sons. Mademoiselle must have been thinking similar thoughts, for she only sighed and shook her head as they stopped before a door marked '*Privée*'.

'This leads to the back entrance hall,' she told him. 'Take the door towards the kitchens and then knock at the first room on the left. That's the office. Ask for Josef.'

'Thank you, Mam'selle.'

'Good luck, Guillaume.'

She removed her hand. Nerves rushed in to take its place and he wished, irrationally, that she would go with him.

19

April 1988

The last thing I wanted to find on my return to Cambridge was a message from Professor Kaufmann. The official summons was waiting in my pigeonhole, bearing my name in her neat handwriting.

On Monday morning, I trudge through town, terrified of being late. I linger in the marketplace, chewing at my already bitten nails. It is busy, as always. A bright sun shines determinedly through the chill breeze, pushing in from across the fens. There are people here lounging, drinking coffee on outside tables, thick mugs at their elbows and cigarettes in hand. I wish I was one of them.

Miserably, I turn into Kaufmann's college. It is one of the oldest and grandest in the university. I walk across the main court, blind to the imposing architecture. I know I should be grateful to be granted time with one of the department's most respected professors, but all I can feel is dread, and a certainty that this is not going to go at all well.

Kaufmann's office is in the cloister. The walls here are permanently cold and shadowed. I hunch my denim jacket tighter and brave the old wooden stairs. The creaking announces my arrival long before I reach the top step; a crisp

131

voice calls for me to enter as I raise a hand to knock.

Kaufmann's room, by contrast, is bright. It smells of lilies, is impeccably organized. The books are housed neatly in tall shelves, and the professor sits at a coffee table that is empty save for a folder of papers and a copy of my thesis. I grimace inwardly. Even from a distance it looks scruffy, the type misaligned on the pages.

'Petra,' she greets, without standing up, 'take a seat.'

I sink too heavily into her sofa. Kaufmann places her glasses upon her nose. She is in her early forties, elegant and polished, her fair hair swept back into a coil. I push my own untidy bob behind my ears.

'I . . . ' I begin.

'Thank you for these.' She speaks over me steadily, picking up my pages. 'I read them this morning. I was wondering if you were confused, however, since you have only sent your most recent chapters. I was expecting the entirety of the draft.'

I wedge my hands between my knees, trying to control my nerves.

'That is it, the draft.'

She looks at me in mild surprise.

'This,' she asks, 'is all you have?'

'Professor Whyke and I — '

'Professor Whyke is not responsible for whether you complete your work on time,' Kaufmann replies, leafing through the pages, 'or whether you take it seriously.'

132

'I am taking it seriously,' I say, rather too defensively.

Kaufmann flips the chapters onto the table before me.

'From the state of these, I disagree. This isn't undergraduate work, Petra. I am not going to baby you through what should be second nature by now. You know that this isn't good enough.'

'I'm working on something new.' I force myself to stay calm. 'No one has documented it before, and there's already interest from the historical community.'

'Ah, yes,' Kaufmann rests her elbow on the arm of her chair, 'Whyke mentioned. A new surprise about your grandfather.'

When I am silent, she sighs.

'Petra, I have been asked to work with you, but I shall only continue to do so if we make one thing clear between us. I don't say this to be cruel, but you must know that far more talented researchers than yourself were not accepted as doctoral candidates by the university.'

I clench my teeth. As much as I want to hate this woman, there's a part of me that knows she's right.

'Whatever it was that prompted the department's decision to award you a place — '

'You mean my grandfather?' I interrupt.

'Whatever it was,' she says firmly, 'you have been given a remarkable opportunity. One that you seem determined to squander.'

'You're wrong,' I protest, but my voice is wavering.

Kaufmann leans forward and picks up her journal, calm as ever.

'Then prove me so. We shall start at the beginning.'

20

February 1910

'Can you read?'

Gui nodded, the stiff collar scraping his neck. For the first time in his life he was wearing an entire outfit of new clothes. White trousers, white jacket, apron, hat, all starched and pristine. They did not belong to him, Josef — the kitchen manager — told him severely, but were property of the pâtisserie and to be treated as such.

He may dirty the apron whilst working, but never the sleeves or the front of the jacket. Each apprentice had two uniforms, which were laundered thrice a week. If he forgot to include his clothes for laundering, his pay would be docked until the next laundry day. Pay would also be docked for dirty nails, dirty hair, muddy shoes or an incorrectly tied apron.

He was to start in the kitchen with the newest apprentices. He was not to touch the ingredients or any of the produce, but would observe and assist by collecting pans, moulds and utensils, washing and tidying after the more senior chefs. He was never to go into the pâtisserie itself unless absolutely necessary.

'You are the lowest rung of the bottom ladder,' Josef told him, demonstrating the correct way to wrap the apron around his waist. 'Keep your head down, your eyes open and maybe you'll learn something.'

There was no unkindness in his voice, but no warmth either.

'You have one month to prove that you can fit into the kitchen and work hard. Do you understand everything I've said?'

Gui nodded, although he had no idea how he was going to remember it all. A foreign land, a strange, bright world, he thought as Josef whisked him into the kitchens, and his heart leaped at the spectacle of it all.

If possible, the place was busier than he had ever seen. There was no sign of the flood that had threatened so recently; everything looked spotless. The workers, too, in immaculate white, were moving so fast it seemed like a dance, chefs weaving between each other, hands finding the objects they needed from memory: Gui could see no one standing still. He had anticipated a leap into the unknown, but he felt utterly lost.

'Service runs straight through the day,' Josef continued, steering through the activity like the prow of a ship. 'The afternoon is a busy time and you will have to be on your toes, because the next sitting begins,' he glanced up at a huge clock hanging at the far end of the kitchen, 'in ten minutes. A roster of breaks will begin at six. You will be in the last group. Ebersole,' he snapped at a balding chef nearby, 'new boy.'

Gui turned to ask what he would be doing, but the large chef was gone, striding towards the front of the room, examining workbenches as he went. The chef he had called Ebersole barely glanced up. He was leaning in close to a tray, inspecting row upon row of what looked like fat pastry fingers. An apprentice followed behind, flipping the fingers over onto their backs. Two more young chefs stood by, conical bags clutched at the ready. Ebersole frowned over the last tray and shook his head.

Gui found the tray thrust into his arms. There was nothing wrong with the pastries, so far as he could see, apart from the fact they look darker than the others. Ebersole barked something at him in German and moved away, clapping the younger chefs into action. No one was watching; Gui's shaking hand strayed towards the pastries, his stomach clamouring.

'Do not even think about eating them,' a low voice rumbled in his ear. 'Put them in the refuse sack. It's by the door.'

The man who had spoken swept past. Gui caught a glimpse of a lean face, a waxed brown moustache and a forehead that shone with perspiration. Reluctantly, he approached the refuse sack. It was full of similar examples of near-perfect baking, muddled together with scraps of paper, eggshells, spoiled cream.

Quick as a flash, he snatched up two pastry ends and shoved them into a pocket, tipping the rest away. Back at the workbench, two apprentices were moving from opposite ends, using metal nozzles to fill the pastry cases with fluffy cream. The chef with the moustache stood in the middle, holding a wide pan of slick, brown chocolate.

Ebersole lifted the filled pastries, floated them

in the chocolate and whipped them out, swiping off the excess with his thumb. The process was repeated until thirty pastries lay glistening on the trays, all in decreasing sizes, all perfect. A completed tray was shoved at him. The scent of cocoa was overpowering, and it was all he could do to stop himself from stuffing one of the confections into his mouth.

'Take them to the cold room,' the helpful chef whispered.

When he returned, Ebersole had vanished and there was something of a lull.

'Thank you,' Gui said to the man with the moustache. 'I don't know any German.'

'Neither did I. And he isn't German, he's Swiss. Try not to get it confused.'

'I will, I mean, I won't.'

'I'm Maurice,' the man added, offering the back of his wrist. His hands, Gui noticed, were coated with chocolate. 'No time to talk now, just try to follow the others. We're making a religieuse, nothing too fancy for a Wednesday.'

Before he could say anything else, Ebersole was back, flanked by apprentices, trays balanced up their arms. The process began again. His arms were piled with rejected pastries; those deemed acceptable were covered with a lighter shade of chocolate until there were just as many as before. Returning from the cold room, he found a hushed group around Ebersole. The man was shaping circles from a soft, creamy clay substance with a tiny cutter wheel.

'*Schablone*,' he demanded under his breath.

Nobody moved. The apprentices' faces were

138

ashen as they stared at each other. Ebersole looked up in frustration.

'*Schablone*, the stencil, we are making a religieuse, no?'

'He means the mould we use for the headpiece,' Maurice hissed. 'Monsieur Clermont commissioned a new one a few weeks back, but I have no idea where they put it — '

Before he could finish, Gui was racing away towards the back of the room, towards the dresser he had piled with boxes, seemingly so long ago.

'Moulds, Goebel . . . ' He scanned feverishly, picturing his trips to and from the handcart, until he saw a little box with the Goebel stamp, 'religieuse' scrawled across it in pencil. He was back before the other apprentices had moved.

Suspiciously, Ebersole glanced inside the box, extracted a small metal mould. Gui received one hard look.

'*Bon*,' barked the chef.

The confection took another hour to complete. Maurice told him that the different coloured pastries were called éclairs and were flavoured with chocolate and coffee. They were balanced upon their ends in a circle until they spiralled upward in rows. A fat, round pastry went on top like a head, crowned with Ebersole's sugar work in the shape of a winged headdress.

'It looks like a nun!' Gui exclaimed.

Maurice gave him an odd look. He was balancing a card amongst the rows of piped cream. The word 'Clermont' looped in gold upon a green background. As soon as he let go, two apprentices lifted the religieuse onto a trolley.

Gui watched it disappear through the doors into the pâtisserie.

'What happens now?' he whispered to Maurice.

'Now, lad,' the older man told him, wiping his forehead on his apron, 'we do it all again.'

21

May 1988

Five o'clock. My shadow lengthens as I cross the courtyard. Inside, it is cool and quiet. I give my eyes time to adjust after the glare of paving stones and river. For once, I am not late. In my bag is a request form from the Newspaper Library. After the business with Hall, I never had a chance to go back and read the article.

For a while, I wasn't sure whether I even wanted to. I'd been driven by the desire to prove Hall wrong, to show him that my grandfather was a good man, that there was nothing shameful in his past. But now I suspect that isn't true. Cass tried to persuade me to let it go; she reminded me that I wasn't responsible for my grandfather's actions or reputation, that I had my own life to think about.

She is right, of course, but at the same time, the thought of Hall unearthing the secret that Grandpa Jim kept for so many years turns my stomach. In the end, I realize that I have already made up my mind. If anyone is going to find out what happened that summer in 1910, it's going to be me.

Which means breaking the promise I made to Kaufmann: that I would give up the research and concentrate on my thesis. I battle my conscience into submission. It can't be helped. I will never be able to persuade her to sign the request form for the Newspaper Library, but hopefully, I'll be able to slip it past Whyke.

My dress flaps around my ankles as I climb the stairs, summer cotton with a flower print. I've made an effort, for once, to appear neat and well prepared, but now all I am aware of is how the buttons strain across my chest. Of course, Whyke won't notice. I could walk into his office naked, wearing a bearskin, and he'd only ask me if I wanted tea.

'Ah, Petra,' he flaps when I arrive, searching for his notebook, 'your end-of-year review has been scheduled. Two weeks from today, like we thought. You might want to make a note of the date.'

My stomach drops as I scribble down the appointment. Whyke is still talking; I force myself to listen.

' . . . by this stage I'd normally expect to see a final draft, but I imagine Dr Kaufmann will take care of that.'

I nod, after the decision I've made, I feel more than a little ill at the idea of another meeting.

'I thought we could use our time on practical things, like your bibliography,' Whyke says, writing in his notepad with the wrong end of a pen. He is more preoccupied than usual, but I decide to take the plunge.

'There's one last bit of research I'd like to check out beforehand.' I try to sound casual as I pull out the request form. 'It wasn't available when I checked, but the library said you'd be able to order me a copy of the microfilm.'

I surreptitiously scrub my hands dry on the dress as Whyke grabs the form and starts to tick boxes. He has reached the signature line when the biro pauses, hovering above the paper.

'Remind me, have we talked about this source before? What is it, exactly?'

'It's an English-language newspaper from Paris,' my heart is hammering. 'There's an article about a society scandal that I want to read.'

Whyke is looking at me closely across the coffee table. I realize that I have made the same mistake many people do in underestimating him.

'Which scandal?' he demands.

The breath dries up in my throat as I struggle for a reply. My carefully constructed answers vanish.

'This is about the Clermont place again,' he accuses, watching me steadily, the form poised on his lap. There is a tightness in his tone I've never heard before.

'Yes,' I have to admit, trying to keep my voice firm, 'but it's important, Professor. I have to find out.'

'You've been told,' Whyke barks, 'time and again, that pursuing anything to do with your grandfather is a bad idea. Which part of that do you not understand?'

'*You* don't understand the significance of this,' I say hotly. 'Some of the things that I've found — '

'Treasures from your grandfather's collection?' he interrupts. 'How am I meant to substantiate that?'

143

'What do you mean?'

'I mean, where is your proof? Whatever it is you've discovered, how am I meant to support you? I don't even know if these things exist.'

Now, more than ever, the memory of the emptied bag makes my hands clench.

'But you've seen the photograph,' I say, 'I showed it to you, and I can get the other things.'

'Then where are they now? Petra, I'm concerned about where these sources are coming from. People will assume that you've — '

Abruptly, Whyke pulls himself back. The unsaid words hang heavily between us.

'That I've what? Made it all up?'

'I never said that.'

I can't stop the angry tears from flooding my eyes as I collect my bag. Whyke is on his feet, looking severely alarmed. At any other time, I might have laughed, but now I push past him.

'Petra, wait.'

'No, I've had enough of this. I shouldn't even be here. Tell Kaufmann she was right.'

I take the stairs at a run, until it's clear that Whyke has not followed me. The tears are spilling over. I swipe them away furiously, feeling empty and sick.

The walk back to college is a blur, but during it, I come to a conclusion. My room is too quiet, cluttered with folders and books, evidence of a year's wasted effort. Slowly, I shuffle some of the papers together. When the phone shrills into the silence, I almost don't answer.

It's my father. I have to stop myself from laughing bitterly. We haven't spoken for over a

144

month, and he chooses this moment to call. I answer in monosyllables when he asks how I am. If I sound strange, he doesn't mention it.

'Dad,' I take a breath, steel myself to say the words: *I'm quitting university.*

'Petra, did you take any of those papers?'

His words slap me out of my daze.

'What?'

'Simon's just had a word with me,' he continues, I can tell he's annoyed and trying to hide it. 'He says that you told him to stay away from your grandfather's papers.'

'I did,' I tell him flatly. 'That didn't stop him stealing them from me.'

'You're being ridiculous. I've told Hall that he has complete access, and that you won't be bothering him any more. Is that understood?'

'Tell him I know what he's doing, and that I want them back,' I snap and slam down the receiver.

I'm shaking with anger and emotion. Cass is out of town for the day, and apart from her, there's only one person I want to see.

Alex meets me later that night in the pub. I hug him tightly when he walks in, hold on for longer than usual. He stands motionless for a second, but then squeezes me in return; his arms warm around my back.

I can tell he's feeling the pressure of deadlines, too. He looks more rumpled than ever, hair sticking up at all angles, a coffee stain on his T-shirt. I can't bring myself to load my problems on him straight away, and listen instead as he complains about lab work, about supervisors and the upcoming review. I know he'll be fine, and tell him so as we nurse our pints.

'Sorry for the rant,' he tells me with a wry smile, 'I came here to see you, not to talk shop all night. What's going on?'

I tell him about Hall, and Kaufmann and Whyke, about the decision I made that afternoon.

'I've been kidding myself,' I say slowly, 'this whole year, I've been falling behind. Now it won't be long before Whyke tells the faculty about me, if he hasn't already, and Kaufmann will back him up; she doesn't think I should be here either. They're right, Al.'

Alex snorts dismissively. 'If tutors reported every highly strung student, there wouldn't *be* a faculty.'

I smile weakly. Alex rolls his eyes.

'Look.' He pokes me in the arm. 'Whyke never said he thought you should quit, neither did Kaufmann.'

'You just don't want me to leave,' I accuse, nudging him with my shoulder.

'Of course I don't,' he declares, and takes a hasty gulp of his beer. 'I'd — ' He hesitates, mouth open to say something. My stomach does a flip.

'You'd what?'

His face drops into a grin. 'Get bored without these weekly doses of drama.'

I try to swallow a sudden wave of disappointment as he pushes my drink towards me.

'See the rest of the term out, at least, P. How you spend it is up to you.'

146

22

February 1910

The hours flew past. Ebersole's team made two more religieuses, one for evening service and one to be delivered to a party. Maurice sweated and swore over multiple pans of coloured sugar icing that Ebersole deemed 'too gaudy', 'too insipid'.

Finally, the colours were correct. Gui peered down into the pan and realized they were just as Monsieur Carême described them: soft, tender lilac and rose pink. When the tower of éclairs was finished, Ebersole looked as though he was going to cry. The religieuse was a masterpiece of pastel shades, ornate swirls of vanilla cream and gold-leaf decoration; but one of the other apprentices joked that it resembled a matron swathed in tight satin.

Ebersole looked devastated. 'They are right,' he said, 'it looks like an old whore.'

'Clermont's is a business my friend, and we must cater to requests,' Maurice placated. 'The Comtesse wanted it to look just so. I'm sure she will be overjoyed.'

The kitchen began to empty out. Maurice beckoned to Gui and pointed up at the clock. It was almost eight. Gui felt lightheaded; he had eaten nothing that day but an end of bread. It seemed a thousand years since he had walked into the café, suitcase in hand.

'Are we finished?' he asked as their group plodded into the communal cloakroom. The younger chefs pulled hats from their hair, talking noisily. Maurice lounged in one corner with Ebersole.

'Not yet,' he mumbled around a cigarette. 'Got to clean the stations and prepare for the morning. Go and get the supper, will you?'

'Supper?' Once again, Gui was bewildered.

'The boys at the ovens keep a few loaves going for breaks. Go and ask them.'

'Be sure to ask for the best white loaf!' one of the younger apprentices called after him.

Gui dodged between bodies in the kitchen. The ovens took up one whole wall; thick, black doors in the tiled walls, secured by brass handles and bars. He approached the least hostile-looking of the workers there.

'Can I get the supper for break?' he asked hesitantly.

The boy ignored him. His pristine white uniform was soaked with sweat as he rearranged shelves in the hot oven.

'It's for Ebersole,' Gui pressed. 'They told me to ask for a white loaf.'

Now he had the boy's attention.

'A white loaf, was it?'

'That's what they said.'

'The *best* white loaf?'

'Yes.' Gui felt his face growing hot. 'The best white loaf. Can I have it, please?'

In a flash his arms were pinned behind him. The first chef grabbed his neck, forcing his head into the open oven. Sweat burst on his forehead, dripping away in an instant hiss. Then the heat was gone and he managed a gasp of air before his vision was filled with white. Powder clogged his nose and mouth and he choked before he was released. Spluttering, he stumbled back, swiping at the flour that clung to his damp skin and stung his eyes. A warm loaf was dumped into his arms.

The cloakroom erupted into laughter when he walked back in. His throat was sticky with flour and humiliation. Gui had heard horror stories about hazing from some of the men who worked the railways. He'd never experienced it himself, so, he decided, he was probably overdue.

'Here's your supper,' he wheezed.

Maurice caught the bread with a laugh and set about pulling off large chunks.

'Guillaume, we all had to endure it. Welcome to the kitchen.'

Ebersole was guffawing quietly as he chewed, cigarette on lip.

'There's a washroom through that door,' Maurice said. 'You might want to use it before you eat.' He caught Gui's glance towards the younger apprentices, who were still doubled up with laughter. 'Don't worry, I'll guard your share.'

'Thanks for supper, snowdrop!' they catcalled.

Gui grinned and curtsied primly to them as he passed and they clapped him on the shoulder and wiped their streaming eyes.

The group had dispersed by the time he returned, dripping with cold water. Good to his word, Maurice handed him the end of the bread.

It was smaller than the share the others had received, but he took it without complaint. He forced himself to eat slowly, but soon it was gone and his stomach remained hollow.

'Still hungry, eh?' Maurice asked, watching him chew.

'Not at all,' Gui lied, thinking of the unwanted pastries he had swiped earlier.

'I saw you sneaking about the refuse sack,' the older man said. 'Hand them over.'

'I don't know what you mean.' Gui looked away, his cheeks burning. Embarrassment was one thing, yet he knew from experience that hunger would feel far worse.

'You have at least two burned pastry cases in your pocket,' Maurice was merciless, 'or did you think it wouldn't be noticed? Come now, or it'll be Josef you have to explain to.'

Slowly, Gui took out the pastries. They were only a little singed at the edges, and still looked delicious to him. In one movement, Maurice swept them from his hand and kicked them under the bench. Gui's jaw clenched at the thought of the waste.

'There now,' the older chef continued, brushing crumbs from his sleeves, 'why would you want those old things anyway?'

There was a napkin in his hand. Gently, he unwrapped the top folds. Within was an éclair, one of the many they had created that afternoon. This one was covered in chocolate, gleaming darkly. He set it on the bench.

'I thought you might be interested in this.' Maurice's voice was nonchalant, but a smile played around his mouth. 'How are you supposed to learn if you don't know what you are making? Now, I'm going outside for a breath of air. We're due back in five minutes.'

For a full minute, Gui couldn't even bring himself to pick up the pastry. It looked so small, lying on the white napkin, yet in the café itself, one of these would cost him a whole day's wages.

Tentatively, he brought it to his mouth. He sniffed deeply, breathing in the mingled richness of baking: of butter and sugar. His teeth sank into one end and sweetness filled his mouth, the chocolate cream airy-light and smooth against his tongue. A shock of bitter cocoa came next, irresistible and bewitching. It was unlike anything he had ever eaten, a strike of joy to his senses. He tried very hard to save a piece, just one mouthful for later, to remind him, but in the end, that too disappeared.

He was checking the napkin for fallen crumbs when Maurice and the other apprentices reappeared. The cocoa and sugar had filled up his body; he could feel them shooting through his veins. Bewildering though the day had been, it was growing brighter, clearer, and he felt his curiosity flare once again.

'On your feet,' Maurice told him, stretching. 'It's back to the grind until ten.'

They set off for the kitchen, smoothing hair under caps, retying aprons.

'What's your story anyway?' the older chef questioned. 'Most apprentices start in the autumn. You are either late or incredibly early.'

'I'm not exactly an apprentice.'

'What then?' Maurice was checking his apron, but Gui could feel the man's attention on him.

'Do you know where I can find a place to stay?' he asked quickly, changing the subject. 'I had to move out of my previous lodgings and was hoping they might know of somewhere here.'

'You are a puzzle, aren't you? Late, out of nowhere, unprepared. Try to ask Josef, after shift finishes. He might know of somewhere. Otherwise, there are boarding houses on the Boulevard Saint-Martin. I know some of the younger men room together there.'

Gui was put on washing duty in the tiny scullery where he had once stood with Mademoiselle Clermont. He had not given a thought to the rack upon rack of pans at the time. All of them were covered in greasy remnants of butter, egg yolks, crusted with sugar, inches thick. There was a terrifying copper cylinder in the corner, all valves and pipes and spurts of steam. The hot water it provided would have scalded Gui's hands, were they not so toughened from the railway's furnaces. Because of this, he worked faster than the other two apprentices, a fact that earned their dislike.

The place was deserted by the time he completed his task. He knocked on the office door but it was dark and he received no answer. Thankfully, the café had yet to be locked up. An old man was pushing a mop around behind the counter. Gui's suitcase was in the cloakroom where the waiter had left it so many hours

152

before, shoved into a corner.

Back in the staff cloakroom, the two remaining workers were changing into street clothes, dropping their uniforms into the laundry hamper. They were the same pair from the sinks, and Gui tried to introduce himself, to ask them about lodgings, but they only shrugged and took their leave without a word.

He had no choice but to follow Maurice's suggestion and head for the Boulevard Saint-Martin. Outside, he asked the driver of a horse-drawn cab for directions.

'Follow your nose,' was the only answer he received.

He found it easily enough. Saint-Martin was busier than the surrounding streets, yet the evening was growing later by the minute. In a bar that remained open, he asked the proprietor for any recommendations. There was a pause in the man's voice as he surveyed Gui's ill-fitting clothes, the battered suitcase.

'Try 106. Madame Pelle. She may have rooms.'

Number 106 was a tall, narrow house sandwiched between two grander buildings. The doors and windows were covered with wrought-iron bars, tightly locked and bolted. Steeling himself, he rang the bell. After an age, light glimmered underneath the door.

'Who's there?'

The voice was shrill and plummy at once.

'I'm looking for Madame Pelle,' Gui called. 'Someone said I might find a room here.'

The door opened an inch. A plump,

153

middle-aged woman in a sleeping cap and shawl blinked out at him, unable to see past her own gas lamp. She reminded Gui of a toy vole he had once seen in a shop window, dressed as a washerwoman in skirts and a headscarf. He suppressed a laugh.

'Have you any notion of what time it is, young man?' she spluttered.

'I am sorry. I only recently finished working and — '

'I regret to disappoint you, but you won't find the type of rooms you require here.'

'Pardon?'

'I cater for respectable clientele. Clerks and secretaries. Not manual labourers who come and go at all hours.'

'I'm not a labourer. I'm an apprentice chef,' Gui declared proudly.

'There are no rooms here, try up in Belleville. No doubt you know of it already.'

'Wait!'

The woman slammed the door on his outstretched foot. Yelling in pain and frustration, Gui staggered back.

On the pavement, a passing man put a protective arm around his lady, hurrying her along. Fuming, Gui seized his suitcase and stalked up the road, quickening his steps as if he knew where he was going. As he walked, the streets became darker and quieter. He turned a corner and realized with a start that he was in Place de la République, where he used to meet Luc and Yves and the delivery carts every week.

Out of the darkness came the clacking of

wood, the syncopated noise of hooves. An omnibus, all but empty, was making its way home for the night.

'Are you going near Belleville?' he called up to the driver as it drew near. Weak gas lanterns did nothing to illuminate the man's face, but the lit end of a cigarette dipped in assent. With relief, Gui hopped onto the back step and perched there, watching the streets sway into shadow.

They were climbing steadily. Lights began to pepper the buildings and Gui heard music, the hum of voices. A group of children streaked past, ragtag creatures in third-hand coats that flapped behind them like broken wings.

'Where's this?' he shouted to them.

'Belleville,' answered one, running alongside. He could not have been more than nine years old, but he stared with a prospector's eye. 'Sir,' he added with a dip of his floppy cap. 'Looking for something, sir?'

'Somewhere to stay.' Gui leaped off the omnibus. It picked up pace, trundling away up the street. 'Clean and cheap enough. Do you know of anywhere?'

'But I do, sir, fine lodgings here, sir.'

The boy had a peculiar accent. He beckoned, so Gui began to follow him. Several bars were still vivid with light. A woman with curves that threatened to split her satin dress eyed him from a doorway and giggled throatily.

'Like what you see?' the boy asked. 'They call her La Balourde, the Turkey, sir, on account of that noise she makes.'

Visions of Ebersole's pink religieuse assailed

Gui as he stared at the woman's quivering décolletage.

'I just want a room,' he said, blushing.

'Of course, of course, we are nearly at a most respectable place.'

The boy stopped, indicating an alleyway about as wide as a coal pit. The stench told Gui that it was a popular place for dumping waste, human or otherwise. He raised an eyebrow, fishing in his jacket for coins.

'Look,' he sighed, 'I shall give you a sou,' the boy's eyes widened, 'but only if you take me to a decent boarding house. I'll give you another if you and your friends promise not to rob me.'

The boy considered the proposition, then grinned, offering his hand.

'I shall treat you as an investment, then, sir. I'm Puce, *homme du monde*.'

'Guillaume du Frère. Puce? You're named after a flea?'

'For my acrobatic talents.' The boy sniffed.

They walked at a slower pace. Further up the road, it was quieter. There were fewer bars and cafés, but more lamps, burning in windows, doorways. Puce stopped at one of these and pointed up a steep wooden staircase.

'You promised not to rob me,' Gui reminded.

'I know for a fact that Madame has a room spare,' the boy said indignantly. 'It's a mouse hole but they're decent sorts, you won't be bothered by *putains* like Balourde.'

Keeping half an eye over his shoulder, Gui risked the stairs. Through a door and a worn curtain he emerged into a small sitting-room.

Several women were reclining, reading books, sewing by the warm fireplace. It would be a genteel scene, were it not for the fact that the women wore very few clothes. Gui tried not to blush but he couldn't stop his eyes from settling where they should not. Eventually, he addressed the coal scuttle.

'Excuse me,' he mumbled as loudly as he could, 'I heard you had a room available but I see I must be mistaken.'

'Where did you find this one, Puce?' one of the women laughed. She smiled at Gui, half-mocking and tired.

'Fresh off the omnibus. Madame, you still got Avril's old room?'

He addressed the eldest of the four women. She sat at a desk, writing a letter. She was fully clothed, a gown hugging her figure like a second skin, right down to the ends of her wrists.

'I do, Puce,' she said evenly. 'She only left two days ago. You are . . . ?'

The attention was turned to Gui. He felt like an exhibit, on a plinth to be examined.

'Guillaume du Frère, apprentice chef,' he blurted out.

'You are looking for accommodation?'

'I am, but . . . ' His eyes found flesh again and he transferred his gaze to the rug. 'But I am not sure whether we have understood each other.'

'I understood you were looking for a room?' said the woman.

'I am.'

'Well, would you like to see the one I have spare?'

An oil lamp threw shadows onto the wooden stairs as they climbed, making the walls full of impossible angles. They circled one landing and then another before the steps ran out. Here, the ceiling was low. Gui imagined that if he punched upward, his fist would emerge through the roof into the cold night air.

'There are three rooms on this floor,' Madame said, searching through a ring of keys. 'The one at the end is occupied by a clerk, the other by Isabelle, one of the ladies you met downstairs.'

The door swung open. A shaft of light from the moon slanted through a narrow window. It looked out onto a vast mess of rooftops, chimneys and walls jutting into the sky. At one end of the room, the ceiling sagged, the wall bulging out to meet it. A metal-framed bed was wedged next to the chimney, the fireplace taken up by a tiny pot-bellied stove. There was a nightstand with a faded bowl and space for little else.

Madame was telling him about the rent, how much per month, how much in advance, where he could find the water closet. The price would swallow up more than half of his pay, and there was still his mother to think of, but all Gui could see was the bed in the corner. He imagined how warm it would be with the stove lit, how quiet; a place where he could close the door and be alone.

'I will take it,' he announced.

Later, he lay wrapped in his blanket on the bare mattress, listening to the wind as it threaded its way through the window in gusts, until he was almost convinced that he could hear the sea.

23

May 1988

I wait nervously outside the university library. I wish Cass hadn't wanted to meet here, when there are certain supervisors I'm trying to avoid. Exams have begun, and the faculties, the libraries are all too quiet, undergraduates shut up for hours on end in the examination halls throughout town.

In the distance I see Cass approaching, pushing her bicycle and looking elegant in a red sundress. I sigh inwardly at my scruffy top and jeans, but beckon her over to where I'm lurking behind the steps.

'You're acting like a fugitive,' she laughs, shifting her books. 'I come bearing gifts.'

We settle on a bench and Cass brandishes a piece of paper in my direction.

'Here. Evan dug this up. He's had it for a week or two, but I didn't see him in the faculty until this morning.'

It's a copy of a photograph. A group of people, dressed in smartly buttoned white. They are arranged in lines outside a shop front, with grand arched windows and ornate stonework. Two darker-clothed figures stand in the middle. One is a tall man in early middle age, the other a young woman. Her face is pale beneath a slanted hat, cold and distant. It is the same girl, once again, and above her, curling letters form a sign.

'Pâtisserie Clermont!' I burst. 'Where did you get this?'

'Evan has a friend at the British Library who works in the photography archive,' Cass tells me. 'He called him, asked a few questions and *voilà!* Apparently the photographic record hadn't been labelled correctly, but his friend remembered seeing it. Explains why your favourite biographer has never come across it.'

'Cass, it's her.'

'The girl from your grandpa's photograph?' she asks, leaning in.

'Yes, and the painting.'

We hunch over the picture, heads touching.

'I knew she was connected with it,' I say. 'Do you think that's her husband, next to her?'

'Too old, her father more like. Look, at the bottom, someone's labelled it,' Cass squints. 'Monsieur J. P. Clermont.'

'Which would make her — '

'*Mademoiselle* Clermont.'

We sit back in silence.

'When do you think this was?' I ask.

'No idea. Judging by the clothes, 1910–1911, perhaps?'

'It must be 1910 or earlier. From Allincourt's letter, it seems that the place closed later that year.'

'You'd have to check with the archive to be sure, only be careful who you ask. This copy didn't exactly come through the usual channels.'

I try to thank her, but she brushes it aside.

'Thank Evan. I think he's rather taken with your mystery.'

'I think he's more taken with you.'

Cass rolls her eyes.

'What about your 'friend' Alex?' she says. 'I hear he stopped you from running off before the end of term. Anything you want to tell me?'

'No!' I laugh. 'We're just friends.'

'Oh yes, that's definitely all there is to it.'

'Nothing's ever happened,' I tell her, though I can't help but remember the way I hugged him last night, the way he almost said something but didn't.

'Not *yet*.' She smiles slyly. 'Look, I have to go in a minute, but there's another thing. I asked a few of the French History professors if any of them had heard of Stephen Lefevre, the man who wrote that book about the letters. Turns out he gave a talk here, a few years ago. He's very old now, retired apparently, somewhere down south.'

I let out a long breath, taking in the information. I thought I was at a dead end, but now, new roads are opening, stretching off into the distance.

'So?' prompts Cass. 'What're you going to do?'

The sunshine is bright in my eyes. I tap the heels of my plimsolls on the tarmac as I think.

'I'll start with Lefevre,' I decide, trying to visualize a plan. 'He might be able to tell me more about those letters. Hall will have read my notes, so he'll know about Lefevre too, but maybe I can get there first. Then I *have* to get hold of that article somehow. I'm starting to think it will answer more than a few questions.'

'You could track Lefevre through his publisher,' Cass suggests, climbing to her feet. 'They'd have his contact information.'

Once she's gone, I race to my room and drag out a duffel bag, throwing in a change of clothes, my toothbrush and the library book. Before I have a chance to think twice, I'm out the door, squashing the bag onto the handlebars of my bike.

Outside, the day is turning blustery, shadows of clouds scudding upon the pavement. My hair whips across my face in fine strands as I pedal through town. *Start with what you know*, I tell myself, *like the gaps in a crossword.*

In a café near the station, I borrow a copy of the Yellow Pages. The cover is ripped and stained from countless late-night patrons thumbing for taxis. Thinking of Cass's suggestion, I look for Lefevre's publisher. There is a matching entry, so I jam a few coins into the payphone.

'Good morning, Kingsley Press?'

It is a woman's voice, quick and abrupt. This might not be as easy as I'd hoped.

'Yes, hello there.' I do my best to match the professional impatience. 'I'm calling from the University of Cambridge. We'd be interested in contacting one of your authors, but don't have any details on record here, I was wondering if you could help.'

'Who did you say you were?'

'My name's Anna,' I lie, hopefully in a convincing manner. 'I'm the President of the History Society.'

'I see. Which author were you interested in contacting?'

I can tell from her tone that she's not inclined to be helpful, but I plough on.

'His name is Stephen Lefevre. I believe he gave a talk here some years ago, we'd like to invite him back.'

There is silence on the other end of the phone.

'Stephen Lefevre?' she asks eventually. 'You're sure?'

'Yes, we'd be very interested in — '

'Look,' the woman is suspicious, 'is there something going on here?'

'I'm sorry?'

'There's been no interest in this author for years, and then I get two calls in the same week requesting his details.'

I clutch the phone, forgetting about the greasy earpiece.

'Two calls?'

'Yes, several days ago,' the woman says impatiently, 'someone researching for a biography — '

'What did you do?' I interrupt.

'Excuse me?'

I bite back the urgency in my voice. 'I mean, did you pass on the details?'

'No, I didn't,' the woman sounds guarded, to say the least. 'I recommended that he contact Mr Lefevre's agent. They should be able to pass on any correspondence.'

'And they are?'

'Hyatt and Smith. Are you going to tell me the real reason you both want to find Mr Lefevre?'

'I'm afraid I have to go, thank you so much for your help.'

My heart is racing as I slam down the receiver. The woman behind the counter gives me a sidelong glance, and I manage a weak smile before I sink back into a chair. Hall is looking for Lefevre too, and he is ahead.

'Shit.'

I kick the table and un-drunk tea slops onto the sticky surface. I try to think rationally. Several days ago, the woman said. That means Hall has at least two days' head start on me. I use the Yellow Pages once again to locate Lefevre's agent.

The answer there is even shorter than the one I received from the publisher. They do not hand out authors' details without prior consent. Any correspondence would be forwarded as appropriate.

Running low on change, I make one last attempt with Directory Inquiries. The phone starts bleeping for me to insert more coins, but not before I hear the answer from the operator as he tells me that the name 'Stephen Lefevre' is listed as ex-directory. At least if I haven't managed to get anywhere, then neither has Hall.

It's only when I reach the counter that I find I've spent all my money on the telephone. I poke aimlessly in my purse. A few coppers, a button.

'Allow me,' says a voice over my shoulder. 'Bring over a couple more, if you would.'

Whyke touches my arm.

'Care to join me?'

We sit at the table that I have just vacated, my

164

previous cup of tea still growing cold in its mug, hard water scum floating on the surface.

'How did you know I was here?' I ask awkwardly. It seems the easiest question.

'I recognized your bike parked outside. Going somewhere?'

The duffel bag sits conspicuously on its own chair. I hadn't realized that Whyke knew what bike I rode, or that I rode a bike at all. The teas arrive and just as I open my mouth, Whyke holds up a hand.

'I think it's my turn to speak, if you'll let me?'

I nod, taking one of the mugs.

'Firstly,' he sighs, 'I'm sorry for the way I spoke to you. I understand why you were angry.' He sips his tea and grimaces, before adding sugar lumps. I know better than to interrupt. 'Why do you think you were assigned to Dr Kaufmann for extra tuition, Petra?'

'I supposed it was because you knew I was struggling,' I answer, as steadily as I can, 'and you reported it to the faculty. Kaufmann has a reputation for whipping people into shape, especially with two weeks until my review.'

A wisp of a smile appears on his face.

'I didn't report anything. I knew you had reservations, but I was confident you would resolve them in time.'

I start to point out the reality of the situation, but Whyke hasn't finished.

'The truth is *all* of my students have been assigned other tutors. The university has put me on probation.'

The words stretch between us, interspersed

165

with the clinking of dishes, the whirr of an electric fan.

'Have you ever looked at the university league tables?' he continues. 'It probably hasn't concerned you much, but my college takes its position rather seriously. The higher we score, the more funding we get. Apparently, not one of my students has achieved a first-class grade in the last five years.'

'But you've never taught for good marks,' I protest, 'everyone says.'

'Do they? That's the problem. This year, if any of my students fail, or get lower than average grades, I will be considered a millstone around the college's neck and sent on my way.'

I start to speak, but his expression stops me.

'It's not so great a surprise,' he says gently. 'It's true; I've never cared much about exam work.'

'Professor, I'm sorry, but I don't think there's any way I'll get a first. It'll be a miracle if I even pass.'

'Listen to me.' Whyke leans forward, more decisive than I've ever seen him. 'I want you to forget everything I said the other day. If I get dismissed it will be no one's responsibility but my own. If you've found something that you think is more valuable than your studies, then I won't stand in your way. I only want to be sure you've considered everything thoroughly, because there will be consequences.'

I nod slowly. 'I have.'

'I thought you might see it like that.' He grins. 'Well then, what do we have to go on?'

I tell him everything, about the clues I've

166

collected so far, the photographs and the girl, the painting, my grandfather's article, the letters and Mr Lefevre. Face burning, I explain about Hall and the whereabouts of the evidence.

'He sounds like a pleasant character,' Whyke says sardonically. 'In which case, I think you'd be right to start with Lefevre.'

I remind him that I've already tried, but he's climbing to his feet, checking his watch and dumping a handful of change onto the table.

'That's for the tea.' He points. 'Now, I take it you were on your way to the station?'

'I was going to go back to the Newspaper Library.'

'Don't buy a ticket just yet. I'm going to locate Mr Lefevre, and you might want to consider paying him a visit.'

'How?'

Whyke is scrawling a telephone number on a napkin with a leaking biro.

'Just be at the station in an hour's time,' he tells me. 'Call my number at the faculty. I should have the details then.'

Before I can question him further he is gone, leaving a mess of sugar and coins behind him.

It feels strange to stand waiting at the station in the middle of the afternoon when I'd normally be studying. The platform clock is pointing at quarter to two as I dial the number Whyke has given me. At first it doesn't work, until I see that one of the scrawled numbers is a three rather than an eight. I try again and it's engaged. There is a train leaving for London in five minutes. The third time I dial, Whyke picks up straight away.

'Petra?' he answers breathlessly.

'Yes, I'm here.'

'Sorry, I had to call someone at the University of Essex.'

'That's all right. Have you found Lefevre?'

'Yes. It took a little more asking around than I thought, but a friend of a friend met him at a conference a few years back. He doesn't have a telephone, apparently, so you'll have to go and see him in person.'

'OK.' I fumble for my notebook. 'Where is he?'

'You're not going to like this . . . '

'*Cornwall!*' I yelp down the phone when he tells me. 'How on earth am I going to get there?'

'Well, unless you want to write to him — '

'I don't have time to write.' I glance up at the departures board, and sigh. 'This is going to be a long day.'

'I suggest you get moving then. Here, have you got a pen?'

24

February 1910

Gui's first weeks at the pâtisserie did not go as well as he had hoped. He was just another skivvy for the most part, the lowest of the order, and the visions he had of becoming a real *pâtissier*, of spinning glorious confections like Monsieur Carême, seemed further away than ever.

He had seen Mademoiselle Clermont only once since his first day. He had been hurrying back to the kitchens after his break when the door of the office had burst open. She had dashed out, her head lowered, and had collided with him before he could step aside. For the space of a breath, his hands had rested upon her arms, hers upon his chest. Her face was drawn and pale, tears reddening her lower lids. He had frowned in concern, opened his mouth to ask her what was wrong, but before he could speak she had shaken her head and pulled away.

He had watched her duck through the private door that led to the apartments above. The warmth that had flooded the space between their bodies stayed with him long after she had disappeared from view.

Gui wondered whether she was still at odds with her father. Sometimes, he thought he could feel Monsieur Clermont's attention on him as he worked in the kitchen, but whenever he looked over, the chef was engrossed in ingredients, or sketches, or conversations with Josef.

The kitchen had its own language, one Gui did not yet understand. He was allowed to work with Chef Ebersole for a few hours a day, but mostly he was shoved aside and left to follow as best he could. Every time he was asked to prepare a bain-marie, or fetch a savarin mould, his stomach turned over. Sometimes, Maurice would give him a nudge in the right direction, but when the older chef was busy, he was at the mercy of the other apprentices. Some of them were friendly, but others were downright malicious.

Before he learned not to listen to them, he handed Ebersole a bottle of cochineal rather than vanilla, and was banished to the ovens for the rest of the week. 'Minding the ovens' was a punishment in the kitchen, the most menial task. He struggled to keep them at a constant temperature; bricks had to be soaked and replaced to create steam, shelves arranged and rearranged. He fared better than most, being used to furnaces far larger and hotter, but by the time the weekend arrived, his hands were red with blisters and scalds.

One night, dog weary, he returned to his new home on the Rue de Belleville. He met his neighbour Isabelle on the landing, and she tutted in sympathy over the burns.

'You work too hard,' she told him, leaning in her doorway.

Over her shoulder, Gui glimpsed walls covered with cut-out paper flowers and landscapes, lace

170

drapes pinned above the bed. Isabelle did not entertain clients here. Madame had a strict rule that all visits took place in the private cabinet rooms downstairs, but even so, he looked away.

'I must work hard,' he said quietly. 'This is my chance.'

Her smile was twisted. She bid him goodnight and went downstairs.

With only one day left of his sentence at the ovens, Gui tried to work hard, to be cautious. Yet the Saturday shift was notoriously long and hectic. Losing concentration, he leaned in too far and scorched a huge hole in the front of his jacket. He swore and batted at himself, but the damage was done.

'Josef will thrash you for that,' his fellow oven worker told him, a boy with a permanently red nose who had taken against Gui from the start.

'He won't if he doesn't find out.' Gui pushed his sleeves to the elbow, but red-nose only gave him a haughty expression and turned away. Gui hitched his apron up around his ribs to cover the hole. A few minutes later, he saw the other apprentice sidling towards the office, and hurried to catch up with him in the corridor.

'Where are you going?'

The young man stopped in his tracks, mouth souring with dislike.

'Nowhere,' he told Gui.

He heard voices then, Josef's booming tones and Clermont's quieter ones, heading towards them. The other apprentice tried to lunge past, but Gui grabbed him and used all his weight to shove him into the cloakroom.

171

The door swung closed behind them just in time. Gui was so intent on listening to the voices in the corridor, on not being caught, that he didn't see the first blow coming. It caught him on the ear and he stumbled backwards, tripping over a pair of boots. The apprentice came on again, fists clenched. His blows were not heavy, but he was wiry and fast; Gui took another to the face before he could surge upward and retaliate.

He shoved the other young man, hard. The apprentice stumbled and fell. Gui heard a tide of chatter coming towards them from the kitchen and took his chance to escape.

He kept his head down as the other chefs passed, arms crossed, and no one noticed the state of his uniform. In the scullery, he threw one of the washing tunics over his ruined jacket. His nose was dripping; he swiped it with the back of his hand and saw blood. He blotted it with one of the rags and prayed that it wasn't broken.

He was shaking, he felt sick and hollow from the fight. It would only be a matter of time before his presence was missed at the ovens. He could not afford to have his pay docked for the damage to his uniform; it was barely enough to cover the rent at Madame's as it was. As for brawling on duty . . .

He plunged his arms into a sink full of water and tried to hide his bloodied nose when two chefs entered, laden with dirty mixing bowls.

'Well, he'd been fighting with *someone*,' one of them said.

'Still, I can't believe that Josef sent him packing without a word,' snorted the other.

'I can. He was on his last warning.'

'Who else was involved, do you reckon?'

'We'll find out when someone gets back from break looking a mess, won't we?'

They dumped the stack of bowls in the deep sink, splashing Gui with suds. He stared down into the water. He couldn't believe that he had been so stupid; his one chance at a future, at something better. He was not going to lose it because of a skinny tell-tale.

He waited until the corridor outside the scullery was empty, then ran down its length to a door at the other end. If anyone saw him walking through it, he would be dismissed for sure.

Thankfully, it was the middle of the day, a quiet time. He encountered no one as he crept up the polished stairs towards the Clermonts' apartment. He knocked, heart thundering down to his stomach, arms clenched tight behind his back to hide their shaking.

The door opened with a gust of warm air. It smelled like flowers and tea.

'Guillaume!'

Mademoiselle Clermont stood there, her eyes widening at the state of him. She wore dark pink today, a lace collar tight and high on her neck. An ornate hairpiece of silk flowers was twined about her head.

'I'm looking for Patrice,' he stuttered.

She seized him by the arm, pulled him inside. Their feet were muffled by thick carpet.

'Who's there, Jeanne?'

Gui froze. There was someone else in the apartment.

'A mistaken caller, Aunt,' said Mademoiselle Clermont loudly. 'They were looking for Madame Bescanon along the hall.' Her voice was cool and even, but Gui could hear the breathlessness below the surface. 'I must just take a moment for myself, if you don't mind.'

'Are you feeling unwell, Jeanne?' the older woman called.

'No, no, I won't be long.'

She dragged him along the hallway to a second door, pushed him inside and followed him in, locking it as quietly as possible. When she turned, her cheeks were burning red.

'What are you doing here?' she demanded in a whisper.

The room was high and airy. Heavy curtains framed the windows, as well as a four-poster bed with an ornately carved headboard. A smooth satin eiderdown covered crisp sheets. With a jolt, Gui realized that he must be in Mademoiselle Clermont's bedroom.

'I am sorry,' he stammered, shrugging off the washing tunic to reveal the blood-spattered, burned uniform. 'I needed help and I thought of Patrice . . . I didn't know who else to ask.'

'What on earth happened?'

'Another boy saw me burn my jacket. He was going to tell Josef, and I tried to stop him, but then he hit me.' Gui sniffed and tasted blood at the back of his throat. 'I didn't want to start a fight, but I can't afford to lose any pay.'

Mademoiselle Clermont had drawn back from the ruined garment, turning towards the door.

'Guillaume, I'm sure that if we explained to Josef — '

Gui snatched at her arm before she could reach for the handle.

'No! If I'm seen with you, I'll be fired on the spot.'

She stared at his fingers, burned and scarred, closed around the fine lace of her sleeve.

'What happened to your hands?' she murmured.

Abruptly, he recalled the feel of her in his arms, her hands locked around his neck as he battled through the floodwater, the warmth he had felt between them in the corridor. He let go. A strange expression flickered across her face. Then she seemed to make up her mind, and pushed him towards a dressing table that was tucked into an alcove.

'Sit down,' she ordered, and opened a drawer.

Gui caught a waft of lavender. She drew out a handkerchief, embroidered with leaves and flowers and the word 'Jeanne'. She shook it free of its folds and wet it with some lotion from a bottle.

'Here,' she handed it to him, 'we should clean up your face, for a start.'

Gui stared in horror at the fine linen.

'I can't use this,' he told her quietly, 'I'll ruin it.'

'No matter,' she said carelessly, searching through a forest of bottles and jars. 'I have hundreds.'

Gingerly, Gui dabbed at his nose, wincing at the rust-coloured smears that came away on the clean, white surface.

'Here.' Mademoiselle Clermont was opening a blue tin, with English writing upon it. 'This will help your hands. It's for treating burns, from America.' She scooped out a small palmful of what looked like lard.

He was not sure whether he should protest or whether it would be rude to interrupt when she took his hand and began to dot the substance over the worst scalds.

'When I saw you the other day,' he began clumsily, to cover his embarrassment, 'you looked upset. Is everything all right?'

She pulled a face, smoothing the balm into his skin. 'I am sorry about that. Father and I disagreed again. He believes that I have forgotten how to behave.'

'Have you?' he could not help but ask.

Her fingers were soft, and he had the uncontrollable urge to touch her, to pull her closer. Something must have betrayed his thoughts, for she looked once into his face, before letting go.

'What can we do about your uniform? I do not have much time. My aunt and I are expecting guests.'

'I need a clean jacket, or they'll know it was me in the fight,' he said hurriedly, grateful to talk about something practical. 'I thought Patrice might have one.'

'He may, I saw him mending one yesterday. Wait here, we shall have to be fast.'

Swiftly, she tugged a bell pull that hung beside the door.

176

'If it's anyone else but Patrice, you will have to hide,' she whispered over her shoulder.

Gui shifted towards the edge of the seat, ready to bolt into the shadow of a huge wardrobe. A minute later there was a knock at the door.

'Mademoiselle?' It was the valet's voice, muffled through the wood. 'Is everything all right? Your aunt is concerned and your guests are due any minute.'

She opened the door an inch. Gui caught a snatch of frantic whispering, before the door was shut and locked again.

'Quickly,' Mademoiselle Clermont told him. 'Take off the old one.'

'It . . . ' Gui stuttered, mouth dry. 'It wouldn't be proper, I've no undershirt.'

The girl made an exasperated noise and crossed her arms.

'I shall look away, if it troubles you.'

Flushing from neck to forehead, Gui fought his way out of the jacket, fingers slipping on the gilded buttons. He gripped the ruined garment, and stood, chest bare. He caught a glimpse of his reflection in the dressing-table mirror, of the muscles in his back and waist above the white trousers, and realized that Mademoiselle Clermont was staring.

A discreet knock on the door interrupted his embarrassment and Patrice was admitted. His eyes flared at the sight of Gui, standing there shirtless, but he thrust a white garment forward.

'Never a dull day when you are around, du Frère,' he said, mouth twitching with amusement. 'My nailbrush sends its regards. Mademoiselle,'

177

he directed reprovingly at the staring girl, though half a smile still lingered, 'the Burnetts' motor car has arrived outside and they will be coming upstairs imminently. If you have finished your examination of young Monsieur du Frère, I suggest you rejoin your aunt in the drawing-room.'

Blanching slightly, she hurried to obey.

'The Burnetts?' Gui whispered, struggling thankfully into the new jacket. 'Do you mean Monsieur Burnett?'

'Yes, his wife and son, they are friends of the family.' Patrice bundled up the old garment. 'Hurry lad, if you leave now you might avoid them.'

Gui grinned and clasped the valet's hand in thanks. Patrice winked and hustled him out into the corridor. As they reached the front door, Gui snuck a look over his shoulder. He was rewarded. Mademoiselle Clermont was looking back from the opposite end. She smiled and they were complicit, until someone called her name.

'Go!' she mouthed with a laugh.

Gui allowed Patrice's nudge to take him onto the landing, where he hurtled down the stairs, ecstatic as a schoolboy.

25

May 1988

London Paddington: I arrive just in time to catch the afternoon train to Penzance. The price of the ticket makes me blanch. At this rate, I'll have to swallow my pride and ask my mum for a loan.

I feel a jolt of anxiety as I board. I'm travelling to the other end of the country on scant information, with little money and no plan, but the train is about to leave and it's too late to worry. I settle back and take out one of my notebooks.

Grandpa Jim was always writing; far more than he ever published. Towards the end, I would sometimes help him make sense of his notes, type them up into articles, but amongst his papers I found whole working journals filled with his untidy scrawl. There were endless lines of musings and ideas, folders full of long rambling pages, hacked out letter by letter upon his old black typewriter.

Slowly, I turn to a new page in my own journal and as the brakes release, I start to write.

Two hours have passed and we're already a long way west of London before I stop. Outside, the suburbs have given way to fields, a thin canal snaking alongside the track. The wind rattles the window in the corridor, clouds race across the sky, making the carriage light and dark with their passing.

My stomach growls; I haven't eaten all day. I wobble through the train to find the buffet car, and wolf down a greasy bacon sandwich and a cup of tea. When I return, the woman in the opposite seat offers me a newspaper. I read it cover to cover, then doze for a while, until I am woken by a poke in the arm.

'You're missing the best part, dear,' my fellow passenger tells me, indicating outside.

Beyond the glass, barely ten feet away, the sea is battering the rail track. The blustery day has whipped the waves into crashing foam, coating the windows with salt. I can almost taste it in the air. Early-evening light streams in, throwing the train's silhouette upon the water. It illuminates every detail: the glass in the windows, the head of an oblivious passenger further down the carriage. I raise my hand to see whether a shadow figure will do the same, but the track curves, flashing through a tiny station and the magic is lost.

Some time later, the woman with the newspaper nods goodbye as she alights at Bodmin. Her seat remains vacant. The train is emptying as we travel further and further south. The ticket inspector gives me a friendly smile when he comes round.

'Penzance,' he tells me, 'end of the line. Heading home, young lady?'

I shake my head. 'Just visiting.'

Finally, the high blue of the sky splits open. A vast sunset spreads from the horizon as we slide into the terminal shed at Penzance.

I am one of a handful of people who step yawning from the train. Those in working clothes head briskly for the car park; others drag suitcases to be greeted by loved ones. Disorientated, I pull the napkin from my pocket and read the address again. In the ticket office, I ask how to get to a village called Mousehole, hoping that they won't laugh.

'Mauzel,' the man corrects me gruffly. 'Blue bus, every half-hour or so, can't miss it.'

The timings sound a bit dubious, but before long a bus does turn up, blue and white with a scrolling panel. It wends its way around the coast road before wedging itself into a tiny fishing village. A harbour forms a protective curve, with rows of grey cottages lining the sea wall.

It is dusk now and gone nine o'clock. Lights are beginning to reflect in the water. It is too late to go calling on elderly academics. Instead, I scrawl out a note. There's a sharp breeze that snatches at the paper and smells of open sea. I lick my lips and taste salt.

The house is easy enough to find. The row of cottages is made from granite, running into each other at odd angles, windows barely four steps from the water's edge. Lefevre's house is at the end, a shabby boat pulled up before it. There are lights on. Before I lose my nerve, I push the note through the letterbox.

The wind has a cold edge in the growing darkness, so I hunch my bag higher and head along the town's one main street in search of somewhere to stay. Heads turn as I let a gust of air into the local pub. The landlady looks mildly surprised when I ask for a room.

'I'll put you in Room Seven,' she tells me with a smile. 'It's cosier for one person.' She hands over a key. 'We close down here at eleven, and breakfast starts at seven. Will you be wanting kippers?'

At least five pairs of eyes follow my progress away from the bar. The room is under the eaves of the building and smells of must. I shove the flaking window frame open and the sea air blasts in, filling the space with coolness. I had every intention of trying out the huge old bath down the hall and going to bed with my notes, but am drawn reluctantly back to the bar by the growling in my stomach. The landlady looks mortified when I ask if there is anywhere to get some food.

'There's not a shop before the next town and we stopped serving at nine, my dear, but if you wait, I'll see what we've left.'

Obediently, I squash into a corner with a glass of cider. A chalkboard menu declares that the special of the day is stargazy pie. I gulp my drink, envisaging withered fish heads gazing plaintively at the ceiling. In the end, I'm presented with a cheese and pickle sandwich the size of my head and a pile of crisps.

I fall asleep in a strange place, with the sea wind whistling through the window, lulling my thoughts until they are as quiet as sand.

26

March 1910

Sundays were slower at the pâtisserie, and Gui came to love their atmosphere, their calm after the frenzy of the week. They ran only one sitting to fit around church-going, so the kitchen operated on half-staff, producing more humble offerings. The towering stacks of profiteroles, the mille-feuille and champagne creams were banished in favour of the sweet and the simple; pans of clafoutis with preserved cherries, slices of tarte tatin and cups of hot chocolate.

Gui put himself forward for all the Sunday shifts available, even the earliest, which meant arriving at the pâtisserie before it was light. It was his job to light the ovens and get them up to temperature, whilst two other chefs proved the dough for that day's baking. One morning, he walked yawning to the back door to see a cart standing empty in the alleyway. A figure was tugging on a rope to secure it.

'Luc!'

The large man turned in surprise.

'Gui?'

Seizing Luc's hand, he shook it warmly, surprised by his own enthusiasm.

'Calm down, lad,' the big man laughed. 'I've had a long night, as you know.'

He greeted Marc and Yves, then stood against

the cart, exchanging news with his former colleagues. He accepted a share of a cigarette, to ward away the morning chill.

'We wondered what had happened, after Christmas,' Yves said pointedly. 'First you disappeared, then Mademoiselle at the end of the month. Thought there might have been something in it.'

'Monsieur Clermont offered me a job here, so I took it,' said Gui, careful not to drop ash onto his uniform. 'It's a long story. What did you mean about Mademoiselle disappearing? I saw her last week.'

'From duties, is what he means,' interrupted Luc. 'End of January, after all the flooding, we brought the delivery as usual, but no Mam'selle. They got another chap now.' He indicated inside, where an old man was staring into the delivery ledger as though it held an almighty puzzle. Gui recognized him as the cleaner. 'Hopeless he is, but we know where to go all right, so we're muddling through.'

Gui remembered Mademoiselle Clermont's words about her father and their disagreement. He wanted to tell the men what had happened during the flood, but he had promised to stay silent. Yves eyed him with interest as he bade them farewell and climbed the back step.

He felt a strange sadness as he watched the cart trundle away, but it was soon eclipsed by the smell of dough in the kitchens. He tended to the ovens, but was allowed to help the other chefs for a few hours, warming butter and measuring out orange blossom water to create

184

trays of rich, buttery brioche.

Monsieur Clermont or Josef were rarely present on Sundays, preferring the company of family and a leisurely breakfast on the day of rest. Usually, the kitchen was run by one of the senior chefs, like Ebersole or Melio, but it was best when Maurice was in charge.

'Let us give thanks to our patron, Saint Honoré!' he yelled across the echoing room. 'We'll need a dozen cakes by the time church slams its doors and ejects those hungry sinners. How long for the creme Chiboust, Gui?'

'Five minutes, Chef!' Gui called back, furiously whisking the egg whites that would be added to another apprentice's pastry cream.

'That should be sufficient, my son. Fetch the caramel, quick, before they finish mass!'

No one in the kitchen could match Maurice with a knife. He sent pieces of sugared almond and dried fruit flying into a tidy pile quicker than Gui could get them out of the jar. Every so often, the older chef would pretend to slip, sending pieces of nut or chocolate skidding down the counter. Gui and the other apprentices fell upon these, grinning, whilst Maurice turned a blind eye.

Gui was learning, slowly, the language of the kitchen. Every night, even when he was exhausted, he read Monsieur Carême's book by the light of his tiny stove, and soon, he could recite it inside out. Proudly, he realized he could nod whenever a silk sieve was mentioned; he had made countless bain-maries, he could whisk egg whites into spires in his sleep.

What was more, he found that he was a natural with pastry dough. Where the other apprentices swore and struggled, Gui's callused hands made deft work of the temperamental substance. One day, Maurice had grabbed his sleeve, pressed his wrist to Gui's palm.

'That explains it,' he declared, testing the other one. 'Your hands are like ice. Warm hands will never make a pastry chef. Did you know that?'

Gui shook his head, inspecting his pale blue fingernails. Perhaps being too poor to afford coal had its advantages. He remained at the bottom of the long ladder of apprentices, but his steps quickened, he laughed more, exchanged jokes with the others.

That Sunday, business in the pâtisserie was slow due to a spring rainstorm and, for the first time, Maurice allowed Gui to leave early.

'Go ahead,' he told him, taking a stack of trays from Gui's arms and depositing them in the scullery sink. 'I'll bet the others have conveniently forgotten to tell you that you're due one day off per week.'

Gui tried to smile gratefully. He knew about the days off, but did not take them. He would rather be at the pâtisserie where it was warm and he was fed, than in his freezing room on the Rue de Belleville.

'Why don't you slip away now?' Maurice insisted. 'It's only a few hours until we close and there are plenty of hands here. Take some time for yourself, go and have fun. Young men should enjoy themselves.'

It would be rude to turn down the offer, so he moved quietly to the cloakroom to dress in his street clothes. It was strange, to leave when there was work still to be done, but as he buttoned his jacket, the excitement of liberation crept upon him. He rarely had the chance to see Paris with its eyes open to the daylight.

In the jumble of the lost-property box he found a rickety umbrella. Several of its spokes had snapped, and it looked more like an ancient crow than a device to keep him dry, but he took it anyway. He sheltered under the pâtisserie's sign, struggling to wedge it open.

There was a commotion in the street before him. A shiny blue motor car stood steaming by the kerb, a man in a chauffeur's uniform poking around beneath its bonnet, water cascading from the brim of his cap.

'Need a hand?' Gui yelled over the rain.

'No, lad.' The chauffeur shook droplets out of his eyes. 'This'll be a night's work to repair.'

'Good afternoon!' a second voice called.

Mademoiselle Clermont was peering at him from inside the vehicle.

'Good afternoon.' He held the umbrella close to the window. 'What's happening?'

'Oh, something has broken,' she said. 'It's a nuisance, I was on my way to visit a good friend, but now I shall have to stay at home.'

She did not look overly upset, smiling through the rain-spattered glass. Gui hesitated, but the feeling of liberty was stronger than his caution.

'How far is it? Perhaps I could escort you,

187

then there would be no need to miss your appointment?'

He wished he could take back the words almost as soon as they were out of his mouth, but it was no use now, they had been said. He steeled himself for her polite rebuttal.

'It . . . it is a very kind offer, Guillaume, but my friend lives near the Musee des Arts. I fear it would be too far to walk in such weather.'

The look of embarrassment on her face was unmistakable. He heard himself speaking again.

'In that case, we might take the metro.'

'The metro?' she exclaimed, glancing towards the chauffeur.

'It is only a short trip.'

Her colour deepened.

'You *have* ridden the metro before?' he asked, incredulous.

'Father believes it is improper, and my aunt has a terror of being underground.' She tapped her gloved fingers upon the door, as if itching to open it. 'I suppose one would take the line from Opéra?'

He nodded. 'There are only a handful of stations between there and Arts et Métiers.'

In truth, he had only ever taken the metro once before, but he had talked endlessly with the other apprentices about it. The fright and the thrill of hurtling through dark tunnels to emerge in another part of the city was something he was desperate to experience again. The boy in him grinned at Mademoiselle Clermont.

'Of course,' he said mischievously, 'if you too are afraid of being underground . . . '

An impish smile was growing upon her face. She reached for the door handle.

'Emile,' she announced to the chauffeur, 'I shall be taking the metro to Lili's. I will telephone later, or ask that their driver bring me home, if the motor is not yet fixed.' She stepped under Gui's rickety umbrella. He took care to swivel it so that the leaks did not fall on her side. 'Don't mention this to my aunt, please,' she told the man. 'It would only worry her unnecessarily.'

The chauffeur nodded, face carefully blank. Mademoiselle Clermont's steps down the road were so fast that Gui had to hurry to keep up. The rain cascaded around their small shelter, until he could not help but stifle a laugh.

'Slow down!' he said. 'I can barely keep up with you.'

'I am sorry.' She was breathless, her smile huge. 'I feel like a prisoner escaping.'

In the warm pause that followed, Gui realized he had forgotten himself, had been addressing her informally. She did not seem affronted, but he switched back to the polite form when he spoke again.

'I met Luc recently, at the back door,' he said, as they slowed their pace. 'He told me that you hadn't been taking deliveries. Was that what you and your father disagreed about, a few weeks ago?'

The smile fell from her mouth.

'Yes,' she answered, 'amongst other things. My aunt told him that it was not appropriate for me to be doing any kind of work. He never listened to her before, but now . . . ' She seemed about to say more, but sighed, gave a half-smile instead. 'These visits to Lili are the only time I am allowed to myself.'

'Is it because of what happened in January?'

She nodded reluctantly.

'I am sorry.'

'Please don't apologize, Guillaume. If not for you, the situation might have been far worse.'

Place de l'Opéra broke open before them, obscured and rain-softened. A few motor cars slicked around the road. They had to leap back as one flew past, sending a sheet of muddy water towards their shoes. Mademoiselle Clermont just laughed, peering in the direction of a set of marble steps.

'There's the metro!' She pointed. 'Are we truly going to take it?'

'If you wish.'

'Of course I wish! Quickly, before my boots are soaked through.'

They ran the remaining distance to avoid motor cars and carriages, bumping into each other as they attempted to stay beneath the umbrella. The marble steps were treacherous with mud and rain. Mademoiselle Clermont steadied herself on Gui's arm, and together they made it to the ticket booth.

'Two single tickets, please,' Gui announced, 'to Arts et Métiers.'

He fished in his pocket for coins. Even a third-class journey would come at the cost of eating that night, but he had never been more willing to part with money.

'Wait,' Mademoiselle Clermont was opening

her purse. Firmly, Gui placed a small, perforated ticket in her hand.

'We are travelling third class?'

'I thought you wished to see the real metro?' he said, and received a smile in return.

They descended grit-spattered steps, and it was as though a hot gullet was swallowing them up. The narrow tunnel curved and Mademoiselle Clermont gripped his arm as they emerged onto the platform. It was saturated with sepia light, a sunset in autumn captured and crammed into the globes that hung from the vaulted ceiling.

The rain was a great equalizer. Men in overcoats mopped their faces and cleaned eyeglasses that were too steamed up to wear. Women removed dripping hats and attempted to brush them dry. No one noticed the young man and woman who stood arm on arm, although a close look would have revealed that they should not have been stepping out together.

The train arrived and Mademoiselle Clermont almost tripped over her skirts in her haste to board. During the short journey she pressed her fingertips to the window and stared in awe through her reflection into the black walls of the tunnels. Gui watched too, taking in the turn of her head and the curve of her cheek. It was with mutual reluctance that they left their seats when the train pulled squealing into their station.

'But I know where we are,' she exclaimed, running ahead as they emerged into the early evening. 'We are by the square. We have come all that way and it feels as though we've barely moved at all!'

'But we have.' Gui smiled, wrestling with the umbrella once more beneath the glass and iron shelter. 'That's the joy of it.'

The walk to Mademoiselle Clermont's destination was over far too quickly. The rain had eased, and it was almost pleasant in the grey, dripping evening. Gui told her about his work in the pâtisserie, stories of initiations and accidents, which had her alternately amused and appalled. She demanded to inspect his cold pastry-making hands for herself, turning them over to touch the burn scars in a way that made his stomach tumble like an acrobat.

'No one discovered you then, when you burned your jacket?' she asked as they ducked past an overflowing gutter.

'I'm safe for now, thanks to you and Patrice,' he said. 'Does that make us even?'

'Hardly.' Her eyes were shadowed beneath the brim of her hat. 'I still feel that I haven't thanked you . . .'

There was a rattling from above and he pulled her to one side, thinking a slate might be tumbling from a roof. Instead, a head appeared from a fourth-storey window.

'Jeanne!' a girl's voice called.

'Lili!'

Mademoiselle Clermont waved at her friend and hastily shook out her skirts, wet through at the hem.

'Lili must have been watching the road,' she said quickly. 'Thank you for escorting me, Guillaume. It was a thrill.'

'It was my pleasure, Mademoiselle Clermont.'

The streets, which before had their own deserted charm, now stretched outward, extending the distance he had to walk alone.

'Goodnight then,' he said.

'Goodnight, Monsieur du Frère.'

Reaching the opposite pavement, he turned. She stood, looking over her shoulder. A doorman in white gloves appeared and held the door open, waiting for her to enter.

'What made you come back?' she called. 'That day in the flood?'

The space between them filled with water and noise as the downpour began again. He tried to reply but his voice was lost in the weather.

27

May 1988

'So you're the one who left the note.'

The woman stands blocking the doorway. She looks like she is in her seventies; her grey hair is closely cropped and her eyes are sharp as flint. It is impossible to tell if she is amused or annoyed.

'I'm sorry to come unannounced,' I say awkwardly. 'There wasn't time to write and I couldn't find a phone number for Mr Lefevre anywhere.'

'We don't have one. We try to avoid communication like that. It's also why we moved here — out of the way, so to speak.'

She is staring, as though she could make me leave her doorstep by willpower alone.

'I read your husband's book, the one about poste-restante letters,' I continue doggedly. 'I need his help, and I think I can explain something about one of his mysteries. I'm sure it would interest him.'

'Perhaps it would.' Her eyes focus out towards the harbour for a long moment. 'Since you've come all this way, you'd better come in. Please try to be quiet for now, he's taking a nap. I'll make some tea while you wait.'

The house smells like old cooking and shortbread and salt-damp from the sea wall. It's a small place, with narrow rooms and sharp corners. In the kitchen, a square window looks onto the waterfront. A mist is clearing, shafts of sunlight breaking through. The kettle whistles on the hob.

'So, what has you turning up on our doorstep like this?' she asks. 'You weren't specific in your note. It must be important.'

Hot water is poured over tea leaves, milk into a jug shaped like a cow. I have spent most of the morning improvising conversations in my head, but now that I am here, I don't know where to start.

'It's to do with my grandfather,' I say slowly. 'I found out recently that he made a terrible mistake when he was a young man. I'm not sure exactly what happened, only that it haunted him for a long time. I think Mr Lefevre can help me find out what it was.'

A noise from the stairs draws her attention. An old man is climbing into the doorway. His eyes are sunken and clouded, but are bright with interest.

'Stephen, this is the young lady who left the note.' The woman adjusts a pair of reading glasses that sit crooked on his nose. 'She's here to talk to you about your work.'

She helps Lefevre into the room. His step falters and I see now that his whole body trembles. I feel a rush of guilt when I think about how I've barged in on this couple's well-ordered existence.

Perhaps sensing this, Lefevre smiles.

'No doubt my wife has tried to grill you over your intentions, young lady. Please excuse her, she used to lecture and has few people to terrify these days.' He extends a hand and I take it, feeling like an eight-year-old. 'Stephen Lefevre. Happy to talk through the book. I'm just surprised you found the damn thing at all. Helen, I think we'll go to the study.'

'I thought you might. This way,' she directs over her shoulder.

Their slow progress takes us into a room at the front of the house opposite the kitchen. The light from the window is darkened by shelf upon shelf of books, built into the walls. They have even been stacked into the corners, volumes of different sizes fanning out like the spine of a fish. An oxblood sofa is jammed beneath the window, one arm buried under newspapers.

'Don't let her get away without a few difficult questions,' says Helen with a smile, closing the door.

The walls of the cottage are thick, and old. Their silence is the kind conducive to study, and hard to break.

'Miss Stevenson,' starts Lefevre, 'please humour an old man. Tell me about yourself, why you're here. In detail please. I meet so few people these days.'

I begin with my grandpa's death, why it devastated me so and how it led to the discovery of the photograph. I tell him about Pâtisserie Clermont, the Allincourt letter, and, finally, the name 'du Frère'.

'In your book,' I say, searching for the library copy, 'when you mentioned the du Frère letters . . .'

Lefevre has gone very still. His rheum-fogged eyes are fixed upon me. I start to worry whether he's still breathing until he lets out a long puff of air.

'J.S.,' he pronounces clearly. 'J. Stevenson. How can you be sure?' He is holding himself back, but I can see the hope in his eyes.

'I can't,' I tell him honestly. 'But if there is a connection between Grandpa Jim and this du Frère, it's through the Pâtisserie Clermont scandal. They were both involved. Whatever happened there, it caused a great deal of damage.'

'I met him once,' Lefevre is in a daze, 'your grandfather. I was a student in London and he'd just brought out his second work, one of his social histories. I never imagined it might be him.'

'I have to know what happened.' I'm surprised by the desperation in my own voice. 'Please, if you know what was in those letters he sent to du Frère, please tell me.'

'Can I see my book?' he asks abruptly.

I hand over the library copy. It falls open on the page I have marked. He peers down almost fondly at the words before tapping one of the paragraphs and motioning me to read.

'*Being one of the best surviving examples of pre-war poste restante correspondence,*' I recite, '*the majority of the collection is held in storage at The Musée de La Poste, Paris, except for one letter, which is in the hands of an archivist. Due to laws surrounding secrecy of correspondence, the seals on the envelopes have never been broken. As such, we are unlikely ever to know the story behind this remarkable collection . . . '*

I look up blankly. Lefevre is levering himself out of the armchair with great difficulty. I catch his arm and he thanks me, limping to a bookshelf where great stacks of box files are gathering dust. He is muttering to himself.

'Mr Lefevre?' I ask. 'Are you all right?'

He is attempting to lift the first file.

'Help me look, will you?'

I reach past him to grasp the box.

'Look for what?'

'For what!' He laughs. 'Dear me, you aren't very quick for a historian, are you?'

'The letter?' I almost drop the file on my foot. 'You have it? *You're* the archivist?'

'Of course I am,' he wheezes, 'what other fool would pay what I did for it at auction? It's filed away in one of these.' He indicates the stacks with frustration. 'I fear I lost heart after the book did so badly, but now you're here, we can — '

A cough racks his chest and he doubles over, unable to complete the sentence. I catch his arm and help him back to the chair, where he slumps down.

'We can open it,' he says eventually, 'the letter. It would be illegal for me to, but you're family, you're,' he gulps in air, 'next of kin.'

I stand uncertain. Lefevre is panting; his eyes squeezed shut in pain. I turn away to fetch his wife, but he catches my hand, points insistently towards the shelves.

He appears to be recovering, so I push up my sleeves and get to work. The files are full of letters, papers, copies of ledgers. They're neatly organized, but finding one envelope among them all will be no easy task. My fringe sticks to my forehead and my nose is itching with dust by the time I start on a third box. I drag it into the light and sit cross-legged to trawl through the contents.

My legs are just starting to turn numb when a loop of ink catches my eye, a familiar scrawl that makes my heart contract.

'Mr Lefevre!'

He is instantly alert, leaning forward as I extract the letter from its plastic wallet. The paper of the envelope is fragile, feels as though it could rip at the slightest touch. It is worn, dirtied by countless hands, but there is no mistaking those untidy characters: *G. du Frère, POSTE RESTANTE, Bordeaux, France.*

'I know the writing,' I tell the old man shakily. 'It's his, it's Grandpa Jim's, I'm certain.'

'Open it.' Lefevre's voice is husky.

My fingers rest upon the edge of the envelope. It feels wrong, to open something so long sealed. Without warning, my eyes are stinging with tears.

'I can't,' I whisper, unable to look up.

'What are you afraid you'll find?'

I cannot answer; the words are too far buried, wrapped around my love for a man who was more of a father to me than I ever realized.

'I'm sorry,' I whisper — to my grandfather's memory, to myself — as I rip open the envelope.

28

March 1910

'I don't think I can get away early,' Gui whispered. 'The delivery this morning was so big, most of us are still trying to catch up.'

Mademoiselle Clermont sighed in frustration. Their Sunday metro trips had become a weekly routine. Her aunt was none the wiser, so it seemed that Emile, the chauffeur, had been as good as his word.

'The delivery will be for the Easter party, next Saturday,' she told him. 'Father has been making the most ridiculous fuss.'

'Are you speaking again?' Gui asked.

'Yes, if you count a one-word exchange as speaking.'

'You will have to forgive him eventually.'

'Not whilst that mop-pushing ape is ruining my delivery ledgers,' she said, drumming her fingers on the doorframe. 'It really is vexing about tonight. Father is dining out and Aunt has tickets to the opera; neither of them shall be home until after midnight. I thought that rather than going to see Lili, we might have visited some of the other stations.'

Gui's heartbeat trebled. Mademoiselle Clermont wanted to spend the evening with *him*. He racked his brain. 'Ebersole is in charge,' he told her, 'so perhaps I can get away by seven.'

Footsteps approached in the corridor and he hurriedly pushed the door between them closed.

'Guillaume!'

Mademoiselle Clermont was peering through the gap, a devious smile on her face.

Metro, seven she mouthed.

Stifling a grin, he hurried back to the kitchen.

That afternoon was a first for Gui; it seemed his talents with pastry had not gone unnoticed, for Ebersole teamed him up with Maurice and set the pair of them making tarte tatin. The other apprentices looked on from their chores with envy, as Gui rolled and folded and re-rolled the butter-filled pastry from the day before, his quick, cold fingers barely leaving a mark on the soft surface.

Maurice was at the stove, creating a dark caramel from butter and sugar. Another apprentice was slicing up a box of apples from the winter store. When the sheets of pastry were the thickness of a sou, Maurice showed him how to score them with a knife into perfect rounds.

Together, they assembled the tarts. When they finally emerged from the oven, they were upturned onto serving plates, deeply caramelized, crisp and sweet. Gui felt a swell of pride as he watched them disappear into the pâtisserie, to be sold to the rich and discerning.

The day flew by, and soon he found himself fumbling with the buttons of his street clothes. Mademoiselle Clermont would be waiting. He had pleaded stomach pains, and Ebersole had allowed him to leave early. There was a fluttering in his chest, as if his lungs had expanded too far.

He was never usually nervous about his trips with Mademoiselle Clermont, but something told him that tonight might be different. He stared down at his second-hand clothes, tight and loose in all the wrong places.

'Maurice, lend me your hat, will you?' he asked the older man.

'Why should I?'

'Come on, just for tonight.'

'Not unless you tell me why,' Maurice baited, spinning the brown hat on one finger. 'I take it your stomach ache is a rendezvous? Aren't you a bit young for the Belleville girls?'

The entire cloakroom had looked around, taking an interest in the exchange.

'She's *not* a Belleville girl,' Gui whispered, face reddening. 'Please, I'll give you my share of supper tomorrow.'

'Respectable lady, eh?' Maurice continued remorselessly. 'Going to take her for a drink, see some singers at the *Folies?* Home for tea with father by ten?'

'Just give me the hat.'

Amidst much laughter, Maurice jammed the felt hat onto Gui's head. It was too big, so he folded up a sheet of newspaper to act as padding. The effect was not all he had hoped, but if he blurred his eyes, his reflection did have a degree of civility.

'If corks aren't popped tonight, I want a return on my investment!' Maurice roared as he made his escape into the street.

As he neared the metro, he made out a slim figure waiting beside a lamppost.

'*Bon soir!*' Gui called.

Mademoiselle Clermont spun. Her limbs relaxed when she saw him, but anxiety remained etched across her face, partly hidden beneath a fine veil. He wondered if it was for disguise.

'Is everything all right?' he said, frowning.

Meeting his gaze, a laugh burst from her lips. It surprised her as much as him, for she clapped a satin-gloved hand to her mouth.

'What is it?' he demanded as she fought to control herself.

'I am sorry, Guillaume, it's nothing, really.'

'It's the hat, isn't it?' he accused.

'No, no, it looks very fine.' Still smiling, she took his arm. 'So, where are we to visit this evening, Monsieur du Frère?'

'I thought we might go to the Left Bank.'

Gui knew he was taking a risk. The Left Bank was everything that Pâtisserie Clermont was not: riotous and gritty, seething with artists and writers, painters, musicians, all ravenous for experience, living in a frenzy of colour and newness and abandonment. Gui was desperate to see it, to show Mademoiselle Clermont a real part of Paris, grime and joy and all. He watched as, with the resolution of one swallowing medicine, she nodded.

'The Left Bank,' she said. 'I've heard that there are women there who wear men's suits.' He could tell she was trying to sound nonchalant.

'How shocking.' He grinned, and some of her anxiety dropped away as she smiled in return.

Arm on arm they strolled towards Concorde. The night felt warmer than usual, a hint of spring to come, although most of the city remained steadfastly bleak and grey. They passed an older couple, out taking the air. Gui touched his hat to them in greeting.

The metro at Concorde was busy. Third class offered obscurity; sitting shoulder to shoulder on the narrow bench, they could have been anyone. There was a moment when the train jolted on its tracks, throwing them sideways. Gui found himself clasping a slim hand. In the flickering light of the tunnel, their eyes met. A hundred words and none passed between them, until Mademoiselle Clermont looked away.

They were still hand in hand when the train came to a stop at Châtelet. They hurried ahead of the departing crowd as best they could, although Mademoiselle was hindered by the narrowness of her skirts. More than once she had to stop and tug at the garment.

'I chose the fabric,' she told Gui breathlessly. In the lamplight, he caught a glimpse of satin, blue-black as a raven's wing. 'My aunt let me, so long as she settled on the design. She doesn't know that I telephoned the seamstress and changed it.'

At the end of the street, the Seine spread itself to the left and right, its surface rippling with gas lamps. The bridge was dotted with people, couples, motor cars, late-night flower sellers offering blue paper roses and more besides. A taxi cab stood juddering at the edge of the pavement.

'I'm not going past the bridge,' the driver was saying stubbornly, pumping the starter handle.

'You'll have to find another cab over there. Or walk.'

A tall young man prowled by the door of the vehicle.

'The journey has been paid for!' he fumed. 'Come now, boss, it will take you less than ten minutes.'

'I *told* you,' the driver said angrily, 'I don't deal with the Left Bank. Now move.'

'You'll have to run me down first!'

The taxi driver clambered up to his seat and began to steer the motor car around in a semicircle. Gui and Mademoiselle Clermont paused, alongside several other passers-by, to observe the scene. To their amazement, the young man planted himself in the path of the taxi.

'*Avancez maintenant*, frog!' he yelled to the approaching headlights.

The taxi trundled forward with increasing speed. At the last minute the man was forced to leap to one side; the motor car shot through a puddle, showering him with a spray of mud before rattling off into the night.

Spectacle over, the crowd began to disperse, leaving the young man to pick himself up from the ground.

'Are you all right?' asked Gui, although Mademoiselle Clermont gripped his arm to stop him.

'Nothing damaged save for pride, all in a night's work,' said the stranger, extracting a handkerchief.

He had an odd accent; Gui guessed at English

or Swiss. He was younger than he first appeared, and thin, like a pile of sticks wrapped in a suit. His clothes were finely made, although there were tell-tale patches of darning, worn elbows that spoke of long hours propped on a desk.

'It would seem I lost my composure,' the young man said, catching his breath. 'If I had not, I might have succeeded in knocking that brute out of his little cab.'

'Well, if you are sure you feel well . . . ' Gui turned away.

'Determined to short change me is what he was.' The young man had fallen into step beside them. Gui felt a pinch on his wrist and glanced at Mademoiselle Clermont. *Now look at what we must deal with*, her stare said. With an apologetic look, Gui turned back to the man's conversation.

' . . . is why one should never pay a taxi in advance. Of course, if they gave me enough cash this would never have happened, but no, it is all pre-approved expenses for staff these days.'

'If you will excuse us,' Mademoiselle Clermont interrupted, 'we were enjoying a private conversation.'

Rather than flinch at the iciness of her tone, the young man coughed out a laugh behind a cheap cigarette.

'Old manners prevail only as far as the end of the bridge, I'm afraid, miss. I'm Jim.' He stuck out a hand. 'Writer, hack, really. Been in Paris a few months. You?'

'Guillaume du Frère. Apprentice chef. This is — '

'You may call me Jeanne,' Mademoiselle Clermont said quickly.

'A pleasure to meet you both, Guillaume and Jeanne. How long have you two been married?'

'A month.'

'We are not — '

In unison, they gaped at each other. Gui cursed himself and Jeanne shot him an impenetrable look before wading into the mire of conversation.

'We are not married yet,' she corrected. 'Engaged for a month, is what he means.'

Jim was not troubled by the confusion, merely took another drag on his cigarette.

'If you insist.'

'What does that mean?' she demanded.

'It means, Mademoiselle, that we have reached the Left Bank. Now the world is whatever we make it.' Their new acquaintance stopped in the middle of the street and spread his arms. 'Where are you two lovebirds heading? Do you have a place in mind or can I pass on an honest recommendation, as a resident of these fair streets?'

'What do you say?' whispered Gui. 'We are for an adventure, after all?'

He squeezed her hand, and her wariness thawed, just a little.

'Very well,' she answered after some consideration. 'We will accept your recommendation, so long as the place is reputable.'

'Of course!' cried Jim. 'What do you take me for? I may be an immigrant but I know a few things about propriety.'

'Where are you from, Jim?' Gui asked as they strolled away from the river. 'You said you had only been here for a few months?'

'England.' The young man swung an imaginary golf-stroke. 'Surrey, to be precise.'

'Your French is excellent,' Jeanne said hesitantly.

'Studied the language in my student days. Learned it from my nursemaid as a child, too. Sylvie. She was from Paris, or Belleville, if you call that Paris. Atrocious accent. Used to get the penny song-sheets sent over to her, and teach them to me during playtime.'

Linking his hands under his chin, Jim bounded forward into the road and began to sing in a high-pitched warble.

'*Tu tressailles sous ma caresse, de si voluptueux frissons, que pour avoir pareille ivresse, rebrouillons-nous, recommencons!*'

A group of passing men and women broke into applause. Jim curtsied and fluttered his hand, and even Jeanne could not keep herself from laughing. Their new-found friend was delighted with the attention and kept up a constant stream of chatter as they walked. Turning a corner, they were confronted by manic fizzing as a tram rolled past. Sparks shot from the wire on the roof as it slid to a halt.

'*Allons-y!*' hissed Jim, sidling up to the back step and leaping on in a crouch to avoid the conductor.

'We'll walk,' Gui announced. 'Mademoiselle can't jump on in her gown.'

But Jeanne was already gone, hoisting her skirt

208

to allow herself an inch or two of movement. Jim handed her up to the step. The tram sparked again and there was nothing for Gui to do but hop on after them and hope for the best.

They hung from the back railing, all in a row, breath misting in the chill March air. Glancing at his companions, happiness rose in Gui's chest and he let out a whoop as the tram gathered speed. The conductor caught sight of them and rolled his eyes. Minutes later they tumbled off in the heart of Montparnasse.

'This is the place!' Jim proclaimed outside a café where, despite the season, tables spilled out onto the streets. Men in evening jackets and ratty waistcoats stood with glasses in hand. Women, too, in loose, printed dresses and furs, trailing cigarettes.

'La Rotonde.' He guided them beneath a flickering electric sign towards an empty table and signalled for a waiter. 'Homes may come and go, but with a few centimes, or shillings in your pocket, you'll find your way from here.'

'What if we aren't lost?' Jeanne smiled, unpinning her hat.

Jim's answer was lost on Gui as he stared. Jeanne's hair was cut short. For the first time it was not hidden beneath flowers and veils. It was dark and smooth and curled simply beneath her earlobes, held back on one side by an ebony pin. A collar still encased her neck, lace rising from the deep blue satin.

'You look . . . ' Gui choked on his own words.

Jim raised his glass a fraction, unexpected interest in his eyes. 'I think my new friend intended to pay you a compliment, Mademoiselle,' he said. 'You do indeed look striking. Truly à la mode.'

'Thank you,' Jeanne murmured, her lips quirking into a smile as she accepted a glass of anisette.

Gui scowled at Jim, but any rivalry was soon forgotten in lively conversation. A dark-haired pianist sidled into the corner, along with a tall cello player. They launched into a swaying melody.

'Would Mademoiselle care . . . ?' Jim started.

'I believe I promised the first dance of the evening to Monsieur du Frère, thank you,' Jeanne said as she stood.

Draining his glass, Gui followed her onto the floor, trying desperately to remember whether he knew anything about dancing. He couldn't make out whether the music was a waltz or a two-step, or something entirely unfamiliar. As soon as he closed one hand around Jeanne's waist, he found that he didn't care.

'You do look wonderful,' he managed to say with an embarrassed smile. 'I am sorry I didn't say so earlier. I mean, about your hair.'

'My aunt will never let me wear it like this in public. I know it must look strange.'

'I like it.' Her eyes were an even brighter blue, up close, and he remembered the electric jolt that had passed through him the first time she had touched his face in the freezing alleyway. 'It's different. You are different.'

'I am not sure I intend to be.'

'What do you mean?'

More couples were joining the dance floor, the crowd shielding them from everything outside, from everything that shunned, that disapproved.

'I did not cut my hair by choice.' She was studying a spot on his lapel with great concentration. 'I cannot grow it any longer. There is scar tissue and the doctor advises against it.'

He was silent as she dropped his hand, and with something like resentment, pulled her high collar down an inch. The skin beneath was angry, stretched and puckered into uneven ridges. Up close, he could see that it reached into her hairline, towards the base of her skull. The bodies of the other dancers were packed in so closely, no one noticed that they had stopped moving.

'What happened?' he whispered.

The fabric at Jeanne's throat beat with her pulse.

'I was in the kitchens with Father,' she said, 'when I was small. One of the chefs forgot about a pan of boiling sugar. I smelled it burning and tried to get Father's attention but he wouldn't listen. I thought I would be able to reach . . .'

Tears were gathering in her eyes, threatening to spill over as she raised a protective palm to her neck.

'I know it's horrible, but I had to show you.'

She turned away, but Gui leaned forward and caught her face in his hands.

'Jeanne Clermont,' he whispered recklessly beneath the music, 'you are the most beautiful girl I have ever seen — '

211

Then her lips were on his. He felt the heat of her mouth, one of her hands grazing his face. The band drew out its final note.

The dancers drifted apart and he stepped back with difficulty, his whole body trembling. They returned to the table hand in hand, eyes bright and faces flushed, where Jim waited with another round of drinks.

'Brava,' he saluted them, 'to the soon-to-be happy couple.'

The evening grew louder. Jim introduced them to all manner of people with strange names and even stranger accents. They even had their likeness taken by a friend of his with a portable photographic camera. At eleven, they made their farewells. Gui loosed a breath of happiness as they stepped into the brisk night.

'Gui! Jeanne!' came a shout from behind them. Jim was leaning out the door, tie loosened, empty glass in hand. 'Where am I to contact you should the occasion arise?'

'Pâtisserie Clermont,' Gui shouted back, already wondering when he could catch another moment with Jeanne. 'Yourself?'

'Here, they'll know where to find me, just ask for Jim Stevenson.'

29

May 1988

The phone rings and rings; I imagine it shrilling into the chaos of Whyke's office. Finally, it clatters into life.

'Hello?' he answers breathlessly. He sounds like he's been running.

'Professor, it's Petra,' I shout. The phone box I'm using is ancient and the line is bad.

'Where are you?' his voice crackles.

'Penzance station. I've just come from seeing Mr Lefevre. They asked me to stay last night. It was too late for the train after we'd finished talking.'

'And?' Whyke sounds as impatient as I feel.

'I read the letter,' I rush, 'it was from my grandfather. And it explains some of what happened, but not all — ' The phone starts beeping urgently. I fumble in my pocket for more change. 'I can't talk for much longer, but I have the letter, the real one. Lefevre gave it to me. I'll show you when I get back.'

'Where are you going now?'

'London, to read the article.'

'I'll phone ahead and make sure it's reserved for you.'

'Thanks.'

'Thank me later,' he says hurriedly. 'I've managed to convince Kaufmann that you've gone home for a 'family emergency', but she's suspicious.'

'I only need a few more days.'

'That's all you have. Do you realize what Monday is?'

I don't need to reply.

'If you don't attend the review, you'll lose your place,' he tells me. 'Are you sure — '

The phone cuts off before I can answer, lapsing into a single tone.

I begin the long journey back to London. In my bag is the letter from my grandfather. Lefevre allowed me to keep it, saying that it was only right.

I read it again and again as the train streams across moorland and coastline. The sun glints on the distant waves. It is written in French, which is unsettling. I had no idea that Grandpa Jim was so fluent. Lefevre's wife, Helen, made a translation for me, but I stare at the original, already knowing its contents off by heart.

Guillaume,

I write to you again in hope of reply. The words I offer are the same, which means that they are worthless, I know. Nothing I can say will restore what I stole from you. Only now do I begin to truly understand.

Conscience is a terrible thing, Gui. Year by year, it grows, like ink on silk, until it touches all of our actions, past and present. Had I known . . . It is pointless to wish. Pointless, too, to ask for your compassion, when I do not deserve it. Yet I

write once more with the words I did not
have a chance to say in Paris: I am sorry.
  Forgive me, please.
  I remain,
  Jim Stevenson

The night I spent on the Lefevres' sofa was a sleepless one. As the moon ghosted over the harbour, I wore out my grandfather's words, whispering them over and over: *Nothing I can say will restore what I stole from you.*

Those words belong to a youth, a stranger. I can't justify his actions or connect him to the old man I loved so dearly. Part of me doesn't want to read the article, wants to keep my precious memories intact, rather than have to deal with the existence of this new 'Jim Stevenson'. And yet, I have to know.

When we finally reach Paddington, I call the Newspaper Library to check that Whyke has reserved the microfilm for me. The woman on the phone is surprisingly curt.

'Miss,' she snaps when I mention the title, 'as I told your professor when he called this morning, that reel has been reserved for research purposes. I advised him, as I am advising you, to request a copy.'

I falter. 'What do you mean, 'reserved'?'

'It's being used exclusively by one of our affiliate publishers,' comes the sniffy reply. 'Like I said, I suggest you request a copy of the item you're interested in.'

'Fine.' I bite back the sharpness in my voice. 'I *am* requesting one. How long will that take?'

'Processing time is ten working days, upon receipt of the signed paperwork and fee.'

Furious, I end the call. This is Hall's doing. Who else would demand exclusive access to one obscure piece of microfilm exactly when I need it? The blood is racing to my head as I hammer my mother's number with my thumb. No answer. I look in my Filofax. My father's number is there, seldom looked at and dialled even less.

Gritting my teeth, I punch in the numbers.

'Can I speak to Mr Stevenson please?' I ask when the call connects. I can hear the sounds of the newsroom in the background, busy shouts and phones ringing.

'Who's speaking?'

'It's his daughter.'

I'm not even sure how my dad will react. Our last phone call wasn't exactly genial. I remember his tone as he told me I was being 'ridiculous'. It's almost enough to make me hang up.

'Petra?' My father sounds shocked and not a little wary. 'What's going on? Is everything OK?'

'Everything's fine.' I struggle to keep my voice light. 'It's about Grandpa Jim's papers.' *The ones you would have thrown out*, I stop myself from saying.

I can almost hear my dad ice over.

'If you're going to start on about that again —'

'No, no.' I steel myself, put on my most contrite voice. 'You were right, I shouldn't have been so possessive. I did take something of Grandpa's.'

'Oh.' My father sounds flummoxed. He'd

216

obviously been preparing for a fight. 'Well, you should return it asap.'

'I will. Listen, I've been in London for research. That biographer, Simon, he lives here, doesn't he? I could go round to his place and drop off the papers, since I'm in town. To say sorry.'

My father agrees, probably because I'm being civil. I can tell he wants to say something more, and wonder whether he feels guilty about his behaviour, but I scribble down Hall's details as quickly as I can, tell him I have to go.

The address is for a street in Putney. I'm halfway there on the tube before my anger subsides enough to wonder what on earth I'm doing. Hall has the photograph, the Allincourt letter, but what will confronting him do? Embarrass him into giving them back? Shame him into letting me take a copy? I feel slightly sick as I step out onto the street, but I force myself onward, without a plan.

The address leads me to a large Victorian house, divided into flats. There are lights on in some of the windows, the sound of water gurgling into a drain. I ring the buzzer, and after a minute I see a shape descending through the glass door. I hitch up my bag, prepared to stand my ground, but it's a woman who answers. She's smartly dressed in suit trousers and a shirt, her dark hair loose.

'Yes?' she says politely.

'Hi.' I grope for any excuse. 'I'm . . . I'm here to see Simon?'

'From the publisher?'

'I'm sorry?'

'The publisher. He's expecting some paper-work?' She has one eyebrow raised.

I'm out of my depth already, but I take the plunge.

'That's right,' I stammer, 'I have it here.'

'I'll give it to him, thanks.' The woman holds out a hand. I step back.

'I can wait, it's no trouble, they sent me with something else that needs to be signed and returned immediately.'

'He's in the shower at the moment,' the woman says a little doubtfully. 'Do you want to come in?'

She leads the way up a dark staircase into a flat at the front of the house. It's a pleasant place, a kitchen-living-room jammed with squashy sofas and books. In another life, perhaps, Hall and I might have been friends. Somewhere in the flat, water is running. I still have no idea what's going to happen when he sees me.

'How is his work going?' The woman leans against the kitchen worktop. The briefcase that Hall was carrying in the library sits open on a chair. If she would leave me alone, just for a second, I could search it.

'Er, great, all on track,' I improvise, trying to peer into the case.

'That's good.' She smiles. 'He's been under so much pressure recently. I suppose you know about the grand-daughter, making waves, trying to steal his research?'

My stomach flips with fear and anger.

'Are you all right?' she asks. 'You look a bit flushed.'

'Fine,' I manage, scanning the exposed contents of the briefcase.

Then I see it. Amongst the papers is an inch of hand-writing I recognize as Allincourt's. The sound of running water stops.

'That'll be Simon out of the shower. I'll tell him you're here before he walks in naked or something. What did you say your name was?'

'Anna.'

As soon as she's through the door I'm lunging for the papers. It's all there: the photograph, the letter, the slip of paper from the gallery. Clipped to them is a page of bullet-pointed notes. I see a reference to *The Word* written halfway down the paper and shove the whole lot into my jacket. There are voices from the other room, questioning tones, a door slamming.

'He said he didn't know that anyone called Anna worked there,' the woman says as she enters, 'but he'll be right out.'

'I'm an intern,' I tell her a little wildly, certain that she'll see the flash of white beneath my jacket. 'Actually, I think I've brought the wrong paperwork, picked it up by mistake. They'll have to send the right version tomorrow.'

I make a break for the door, heart thudding against the pages.

'Well, if you wait a second — ' she tries.

'Thanks, but I've got to run.'

I don't care if it's suspicious; I have to get out of there. In the hallway a door opens to my right. I catch a flash of a figure in a dressing gown before I'm skidding down the stairs in my haste to reach the front door.

There are voices behind me. I won't make it onto the road without being seen, and my brain is so sizzled on adrenalin that without a second's hesitation I clamber over the side of the steps that lead to ground level, landing heavily in a pile of rubbish, old branches and brambles.

The wall is slimy and damp with weeds, but I press against it as the front door flies open above me. I can just make out the back of Hall's head as he begins to swear.

'She's taken them,' he barks. 'Why the hell did you let her in?'

'She said she was from the publisher,' the woman sounds equally peeved. 'Maybe she just got nervous.'

'Was she blonde?' he demands.

'What?'

'Blonde, slim, in her twenties?'

'Why?' The woman's tone has taken on a hostile edge. 'Who is this girl, Simon? Why are you so angry with her for turning up here?'

'Carol, wait, I told you . . .'

Their voices fade as the front door is slammed. Grinning stupidly, I zip the papers into my bag.

30

April 1910

That morning, the bells woke Gui, louder and more vocal than he had ever heard them. Rather than pulling the blanket up over his head and shivering at the thought of his night-cold clothes, he rushed to the window, shunting it open to let in a blast of morning.

His head jutted out from the roof and he felt like an animal emerging from a burrow. There was life in the air. Gui wondered if Jeanne was leaning through her curtains. Raising his head, he let out a crow, pictured it bouncing from wall to wall across the city to greet her.

There was scraping from along the roof, and Isabelle's head also appeared, tousled from sleep.

'I thought it was a dog, howling at the moon,' she called, 'but here I find you.'

'Happy Easter!' he laughed. 'Did I wake you? I am sorry, I couldn't keep it in.'

'Don't apologize, it's rare that I'm woken by such a happy sound.'

Back in his room, Gui lit the fire and balanced a kettle on the tiny stove for hot water. He enjoyed his morning routine. With his few belongings stowed neatly, the mouse-hole room was almost cosy. Some of the hot water went into the ewer, some into a battered tin pot with a sprinkling of tea leaves.

He washed carefully, paying particular attention to his nails. Today was the day of Pâtisserie Clermont's grandest event: the Easter celebration. The kitchens had been a hive of activity. Monsieur Clermont had been present every day, experimenting with ingredients to create an opulent centrepiece. Everyone in the cloakroom speculated about what it would be, gossiping like washer-women. One junior chef had even started a pool for those who cared to place money on their opinions.

Whatever it was, Gui knew it would be magnificent. He had spent a joyous day melting chocolate and moulding it into shapes, another making batches of the delicate pastry he was developing such a talent with. He sincerely hoped that Maurice would be in charge of his section and that they would be able to work together to create something wonderful.

Locking his door behind him, Gui heard a rustle. It was Isabelle, smiling.

'We used to do this when we were children,' she said, patting something onto his back. 'It's supposed to bring you luck.'

Gui's fingers found thin paper, cut into the shape of a fish, fixed to his jacket with a pin.

'I don't believe I'll need it,' he said and grinned.

Although the sun had barely risen, the omnibus at the bottom of Rue de Belleville was crowded with worshippers, all heading to the larger churches for a special service. Eventually, he gave up his seat to an old lady and walked. By the time he got to work, the cloakroom was packed. The night shift had just come to an end, and apprentices jostled for space, balancing cups of coffee and cigarettes, trying to find a seat before they returned to the kitchens.

Maurice was napping in one corner, an apron spread over his face. Gui reached out to sneak a few sips from the steaming cup of coffee that sat forgotten by his elbow.

'Don't even think about it, you southern rat,' the chef's voice rumbled from below the apron. 'I need that like I need my blood. That bastard Melio's gone and caught himself the black lung. They've put me on his shift.' Wearily, Maurice removed the garment and blinked up at Gui. 'Going to need your help today, lad.'

'You mean . . . ?'

'Welcome to the next rung. You'll be my commis chef for the day.'

'What will we be doing?' he pressed.

Maurice tapped his nose mysteriously.

'All will be revealed. I just hope you remember how to handle choux.'

A clock chimed in the hall, and the chefs filtered back to work. Hurriedly, Gui shed his clothes and crammed the white hat over his hair, grown back into its thick curls. When he reached the kitchens, he found the entire staff being ushered through the empty café towards the front of the building.

'What's going on?' he whispered to a neighbouring apprentice.

The boy was trying with great fervour to push a tuft of hair beneath his cap. 'A photograph,' he said breathlessly. 'Josef announced it this morning. It's for the newspapers.'

Eyes wide, Gui began his own frantic grooming, thankful that he had paid extra attention to washing that morning. Outside, the sun was growing warmer. It was the first true spring day, breezy and cool yet brimming with the possibility of a new summer.

A man with clipped-up sleeves was struggling with a tripod, while another assembled something that looked like a big, black accordion. Gui felt a rush of excitement, remembering the last time he had had his likeness taken, in La Rotonde with Jeanne.

Josef instructed them to line up, to cross their arms one over the other in the same fashion, and to await the photographer's instructions. No smiling, he commanded solemnly, no monkey business or japes, or he would know about it. They had been standing silently for ten minutes when Monsieur Clermont finally arrived.

Gui's heart quickened its pace; Jeanne was accompanying her father.

She was dressed in sober clothes, a dark dress with delicate cream lace that, as always, encircled her neck up to the chin, hiding the scar he now knew was there. Her short hair was disguised by a slanting hat and a coiled hairpiece. Silently, she followed her father and took her place at the centre of the group.

She looked so distant, cold even, that he could not believe this was the same girl who had hitched up her skirts and stolen a ride on a tram just days before. Joy and uncertainty burned his throat as he remembered the kiss. Had it been the same for her?

A horse-drawn carriage rolled up to the pavement, almost scattering the group. The photographer was apoplectic and Josef had to be dispatched to urge the driver on his way. In the confusion, Gui lunged out of his place and dashed down the line, squeezing in beside Mademoiselle Jeanne and stepping hard on a fellow apprentice's foot as he tried to complain.

There was a whisper of fabric as she adjusted her shawl. His breathing was coming fast. The photographer was shouting instructions, counting down. As he reached zero, Gui reached out towards Jeanne.

Her hand was waiting. They locked fingers just as a flash exploded into the morning. For one single, glorious instant, they held on to each other. Then they were blinking the brightness from their eyes and her fingers slipped from his, as if it had never been. Slowly, Gui mingled with the crowd as they made their way back into the kitchens.

They lined themselves up before the workstations to await their orders. Clermont surveyed his army, taking care to meet each pair of eyes. Gui felt that his gaze was held for far longer than anyone else's. Images of Jeanne crowded into his mind. He fought to keep his face blank as Clermont started to speak.

'As you know,' the older man told them, 'Easter Sunday is an important day for us. It is a return, a renewal and a celebration. Many of the guests attending today's special gathering do so after a long month of abstinence. Can anyone tell me, what does abstinence lead us to crave?'

There was an awed, schoolroom hush from the assembled chefs, until an eager voice piped up: 'Luxury.'

Clermont nodded, waved his hand for more.

'Glamour?' someone else supplied.

'Beauty.'

'Sin.' Gui heard the word falling from his mouth and blanched. Monsieur Clermont, however, only nodded.

'Luxury. Glamour. Beauty. Sin. We must create all of these today.' An unnerving smile twitched his mouth. 'I've heard that there is something of a wager running on what the centrepiece will be. Would someone care to tell me the assumptions?'

No one spoke. It was impossible to tell whether Monsieur was furious or amused.

'No? Josef, put them from their misery.'

'We make croquembouche!' the blond chef boomed.

A ripple ran through the kitchen, excitement, apprehension.

'Croquembouche?' Gui whispered. He was sure he had seen the word somewhere before.

'Just wait,' Maurice said, 'you will see, when we find out which part we are to play.'

Josef called upon the more senior chefs one by one, starting with Ebersole and working down the chain. Maurice came about halfway. He beckoned his small team forward. Under the watchful eye of Monsieur Clermont, they were talked through a series of techniques, ingredients

226

lists, preparation times. Finally, Josef turned a page to show them a sketch of the finished confection.

'But that's Monsieur Carême!' Gui burst out before he could stop himself. He had seen the illustration a hundred times over in his tattered book. It showed a spiralling cone of little choux pastries, held together with caramel and spun sugar, decorated with sugar ribbons and flowers.

Josef had stopped speaking. Monsieur Clermont's stare was cold. Eventually, talk resumed and they were dismissed to their station.

'What was that?' Maurice demanded. 'I thought you were smarter than to spout every thought that comes into your head.'

'I'm sorry,' Gui winced, 'but I've seen that drawing before, the exact same one, in a book I have, by Monsieur Antonin Carême.'

'A word to the wise,' Maurice murmured, 'and I shall only say it once, because you won't get another opportunity to listen. Never compare Clermont's work to that of another chef. As far as we are concerned, it is original, it is brilliant and it is our job to keep quiet and make it happen.'

Gui frowned. He had thought that Clermont was a master in his own right, an architect, not a copycat. Perhaps Clermont, too, loved Carême, Gui told himself, wanted to pay homage to the great man with his creation. All the same, the realization bothered him.

Josef set them making a range of caramels, some soft and tempered with cream, some dark and brittle as glass or flavoured with essence of orange and vanilla. Watching yet another pan of sugar melt into a bubbling mass, Gui thought of Jeanne, of her story.

'Ever burned yourself with sugar?' he asked Maurice distractedly. The other man was busy spinning sugar through the air, until a nest of fine strands rested in his palm. He balled it up and threw it towards the refuse.

'No good,' he called to another chef. 'It needs to be darker. Sugar burns?' he replied, wiping his hands on his apron. 'Nasty things. Sugar sticks to the skin and keeps burning. By the time you wash it off, half the flesh comes with it.'

Thinking of Jeanne's neck, Gui blanched.

'Been talking to Mademoiselle?'

The comment was so offhand that Gui almost answered in the affirmative, before he caught himself. Maurice's face was turned away, but there was something observant in his posture.

'Just a story I heard,' Gui tried to sound indifferent. 'One of the other boys said that she got burned when she was a child. I wondered about it, that's all.'

'Well, you heard right,' Maurice said, 'though there's not many here who know about that. Who told you?'

Gui tested the sugar with a spoon. 'Can't remember.'

'I reckon it's why Monsieur let her run around like she owned the place for so long,' the older chef reasoned. 'Of course, he's had to rein her in now. It's lucky she's a girl of means, or else he'd have trouble getting her married off.'

'What?' Gui asked, a little too sharply.

'Well, who wants damaged goods when there are better ones on offer?'

Whether he saw the anger in Gui's face or not, there was little time to talk after that. Gui wrestled his temper under control, for the day was advancing and there was work to be done. Clermont had finally settled on the right caramels, and together, he and Maurice measured the ingredients into different pans.

The activity in the kitchen began to build. Each team approached the front, bearing trays of produce. Their work, Maurice explained, was crucial. The caramel was the mortar that would hold the creation together. They delivered the first pan to the front, and returned immediately to the stove, to make another batch before the first one cooled and became too hard to use.

Before Gui's eyes, a tower rose, cream-filled choux pastries the size of billiard balls marching upward in a spiral. When the last pastry rested at the top of the cone, almost a metre high, they were called once more.

Josef was the only one tall enough to reach; he dipped a spoon into the copper pan and gently raised a ribbon of molten caramel. He whipped this through the air like a magician, allowing it to fall over the whole confection. It settled in golden strands, as thin as silk. Gui stared in awe, but was hustled away, to clean up before the afternoon.

'You will see it later.' Maurice nudged him towards the scullery, where almost every pan awaited cleaning. 'Better get busy, you lads are on serving duty.'

Emerging damp and sweaty into the cloak-room, Gui had just enough time to cram in a mouthful of bread, before Josef called his name.

'Serving uniform,' he grunted, shoving a stack of pristine new clothes into Gui's arms. 'Dirty them and you'll wish you hadn't been born.'

The outfit was similar to their everyday whites, but with gold buttons marching down the double-breasted front, gold trim on the shoulders, a gold stripe down the leg and a starched cap, embroidered with the Clermont logo in green and gold.

'This is ridiculous,' Gui muttered, peering into the mirror along with several other boys. 'How are we supposed to do anything without getting dirty?'

'I'm not even going to move,' said one, staring terrified at the snowy apron, 'let alone go near all that chocolate.'

But of course the time came for them to return to work. They passed back through the kitchens, enduring whistles from the other chefs. Maurice tipped him a wink. He was shaping two letters out of a substance that looked like gold clay. The confection stood almost finished. Gui gazed at it as he passed: a towering masterpiece of caramel and pastry, adorned with sugar-work, glimmering beneath the lights.

He would have given anything to remain in the kitchen, but instead he was obliged to endure the commands and prods of the pâtisserie's Maître d', a coiffed man who told them — in no uncertain terms — that they were little more than walking cake stands. The only thing that kept his mood from plummeting was the thought that he might see Jeanne at the party. Perhaps they would be able to sneak a moment alone together.

Before long, the door swung open, bringing with it a gust of spring air. The first guests had arrived. Afternoon sunlight clung to their coats. Slowly, the room filled and attendees began to drift past him, occasionally stopping to nibble at one of the chocolate shapes he offered up for their gloved fingers. The champagne flowed, laughter was pitched a tone higher than everyday speech, pearl beads struck silk hems. Gui had never seen so much wealth in one room, so much opulence; it was grotesque and exquisite.

Then he saw her, amongst a group of other women. She was dressed in a delicate gown, rose-pink. Silk flowers were pinned to her dark hair, hiding the cropped cut.

She was staring around the room for something. His heart leaped in delight when he realized that she was looking for him. He caught her eye and smiled, waving a hand to indicate his trussed-up uniform. She stifled a laugh.

Over the next few minutes, she managed to steer her aunt closer to where Gui had been stationed. He in turn edged further into the room. Finally, she contrived to linger over the tray of chocolates, as if contemplating which to choose.

'Mademoiselle,' Gui murmured with a smile.

'I like your uniform, du Frère,' she whispered, looking up through her lashes.

'Can you get away?'

Their faces were separated only by the width of the tray.

'Someone will see.'

'I thought you liked an adventure? Besides, who will notice?'

Jeanne shot him a shrewd smile.

'Aunt,' she called, as if bored, 'will you excuse me? I think I feel some of my hairpins coming loose.'

'Honestly, after how long it took!' the older woman fussed. 'Would you like me to see to them?'

'No, no,' Jeanne said, 'I shall fix them myself.'

She walked away sedately, patting her hair as she headed for the corridor towards the cloakroom. Gui had to be fast. He edged along the wall. Thankfully, the Maître d' was nowhere to be seen. He shoved the tray of chocolates under a waiters' station and followed Jeanne, fully expecting to hear an angered shout behind him.

The corridor was thickly carpeted, hung with heavy brocade curtains that framed alcove windows. As he passed the first one, a hand shot out to grasp his sleeve.

'Help me!' Jeanne commanded. She was loosening two huge, ornate tassels.

They came free and the curtains swung closed, hiding the couple from view. They were safe. Jeanne's cheeks were pink, breath quickened by daring.

'You look magnificent,' he whispered, his hand hovering at the shoulder of her elegant gown. 'I'm almost afraid to touch you.'

'I hate it.' She stepped nearer, reached up to brush his face. 'None of it is real, Gui.'

'What would they say if they saw you on the Left Bank?' He grinned. 'Stealing rides on trams, dancing at La Rotonde?'

Her laugh had a wild edge to it. He hesitated, then leaned in to kiss her, lightly at first but with growing intensity. His body thrilled at her closeness, at their stolen time together. She must have felt it too for she was kissing him back, shy no longer, her hands locked around his neck.

Her dress of silk and lace betrayed the warmth of her limbs. He gripped her tightly, one hand slipping down the side of her neck. Abruptly, she broke off, eyes bright and guarded. Maurice's cruel words came back to him: *Who wants damaged goods when there are better ones on offer?*

He placed his hand upon her neck, above the scar she tried so hard to conceal.

'I love you, Jeanne,' he whispered, his forehead against hers.

'I . . . ' She was swallowing back tears. 'I love you . . . '

'Then marry me.' The words dropped from his mouth before he could think twice.

She pulled away, dazed.

'What did you say?'

It must have been the elation of the moment for he could only laugh and kiss her and laugh again.

'I don't know,' he managed eventually. 'I think I just asked you to marry me.'

Footsteps approached in the corridor and they

fell silent, clutching each other.

'Jeanne?' someone called, dangerously close. Feet passed, inches away, before receding.

'It's my aunt.' Jeanne was trembling. 'Hurry, you must go, I will distract her. Now!' she told him. 'Please, Gui, go!'

How he was able to make it through the door and step out into the pâtisserie without notice was a mystery. His heart was thundering. A nervous sweat coated the inside of his clothes; his blood had turned to champagne, bubbling through his body in wild haste. He could still feel her lips, pressed to his as he asked her to marry him.

'What in God's name are you doing?' hissed Maurice, face like thunder, as he hauled Gui to the edge of the room.

'I'm sorry,' Gui stammered, too distracted to wonder why the chef was there. 'I was — '

'I know what you were doing, you brainless fool. I saw you both, sneaking in there. What are you thinking?'

'I don't know what you're talking about.'

Gui noticed now that everyone, save for him and Maurice, were grouped together, the staff in orderly lines and the guests corralled, awaiting an announcement.

'You had better pray to God that I'm the only one who noticed,' whispered the older chef as they crept over to join the staff. Over his shoulder, Gui saw Jeanne emerge from the cloakrooms. Her aunt was whispering rapidly in her ear, towing her towards the centre of the room.

'It's none of your business,' Gui snapped as they slid into line, half hidden at the back.

'It is if you're going to ruin your life.'

'I'm not. I've asked her to marry me.'

Maurice's face went pale with shock as a glass chimed and a hush fell rapidly across the room.

The towering confection had been unveiled, the centre of attention. It sparkled with sugar, bright as amber. Two gold letters adorned the top: an 'L' and a 'J' interlocked.

Monsieur Clermont raised a hand.

'I bid you a warm welcome, one and all,' he announced. 'First and foremost on this happy day, I am delighted to make public a long-awaited engagement. Please raise your glasses in congratulations to my daughter Jeanne and her husband-to-be, Monsieur Leonard Burnett.'

31

May 1988

'May 1910,' I read aloud, 'Mademoiselle Clermont and du Frère in Stevenson's article, 'A Boulevard Sensation' leads to closure of Pâtisserie Clermont.' I throw the page down and rub at my eyes. 'But years later, my Grandpa Jim is *still* writing to this du Frère person. What does it all mean?'

I'm sprawled on the carpet in Alex's room. I know that there's something important in Hall's notes, in the collection of scraps and clues, but so far, any answers have eluded me.

'Well,' Alex says, 'I think we can be fairly certain what your scandal was, 'Mademoiselle Clermont and du Frère'? It has to have been a love affair, right?'

'Yes, but how do we know for certain? Without the article itself . . . ' I trail off, staring glumly at the floor. Alex swivels to and fro on his desk chair.

'OK.' He spins in a circle. 'Run it past me again, what else do we have?'

I lay it all out before him on the floor, explaining as I go. The original photograph of my grandfather, with its reference to Clermont; the slip of paper from the gallery with an address for 'du Frère' in Bordeaux. I give him Allincourt's letter to read, and the paragraph in

236

Lefevre's book. I explain how the group photograph taken outside the pâtisserie came into my hands. Finally, I pass over the poste-restante letter from Grandpa Jim to Guillaume du Frère.

Alex takes it all in, examining each piece carefully. I can't help but smile as I watch him thinking, brow creased in concentration. As he passes me the letter, our hands touch. I am definitely not imagining the strange jolt that runs through me.

'All right,' he says, 'read me Hall's note again, about when the article was written.'

'It says it was May 1910,' I tell him, a little flustered. 'Why?'

He joins me on the floor and scoops up the photograph of the group outside the pâtisserie.

'This picture,' he squints, 'when do you think it was taken?'

'Not sure,' I peer closer. 'Some time in 1910 as well?'

'Yes, but it must have been taken *before* May of that year.'

'The tree,' I realize, tracing the shape at the edge of the frame, 'it's only just in leaf, so this must be spring, early April perhaps.'

Alex leans in beside me. His hair is sticking up at impossible angles and I have the uncontrollable urge to straighten it, to let my hand rest upon his back. He pulls the two photographs towards him, places them side by side.

'Here.' He jabs the pâtisserie shot, then the two strangers in Grandpa Jim's photo with his finger. 'There's our Mademoiselle Clermont, in

237

both photographs. If we assume the chap next to your grandpa is du Frère ... '

I'm still trying to get my feelings under control when Alex jumps to his feet and begins to rummage through the desk drawers. Eventually, he extracts a dusty magnifying class.

'What's that for?' I ask.

Alex doesn't reply, kneeling down in front of the group photograph.

'I knew it,' he whispers, nose almost touching the paper. He shoves the magnifying glass into my hand, pulls me closer. I can feel every place our bodies touch, hip to shoulder, but I try to concentrate. 'There, next to the mademoiselle, what do you notice?'

Beside the girl is a young man, dressed identically to all the other chefs. I catch my breath and look between the two pictures; it is him, du Frère. He has the same dark curls, beneath the white chef's cap on his head, the same infectious half-smile, as though about to break into a grin. Yet in the pâtisserie photograph he is the odd one out: his arms are not crossed like the others, but are blurred with movement. Next to him stands Mademoiselle Clermont.

'They're holding hands!' I burst. 'They *were* together, this is the proof.'

Alex and I nearly bump heads as I look up. Our faces are separated by barely an inch.

'Didn't I say?' His voice is soft, eyes flitting over my face. 'They were in love.'

I can feel my whole skin tingling. Then the phone rings, horribly loud and shrill. Alex leaps away to answer.

'What? Yeah, she's here.' He is beetroot red as he holds out the receiver. 'It's your friend Cass, I'll give you some privacy.'

He has fled through the door before I can protest. From the other end of the phone, I hear Cass laughing.

'Am I interrupting?' she asks innocently.

32

April 1910

Something pounded in his ears; the noise of applause, sickeningly loud. Maurice had hold of his arm and was pulling him away. Through the crowd he saw Jeanne, another man's hand claiming her own, his lips meeting her cheek, all to the appreciation of the partygoers.

Maurice shoved him towards the kitchen door.

Through the chaos of silk-draped shoulders, Jeanne met his gaze. A smile was falling from her mouth. What did it matter, whether it was forced or genuine?

'You knew,' Gui spat at Maurice. 'You knew all along while you sneered at her, you bastard — '

He flailed at the older chef, trying to break his grip, to run towards Jeanne, but Maurice was hustling him out of sight, through the double doors and into the kitchen.

'I am saving your hide, you fool,' he hissed. 'Of course I knew she was to be wed! Everyone here knew! The Burnetts have been hanging around for weeks waiting for Clermont to palm her off.'

'Don't speak about her like that,' Gui croaked. He felt tears burn his eyes, but he didn't care. 'You're lying, she would have told me.'

'Told you what? That she would turn down marriage to one of the richest families in the city for the prospect of burned scraps and a room

240

with the prostitutes in Belleville?'

Gui struggled, but Maurice was pushing him, through the corridor to the back entrance, down the steps and out into the alleyway.

'Get out of here.' The older man was breathing heavily. 'Don't come back until you see sense. I'll say you're sick, which you are. Get your head straight and with any luck you can carry on as before.'

'Go to hell,' Gui choked, as the tears streaked his face.

He had no choice but to leave. The streets outside were crowded with Parisians, young and old, carrying baskets brimming with gifts, stuffing Easter sweets into their mouths and pockets. He hated them all: the pampered children with their sailor suits, the men in sleek moleskin, stomachs preceding them, the women, pale and joyless as ivory.

A small boy was staring at him from the pavement. His hand bulged with Easter favours; there was a smear of jam on one fine linen cuff.

'What?' Gui yelled, voice hoarse with pain.

The child's nursemaid threw him a filthy look. As Gui moved away there was a flash of white and he caught his reflection in a shop window. He had forgotten that he still wore the gilded Pâtisserie Clermont uniform. He cursed, ripping the hat from his head and flinging it into the road, to be crushed and muddied by hooves and heels. He could never go back there, not if it meant watching in silence from his lowly position in the kitchen as Jeanne became another man's wife.

It was a relief to escape the streets of the Opéra district. He stalked through the Place de la République towards Belleville. *Towards his people*, he thought bitterly. The road on the far side was blocked by a gaggle of children, chasing eggs down the gutters, to see whose made it the furthest without breaking. At any other time he might have smiled, but now he hurried past, trying not to hear their high, joyful voices. He almost walked head first into a man on the opposite pavement.

'Sorry,' he mumbled, stepping aside, but the figure grabbed his arm.

'You will be sorry, my boy . . . '

In alarm, Gui glanced up.

'Jim?'

The writer's face split into a wide smile as he released Gui's sleeve.

'I believe you were going to ignore me, du Frère. Where are you off to, with your head in the clouds, dressed all white and fancy like a communion wafer?'

Gui couldn't smile; he couldn't even find the words to answer properly.

'What're you doing here?' was all he could ask.

'The paper sent me out to cover the Easter parade.' Jim frowned, his good cheer faltering. 'What is it, du Frère? You look terrible.'

To his shame, Gui felt the tears returning, scalding his eyes and threatening to spill. He blinked hard and turned away.

'I can't talk about it,' he mumbled. 'Sorry, Jim — '

'No you don't!' The writer hooked his arm

through Gui's and wheeled him around. 'Never lie to a reporter. I've seen that look before on a young man, and if it is what I think it is, then moping will do you no good.'

'You don't know anything about it,' said Gui, his voice falling short of anger. 'Let go, please.'

Jim released his arm and stood, facing him in the crowded street. Unanimated by jokes or mockery, his grey eyes looked almost sad.

'Whatever it is, it must be important for you to walk out of your work, still in uniform,' the writer said seriously. 'In which case, I am guessing that it involves Mademoiselle Jeanne.'

Gui stared at him. Fight gone, he nodded.

There were few bars open on Easter Sunday, but Gui knew for a fact that the Chapeau Rouge on the Rue de Belleville never closed its doors. Jim dismissed his assignment with a wave of his hand, and told Gui to lead the way.

As they walked, he told Jim about what had happened, as best he could, without giving Jeanne's name away. He talked about her protective father, who treated her like a precious object, about how their engagement would be met with universal disapproval. He tried to mention what had happened that afternoon, but he found that there was a lump lodged in his throat that refused to be shifted. He lapsed into silence.

Jim didn't interrupt, only loped along the pavement with his scarecrow legs, smoking quietly.

'You don't seem surprised by any of this,' Gui ventured, as they neared Belleville.

243

Jim's smile was wry. 'A foreigner I may be, du Frère, but you forget I am a reporter by trade. Any hack worth his salt would've spotted that you two were stepping out clandestinely.'

Gui felt his jaw tighten, whether through shame or concern he wasn't sure. Jim laid a placating hand on his shoulder. 'Clandestinely and head-over-heels for each other, of course.'

Balourde guarded the doorway of the Chapeau Rouge, swaying languorously to the sound of the church bells that drifted down the hill. When she saw them, a giggle built and began to tremor in the expanse of flesh on show.

Jim's eyes were wide. 'Reminds me of a plate of blancmange,' he whispered as they squeezed past. Gui found a smile, but it was weak.

The bar was relatively empty. Even the residents of Belleville had families to spend time with on a holiday. Belatedly, Gui thought of his mother, that he should have sent her an Easter greeting along with the last money-packet, but the guilt died as Jim nudged over a glass of pastis.

'So, what has happened?' he asked gently, when they were seated in a corner.

Gui took one large sip, then another. The liquorice sweetness clung to his throat, reminded him of Jeanne, of her lips as they kissed on the dance floor of La Rotonde.

'She . . . she is supposed to marry someone else, someone her father chose. I found out today. She must have known, all this time, but she never told me.' Gui took up the glass, tossed back the rest of the drink as quickly as he could.

It burned, and he coughed.

Jim sighed, leaned back in his chair.

'This other man, is he . . . ?'

'White silk tie.' Gui laughed bitterly. 'Hair oil, kid gloves.'

'A classic bourgeois ass.'

Gui stared down into the dregs of his glass.

'How can I compete with that? I have nothing to offer. Why would she choose me?'

To his astonishment, Jim was smiling, shaking his head.

'Don't lose heart, du Frère. The world of the bourgeoisie is not all it seems. Take it from someone who knows. I left the best university in England to come here, to be penniless and scrabbling in Paris. And you know why?'

Gui shrugged, his eyes on the table.

'Because I didn't want the life they had planned for me, Gui. Here, I might not know where my next drink is coming from, but at least I know I'm alive.' He fished in his jacket for cigarettes. 'I'll wager your Jeanne knows this too. I'll wager she wants a life for herself, not an eternity of sitting in a parlour.'

Before he took his leave, Jim made Gui promise that he would make things up with Jeanne as soon as he got the chance.

'Who else am I to drink with on a Sunday?' he called, as he ducked past Balourde's arms. 'Besides, I have a photograph of the three of us — that makes us friends, du Frère!'

Gui's smile faded as he watched' Jim stride away. Despite his promise, he could not see a way back to Jeanne. Even now she would be graciously accepting the congratulations of friends and family, Gui thought, showing off the ring upon her finger — the likes of which he would never be able to afford.

The glasses upon the table were long drained. Gui sloped over to the bar.

'What cause for the costume?' the bartender asked, indicating Gui's whites.

Gui ignored the question. 'What's your cheapest?' he asked. With Jim gone, he was in no mood to share his drinking, especially not with the group of drunks who were conversing with Balourde. The bartender pulled a bottle down from a shelf and hovered near the edge of the counter.

'How will you be paying?'

Cursing, Gui remembered that Jim had paid for the previous drinks. All of his money was in the pocket of his jacket, back at the pâtisserie.

'Look, I'm good for it,' he tried. 'You know where I live. I'll bring it to you tomorrow.'

Face hardening, the man put the bottle back on the shelf.

'Wait . . . '

Gui tugged appraisingly at the large gold buttons of the uniform. What did if matter if he ruined it? Without Jeanne, without the pâtisserie, he had nothing. He would have to beg the railway for his old job back.

'These are fine work,' he told the barman, his voice heavy. 'Fetch a good price at the haberdasher's.'

The bartender brought the bottle down again, eyeing the jacket suspiciously.

'Let's see.'

He took out a knife and sliced one of the buttons from the fabric. It gleamed on the dull surface of the bar. Mouth turned down into a speculative arc, the man scooped it into a pocket.

'Fine,' he sniffed.

Gui stripped the rest of the buttons without ceremony and took the bottle.

In his room, it was too quiet. Slowly, he shrugged off the ruined uniform, not caring that it landed in a crumpled heap. He would have burned it, had he the coal.

He pulled on his old trousers, the ones he had barely worn since the night of the flood. They made him think of Jeanne, of wading through endless streets with her in his arms. Gritting his teeth, he reached for the bottle.

There was a knock on the door. He weighed in his mind the small handful of people it could be and decided to ignore it. A few seconds later, the knock came again.

'Go away,' he murmured, struggling with the cork.

The door opened. It was Isabelle, half-dressed, a floral robe thrown over her undergarments.

'Gui, what's wrong?' she ventured. 'Why are you home so early?'

'Nothing at all.'

'You trudged up those stairs so hard I thought the ceiling would fall through into Madame's parlour.' Uninvited, she stepped into the room and leaned against the wall. 'What has happened? Did you lose your job?'

The cork wouldn't budge, no matter how much he twisted it.

She took the bottle from him and placed it on the floor. 'You were so happy this morning,' she said softly.

He hadn't realized that his hands were shaking. With Isabelle's proximity came an image of Jeanne, breathless in their secret alcove, her mouth on his, telling him that she loved him. Now, another man's lips would be touching hers.

'Please don't ask me,' he whispered.

'Very well,' Isabelle said eventually, 'how about I keep you company for a while?'

Gui nodded, grateful. Isabelle picked up the bottle. ' 'Parrot's' Absinthe,' she read with a laugh. 'I wonder if that old fraud knows it's supposed to be 'Pernod's'.'

Sitting in front of the tiny stove, the day grew old and died as they drank. As good as her word, Isabelle did not ask him what had passed, but talked about herself, her own misfortunes and hopes. He was glad; it helped to keep his mind from Jeanne. Isabelle told him about her childhood in Rouen, and how she came to Paris. He tried to listen, to ask the right questions.

Finally, Isabelle sat back and lapsed into silence. She poured them both another drink. Gui's courage flickered. He knew he should tell her about that afternoon, about everything he had lost, but he did not want to live through it again. Before he could begin, there were footsteps in the hallway.

'It is most likely the clerk from the end room,' Isabelle soothed, but the footsteps did not stop.

They came towards his door.

'Wait here,' he murmured, and crept to the frame.

There was a pause — someone outside listening — then a knock. He opened the door an inch, prepared to slam it shut if necessary. Puce's face beamed up at him out of the darkness. The boy had lost a tooth since Gui had last seen him.

'Monsieur du Frère,' he announced, 'glad you are at home. In my occupation as guide and general watchman of these fair streets, I stumbled across something that might interest you.'

'What is it, Puce?' he said with a sigh, opening the door further. Isabelle waved from her place by the stove, and the boy blushed.

'Ah, I didn't know you had company . . . '

'What is it?'

'Well,' Puce hedged, scuffing at the doorjamb. 'I was asked — '

'I told him that I was looking for you,' came a voice from the darkness. Jeanne stepped forward. Her eyes were red in a pale face.

'I am sorry if I am interrupting,' she directed at Isabelle, 'but I must speak with Monsieur du Frère alone.'

33

May 1988

'It all makes sense, Professor, it has to be the explanation,' I tell Whyke as he moves along the counter with his tray.

He ignores me. 'Kaufmann phoned again this morning,' he says miserably. 'Told me she was going to report you to the faculty if she hasn't heard from you by the end of today. Thank you,' he directs at the cashier, absent-mindedly patting his pockets. 'Sure I can't get you anything, Petra?'

Repressing a sigh of frustration, I order a cup of tea and join him at a table. He begins to eat his baked potato, tuna and beans with a resolute expression.

'Sugar?' he offers cheerlessly, pushing it my way.

'No, thank you.'

'I thought you took two?'

He looks so hangdog that I don't have the heart to tell him I've never taken sugar in my tea and let him drop two lumps into the bottom of the cup.

He sits back and stares at a baked bean that has escaped onto the table.

'What are job opportunities like these days for an ex-don?' he mutters.

Seizing the plate, I shove it away, where it

stops just short of falling to the floor. Finally, Whyke looks up.

'That's my lunch.'

'Professor, I need you to listen. Then you can go back to eating tuna and being defeatist.'

'Two things I'm very good at.' He gives me a hint of a smile. 'Please, go ahead.'

Swiftly, before his attention strays back to his abandoned lunch, I explain Alex's discovery from the previous night.

'So there was an affair,' Whyke says with interest. 'It would certainly be the most obvious material for a scandal, especially in the case of a class divide. Such things were known to happen — seduction, blackmail and the like.'

His words take me by surprise. 'What do you mean?'

'If your du Frère was a chef, then no doubt he was from a lower social class than Mademoiselle Clermont. In which case, he could have seduced her in order to extort money from the family. A scandal suggests irreparable damage to her or her reputation, rather than an embarrassing dalliance.'

I'm silent: part of me baulks at the idea, even though I can see the sense in it.

'Well, we can't know for sure,' I point out somewhat stubbornly. 'All this is conjecture without that article.'

'But I asked them to send out a copy,' Whyke frowns. 'I telephoned the reprographics team directly. When I told them how important it was, they pulled some strings and rushed it through.'

'When was this?' I ask, stunned.

'Yesterday,' he reaches for his lunch once again, 'after I spoke to you. I'm not one hundred per cent sure that it will have arrived, but he did promise he'd try to get it in the last post.'

I don't hear the rest of the sentence, because I'm scrabbling for my bag, nearly knocking over the mug of tea in my haste to get out of the chair.

'Thank you, Professor,' I yell, already halfway out of the door. 'I'll phone later!'

'Petra!' he calls. 'Your review is in three days!'

The journey back to college is a blur. I veer across junctions on my bike and pedal furiously past other students, all celebrating the end of exams. I dump my bike in the rack without bothering to lock it up and charge into the porters' lodge.

My pigeonhole is filled with the usual rubbish. I fling it all out onto the floor, earning a frightened look from a passing first-year. There is nothing. No delivery slip announcing a registered letter, no unfamiliar envelopes. In desperation, I check the pigeonholes around mine, hoping it might have been placed in one of them by mistake. My excitement fades as quickly as it arrived. I scoop the papers from the ground and jam the fistful into the bin.

'Miss Stevenson?' a voice stops me. One of the porters is leaning out of the office, waving a flat, brown envelope in my direction. 'This arrived earlier, registered post for you.'

I grab it and start tearing open the paper.

'Something important?' he asks mildly.

It's the article.

34

April 1910

'How did you get here?'

The question shattered the frosty silence.

'I hailed a taxi cab.'

Her voice was stiff; she no longer seemed so sure of herself. Gui realized that she must have walked past Madame's parlour in order to reach his room.

'Found her at the bottom of the road, Gui,' said Puce, 'near the Chapeau. Not wise to take a cab into Belleville at night, Mam'selle.'

'Thank you, Puce,' Jeanne said softly.

'I'll go.' Isabelle wrapped her gown tighter about herself. 'I believe that you and the mademoiselle have matters to discuss in private.'

'That would be welcome.' The coldness in Jeanne's voice was unmistakable, but Isabelle merely nodded, taking Puce with her.

As the door swung closed, Gui heard Isabelle promising to find Puce some sugared treats as a reward. They were alone. Jeanne's eyes were bright, fixed on the small stove. The coiled worm of anger in Gui's gut began to stir again when he saw that her engagement finger remained bare.

'You didn't need to be so rude,' he snapped, retreating to his place in front of the fire. 'Isabelle is a friend.'

'I know what she is.'

'What does that mean?'

Jeanne was silent, resolutely looking anywhere but at him.

'I said, what does that mean?' he pushed.

'For God's sake, Guillaume, she was barely dressed,' Jeanne burst. 'I knew you lived in Belleville, but I didn't think you shared a roof with . . .'

'With who? Say it, Jeanne.'

'With prostitutes and criminals and who knows what else!'

'Can you hear yourself?' Gui was on his feet again. For some reason, the sight of her fine clothes in that shabby room enraged him more than her betrayal. 'Isabelle is my friend, yet you treat her like she's nothing, like you're better. You're acting like one of *them*.'

'I am 'one of them'!'

He turned away then, overcome by the hopelessness of it all.

'Are you engaged to that man?' he said.

'I came here to try to explain.' Her voice was taut with emotion. 'It was arranged such a long time ago, I never thought — '

'Are you engaged to him? Yes or no?'

'That is not what I am trying to tell you.'

'Answer the question.'

'Yes,' she broke, almost defiantly. 'At this moment, I am engaged to marry Leonard Burnett, and it seems that I might as well go through with it.' She fumbled with the door, wrenched it open. 'I am sorry to have disturbed you and your 'friend'.'

The door drifted closed, the sound of her

rapid footsteps disappearing down the stairs. *Let her go*, a voice in his head told him. It sounded like Nicolas. *Better that it should end here, for both of you.*

Gui dragged the cork from the bottle and took a swig of the cheap liquor. It stung his nose and he coughed, trying to rid his throat of the burning sweetness. Nearby, in another attic room perhaps, a gramophone was playing, the melody warbling across the roof like a lost soul.

He saw what could have been. A place for them to be alone, truly alone, closed off by four, rickety walls and the orange light of a stove. What did the rest of it matter, here? The night could have been theirs, stolen and hidden away, to burn itself up like the last pieces of coal in the hearth.

Cursing, he threw himself through the door, taking the steps two at a time. He flashed past Madame's parlour, where a first client was taking tea. Pushing aside the curtain he stumbled down the stairs, out into the street. It was empty. He swore again.

'Did I forget something?' a voice asked bitterly.

She was standing behind him, a handful of change in her gloved palm. Her eyes were rimmed with red. His arms went around her then, and at first she stood stiffly beneath his embrace.

'I am sorry,' he murmured into the soft fabric of her shoulder. 'I just want you. I don't care about the rest of it.'

'Of course you do.' The tears she had kept

tightly held began to unravel. 'I saw your face, at the pâtisserie, after the announcement. It frightened me. I wanted to scream at them all, tell them to go to hell.'

He laughed, pulled away.

'That would have made me proud,' he said. 'Can you imagine — '

She kissed him then, a heedless kiss. He tightened his arms with growing urgency, before managing to drag his mouth away. The coins had spilled from her hand and lay like quicksilver at their feet. Several Belleville children were already creeping forward.

'Come on,' he smiled, pretending not to see, 'we can't stay out here.'

Before the stove, her bare shoulders looked like a painting; oil upon ochre. The chemise fell from one arm, then another. Her hair was loose, tangled above her chin. She held his gaze. The burn stretched from neck to collarbone, an uneven V-shape of scar tissue arching across smooth skin.

The bottle of absinthe was three-quarters empty, but even so they trembled, as if from cold. They were sheltered from the world by a flimsy lock, by the anonymity of the poor. It would be enough to protect them, if only for tonight.

Jeanne took his arm, pulled him with her until they were laying side by side, length against length upon the floor.

'Gui,' she said. Her breath was on his face, aniseed and so familiar that it made his heart contract. Outside, the bell at Ménilmontant struck midnight, its voice lingering against the glass.

'You will be missed,' he whispered, stroking a few strands back from her cheek.

'I want to stay.' She shuffled closer to him, hesitating an inch apart. 'Let me stay.'

'What of your fiancé?' he forced himself to ask.

'It should never have been. I was too young to know.'

'Know what?'

'That there would be you,' she said. 'That I have a choice.'

He wanted to tell her that he was no choice, tried to find a voice of reason for her sake, but all of it dissolved as she kissed him again. They could barely breathe for sharing each other's air.

'You asked me to marry you,' she told him. 'I am, now. The rest is just words.'

35

May 1988

The article flutters in my hands, a thin sheet of paper. My grandfather's name — my own surname — glares up at me. Two columns squashed onto a page, but enough to lay waste to a reputation. Heart pounding, I begin to read:

A BOULEVARD SENSATION
*Respected Business Rocked
by Blackmail Scandal*

The sole topic of conversation amongst the well-heeled this week has been a revelation concerning that most reputable of meeting places: Pâtisserie C. A case of seduction and exploitation, I — your humble reporter and ear to the boulevard — discovered the stunning details of this story in a most remarkable manner, and felt compelled to report them exclusively for *The Word*.

It came to my attention when, on the streets of the Left Bank, I met Monsieur G. du F.: an apprentice chef and resident of the notorious Rue de Belleville. I came to discover that this miscreant had, over the course of several months, inveigled his way into the affections of Mademoiselle C., the only child of Pâtisserie C.'s illustrious proprietor. His intent? The extraction of money.

This story itself is not so unfamiliar to daughters from wealthy families, who daily run the risk of being swept off their feet by charming, avaricious vagabonds. Indeed, the affair in question may have stopped short of harm, were it not for the fact that an engagement already existed between Mademoiselle C. and Monsieur Leonard B., youngest son of the celebrated lawyer and financial trader, Monsieur Edouard B.

'Unfortunately, Mademoiselle is a clever young woman,' an informant from inside the pâtisserie confided. 'She went to great lengths to conceal the affair, believing herself to be in love with the youth.'

Thus, our source relates, the coquetry went beyond any point from which it could respectfully be retrieved. Monsieur C. was to discover this in a most unenviable manner, upon surprising his daughter in the company office, stealing funds in order to elope with the kitchen hand.

'Monsieur C. was in a rage, understandably,' tells our chef, who witnessed the entire confrontation. 'He dragged du F from the premises and had him restrained outside whilst he telephoned for the gendarmes.'

* * *

One can only imagine the chaos amidst the kitchens; Monsieur C., shaking the young Bordelais the way one would a pup. We are informed by the local Gendarmerie that du F. fled the scene before they could arrive to quell the dispute.

Prior to employment at Pâtisserie C., *The Word* has learned that du F. worked as a labourer for the National Railway.

We can only regret Mademoiselle C.'s lot, for although her only crime was naivety, du F. has now vanished, leaving her with a shattered reputation that may bear further fruit.

At the time of going to print, Pâtisserie C. has not yet reopened its doors and we must wonder, after such a scandal, if it is at all likely to again.

— *J. G. Stevenson*

★ ★ ★

'I don't know what to think,' I tell Alex over the phone. 'Perhaps du Frère *was* just trying to get his hands on her money.'

'Is that what the article says?'

'Yes, but then there's Grandpa Jim's letter. All that regret.'

There is silence on the other end of the phone as we both ponder the situation. After everything, I've found an answer, but it isn't the one I've been searching for; it still doesn't explain why Grandpa would keep his time in Paris a secret from me, why he wrote hundreds of letters to du Frère, even though he never received a reply. I feel as though I have unravelled a piece of string, only to be confronted by another unfathomable knot.

'What about the man who bought the

painting?' Alex says abruptly. 'The 'du Frère' from Bordeaux? Could it be the same man? Why don't you just ask him.'

'But he'd be — what? — in his nineties? He's probably long dead.'

'You have the address, right?'

'Yes, but what can I do? Call up Directory Inquiries in France and ask to speak to someone I've never met?'

I can almost hear Alex's answering grin over the phone line.

In the French language section of the library I find what I'm looking for: a telephone directory, several years out of date. I dial the number for Inquiries, working up the courage to ask for what I need in French.

The operator is impatient as I falter my way through a request, but quickly gives me a telephone number in Bordeaux for a G. du Frère. I am being put through before I can even think about what to say.

My heart thunders as the line clicks into life and starts to ring. Somewhere in France, in a house or a flat or a shop, a phone is trilling away. Four rings, five . . . then the sound changes. Someone has answered. A man.

'Monsieur du Frère?' I hear myself ask.

'*Oui, c'est moi.*'

The voice is that of a young man, not a pensioner. I feel as though I've stepped into a dream, that my voice is travelling down a wire to emerge from a metal earpiece in 1910.

'Monsieur *Guillaume* du Frère?'

'*Oui, qui est-la?*'

Suddenly, it's too much. I'm making a terrible mistake. I'm digging up history that should never have been disturbed, hunting down people who did not want to be found by my grandfather seventy years ago. The young man repeats his question, more forcefully this time.

I slam down the phone.

My forehead is clammy with cold sweat. It *couldn't* have been him, the same Guillaume du Frère who is staring up at me from my grandfather's photograph. It's a good few minutes before I can pick up the receiver again.

Shaken as I am, the telephone directory has given me an idea. Perhaps there is another way to uncover what happened to Mademoiselle Clermont and du Frère.

This time, I ask Inquiries to put me through to the newspaper archives in Paris. I'm transferred to the library at the Rue de Richelieu. The receptionist there is much more helpful. Yes, they hold copies of newspapers from 1910, she tells me politely; yes they are available on microfilm, but they must be accessed in person.

I hang up. For a long while I sit staring at the silent phone. *Accessed in person.* Fifteen minutes later I'm standing outside Alex's door, a bag of Chelsea buns in hand.

His face lights up.

'P! What're you doing here? I thought you were on the phone to France.'

I can feel a mischievous smile growing on my face as I hand over the bag.

'I was. And then I had an idea.'

Alex stops with a bun mid-way to his mouth.

262

'Oh no,' he says, 'I know that look. What do you want?'

'Nothing much,' I tell him. 'I was just wondering whether you still have your moped.'

36

April 1910

'Do you think anyone will suspect?'

They stood hidden in a doorway. There was not another soul on the streets, in the hinterland of dawn. Jeanne fiddled with a loose thread of her coat.

'I do not believe so,' she murmured. 'I said that the excitement of the party had worn me out. I locked the door. Patrice has the only other key, he promised to tell Father that he had checked in on me.'

'Does he . . . ?' Gui began, alarmed.

'He knows,' Jeanne looked him in the eye. 'I needed his help to get away yesterday. I think he suspected from the beginning, in a way.'

The pâtisserie loomed above them. He wanted to take Jeanne in his arms, but the coming dawn had sobered them both, was transforming her into 'Mademoiselle Clermont' again.

He tried to smile. 'I wish you could have stayed longer.'

Sadness lurched across her face. 'I do too, more than anything.'

'We could have gone to Pigalle.'

She laughed then, but it was a lonely sound. A second later they were in each other's arms.

'What will we do?' whispered Jeanne.

'Let's leave now,' he said desperately. 'Take an

early train and disappear. We can stay with my mother in Bordeaux.'

'I can't,' she captured his face in her hands, 'not yet, Gui. There may be a way to solve this without running like criminals. I just need to think.'

'If you go back in there, they will treat you like *his* fiancée.' He could not keep the anxiety from his voice. 'There will be wedding dress fittings and presents and fine jewellery — '

'Listen to me.' Her ice-blue eyes held him. 'We promised last night. You cannot back away from me now, Gui. I will not, no matter what happens.'

'I could never,' he swore.

'Then allow me a fortnight. Either we will think of a way to tell them or we will leave, but at least that will give me time to gather some money, make a few plans for our future.'

'Our future,' he repeated, almost laughing.

One kiss became another, until finally Gui had to turn away in order to let her go. She lingered on the step, looking back at him. It took all of his willpower not to follow her.

The sun was not yet up as he wandered the city. The grand boulevards were his own, the streets bare of their finery. He walked slowly, wanting to see every second of that blessed day through.

Back in his room, he was reluctant to disturb the air. The bottle of absinthe stood almost empty beside two glasses, sticky residue drying on the rim. A faint scent lingered, blossom and sweat. He pulled his blanket over his head and imagined that she was with him.

The next day he returned to the pâtisserie. Easter and its celebrations had vanished like a snow flurry in July. He shrugged away the lost uniform, pleading ignorance, and although his pay was docked for it, no one commented on his absence.

'Feeling better, lad?' Maurice asked loudly for the benefit of the cloakroom.

Gui nodded stiffly, until he realized that Maurice had probably saved his skin by booting him out of sight when he did.

Besides, the anger he felt then was long gone, replaced by a fragile happiness. In the days that followed, he volunteered for all the tasks that would take him into the pâtisserie itself, found excuses to linger behind the counter there, in order to catch a glimpse of Jeanne. She too had begun to appear downstairs more frequently. Three days after their night together, and even the quickest glimpse of her face was like cool oil for his burning chest.

He watched her drink chocolate with acquaintances, perusing the fashion plates and drawings of bouquets, as any bride-to-be might. Their wedding would be very different, he thought with a stab of guilt. No guests, no flowers, no silk dress covered with pearls. It would be anonymous in some forgotten parish church, on the run to the south.

She came to the counter, pretended not to see the waiter so that she could order from him instead. Their hands brushed as he passed her a tiny plate.

'Thank you, Mademoiselle,' was all he could murmur.

Gui's attention in the kitchen began to suffer and twice he was penalized for ruined dishes. Ebersole put him on washing duty, but he didn't care. At least by the sinks he could be alone.

When there was a week to go, he found a note slipped into his jacket pocket, elegant writing signed with a 'J'.

Gui,
Last night I spoke to my aunt and my father about severing the engagement to Monsieur Burnett. My father was furious, and threatened to keep me housebound until the wedding, and the very notion sent my aunt into such hysteria that I dare not mention it again. This morning I told them it was only a case of nerves, and I believe I have reassured them, but I must be careful, in case my father decides to make good on his threat. I shall start making plans for us. One week, my love.
J —

He read it through at least five times, his nerves vanishing into a wave of happiness, at those two words, in her writing: *my love*. He desperately wanted to see her, to smile at her and mouth the words in return.

He had to find an excuse to slip into the café. She was there, he knew. She had breezed through the kitchen earlier, a delicate violet and cream gown rustling as she moved; it must have been after she left the note for him. Even the thought of it made him want to leap.

Maurice had been set to making rose-scented *macarons* that day, and Gui pleaded with him, grinning and cajoling until he was allowed to help. Soon, his excitement settled into concentration. The mixture was fragile, could crack and split in the ovens at the slightest mistake.

By the time the afternoon break rolled around, they had created thirty-six perfect shells. Maurice slapped his shoulder, satisfied. Gui could tell that he was itching for a cigarette. Before them stood the remaining *macaron* mixture, waiting to be coloured and piped. Eyeing it, Gui had a wild idea.

He told the older chef go ahead and take his break first. If Maurice was suspicious, he didn't say anything as he left, already patting his pockets in search of cigarettes.

As soon as he was out of sight, Gui pulled the *macaron* mixture towards him, and took a deep breath. He whipped it back and forth, beads of sweat springing on his forehead as his arm muscles released and contracted. When it was almost ready, he reached up for the shelf where the spices and colours were kept. Carefully, he brought down the bottle of *crème de violette*, the jar of delicate, dried violets, their petals sparkling with sugar.

In tiny drops, he measured the purple liqueur into the mixture. He was acting on impulse, yet at the same time he felt certain, as though his first teacher, Monsieur Carême, was with him, guiding his steps. The scent reached up as he stirred, heady and sweet as a meadow, deep as lingering perfume in a midnight room. Hands shaking, he piped the mixture onto a tray in tiny rounds, enough to make six, one for each day that he and Jeanne would have to make it through before they could be together for the rest of their lives.

Maurice was delayed talking to Josef, and by the time he returned, Gui was putting the finishing touches to his creations, filling them with a vanilla cream from the cold room, balancing one, tiny, sugar-frosted violet flower upon each.

'What on earth are those?' the chef demanded, leaning in to inspect Gui's work. 'They look marvellous.'

'Special order,' mumbled Gui non-committally, though he couldn't help smiling with pride as he placed the delicate confections onto a tray and hurried for the pâtisserie door. Maurice called his name as he went, but Gui pretended not to hear him.

His heart was thumping as he stepped into the opulent café, a wave of chatter rushing up to meet him. The tray of *macarons* rested on his hand. How could he get them to Jeanne? He looked around for a waiter, but they were all crowded around one particular table. A party of guests there had ordered a bottle of the best champagne. Glasses were being brought out, attention lavished.

He scanned the party. Jeanne's aunt was there, draped in furs. There was a red-haired woman, baring her teeth in laughter, a young blond man and there, dressed in her pale violet, was Jeanne. She was smiling, accepting a glass of champagne from someone. It was Leonard Burnett. He wore a fine-fitting coat, a pristine starched shirt, his black hair oiled. He had the look of his father. Taking Jeanne's fingers in his own, he kissed them lightly, before leaning in to speak to an older woman.

Gui's stomach started to roil. He felt grubby, peering through a window at a foreign world. The burns on his hands, the stains on his apron from a morning's work made him want to curl in on himself, even as jealousy howled. He did not see the man approaching until it was too late to turn away.

'Afternoon,' Burnett said easily, refolding the handkerchief in his jacket pocket. 'What are those things?'

Gui bit the inside of his mouth hard. He had no choice but to answer.

'*Macarons*, sir.'

'Fine, fine, I'll take them. Although I suppose she's eaten them a dozen times already.'

Mistaking Gui's hostile silence for polite interest, he glanced up, smiled. 'Mademoiselle Clermont,' he said. 'She only asked me to fetch her a *chocolat chaud*, but those little things will match her dress perfectly.'

Across the room, Jeanne was staring. Even from a distance he could see how white her face had become. There was bile in his throat.

'They're not for sale — '

A waiter returned and hurried towards them, horrified.

270

'What are you doing?' he hissed to Gui. 'Get back to the kitchen! I apologize, monsieur,' he gushed to Burnett, wrenching the tray of *macarons* out of Gui's grip. 'What can I get for you?'

'I just told this lad.'

'He is only a kitchen hand, sir,' the waiter continued, 'he is not permitted to serve the counter. I would be delighted to help.'

'Well, why didn't you say?' Burnett directed at Gui, fishing in his pocket. 'I didn't mean to interrupt your work. Here.' He flicked a coin towards him. 'Now, I'll take those six violet fancies . . . '

Burning with rage and frustration, Gui returned to the kitchen, Burnett's coin stinging his palm. He took over the oven duty without being asked and worked so furiously that even Ebersole told him to take a break before too long. He couldn't bear the cloakroom, with its endless jibes, so he left the apprentices to their food and escaped into the alleyway.

It was here, he thought as he sat on the step. This is where we first spoke. How distant she had been then, with her pencil and ledger — cold and sharp like one of the best kitchen knives.

Burnett's coin was still in his pocket. He flung it angrily to the stones, where it ricocheted away into the main street.

The spring afternoon calmed him. There was a breeze in the shade; it helped him remember Jeanne, her face close to his, tired and happy in the cold dawn as they pledged themselves to each other. He had closed his eyes when someone shouted a greeting. The sun was bright beyond the walls, turning the figure into a silhouette.

'It *is* you!' exclaimed Jim, striding forward, hand outstretched. Gui smiled in surprise and clambered to his feet to greet him. 'Nice whites.' The writer winked, jamming a cigarette into his mouth. 'You're looking a good deal cheerier, du Frère. And how is your delightful Jeanne?' Stevenson blew out a plume of smoke. 'Did you two lovebirds make up and get everything squared?'

Gui laughed, accepted a cigarette from the box and tucked it behind his ear.

'Yes, although she was the one who made it right, in the end. I'm doing my best to deserve her. I need to thank you, though, Jim, for listening.' Gui paused. If all went to plan, it might be a long time before he saw the writer again. 'I hope I can repay the favour one day.'

'I'm glad to hear it. And no need to wait for 'one day'. I'm about to visit your place of employ. You can make good on your account by slipping me an extra plump cream cake. Put a little note in it — 'du Frère was here' — so I can admire your handiwork.'

'You're going in there?' Gui felt his stomach plummet.

'Certainly am,' Jim said cheerfully. 'Meeting a friend, an English chap I know from the embassy. He has a notorious sweet tooth, so I thought I'd look your establishment up. It's *quite* the place to be seen of an afternoon, from what I gather.'

Jim was laughing, but Gui felt sick. Jeanne was inside, at the best table in the house, seated next to Burnett. His brain was whirring, trying to think of something, anything, to dissuade Jim.

'You can't — '

'Can't what, pay? Christ no, I'm leaving that to Lionel. He's taken me under his wing, rather.'

A squeal of brakes interrupted, as a taxi cab pulled up and drifted past the alleyway.

'Speaking of which . . . ' Jim took a deep drag on his cigarette and threw it to one side. 'Good to see you, Gui. Come over to the Left Bank again soon, you and Jeanne. We'll get horribly drunk on cheap brandy and dance till we drop.'

He was already striding away.

'Jim, wait.' Gui scrambled after him. 'Jeanne is in there.'

'Is she? How extraordinary. I shall have to say hello.'

'No, please — '

'Don't worry, du Frère, I won't embarrass you.'

'You don't understand.' Gui pulled roughly on his arm. 'She's Jeanne Clermont, *Mademoiselle* Clermont.'

Jim halted, an inch from the street.

'Her father owns the business,' Gui continued shakily, cold sweat breaking out on his neck. 'I told you, he promised her to another man, but she won't go through with it. She's going to marry me. As soon as she can get some money — '

'Some money?'

'Yes, she said she has a little of her own, some

jewellery, too. It's enough to live on, for a while.'

Jim was turning pale. 'You told me you loved her . . . ' he accused.

Before Gui could protest, voices sounded on the street, horribly familiar. In two strides, Jim was gone. Gui clutched at empty air, too late. He could not see around the corner to witness the scene. There was a silence, too long by a beat.

'Jim,' Jeanne stammered, 'I mean, Monsieur Stevenson, what a pleasure. This is Leonard Burnett, my . . . fiancé.'

'A pleasure to meet you, sir.'

'Likewise, Mr Stevenson.'

Gui edged along the wall as far as he dared. He caught a glimpse of the two men shaking hands. Jim looked over his shoulder, back down the alleyway. Gui met his hard gaze, then let his head fall back against the wall, eyes clenched to the sky.

'Mademoiselle,' he heard the writer murmur, 'I believe I see my friend. If you will excuse me?'

37

May 1988

'You are mad,' Alex complains, fishing a helmet out from under the cracked seat. *'I'm* mad for even considering this.' He surveys the old motorbike with a mixture of pain and affection. 'I don't even know if she'll make it. I haven't ridden her since the start of term.'

'Her?' I laugh. 'Your moped is a girl?'

'It's not a moped.' He picks a spider from the handlebar, depositing it on a nearby bush. 'It's a motorbike, a CB 400 Hawk.'

'Fine. Will it get us to Dover?'

For the hundredth time that evening, Alex rubs at his forehead. He is not a spontaneous person.

'Petra, what if you don't find anything? What if there isn't any record of Mademoiselle Clermont's marriage? Then what happens if you get stuck in France? How will you be back in time for the review on Monday?'

I reach up and grab Alex's face between my hands. He stops speaking instantly. I smile, strangely calm. All of my anxieties and fears have distilled into a fine beam of light, pointing inexorably through the next three days. All I have to do is follow.

Eventually Alex sighs, a long, resigned sound.

'OK,' he concedes, placing his hands on my

shoulders, 'but don't blame me if we break down in the middle of Kent.'

Alex's thumb brushes my cheek, as if smoothing away something there.

'You know I wouldn't do this for anyone else, don't you, P?' he murmurs.

A few minutes later, he kicks the bike into life. It snorts and splutters, smells strongly of oil, then settles into a disgruntled wheeze.

'All right, jump on!' he shouts over the noise.

Several residents of the street are peering through windows, looking for the source of the commotion.

'Are you sure?' I yell back, adjusting my rucksack.

'This was your idea. Do that helmet up properly.'

Grimacing, I tighten the strap, trying not to think about where it's been. It smells like damp foam and petrol. Satisfied, Alex nods and I climb on. He is wearing a leather bike jacket, sunglasses. The jacket is a little short at the wrists, but even so, it suits him. He looks like a messy James Dean, if James Dean had ever decided to change career and study for a Physics Ph.D. I close my arms around his waist, and feel him jump. A second later he revs the accelerator.

We shoot through the streets of Cambridge. Landmarks pass in a blur, made unfamiliar by speed. Instead of heading for the motorway, Alex turns instead towards the centre of town, slowing to a halt outside a familiar faculty.

Cass bounds down the steps, wearing an expression that is more than a little mischievous.

'Thanks for stopping by, Al.' She leans against the railings, grinning. 'As for you, you were going to run off to France without even a word?'

I stammer an apology, mortified. In all the excitement, it hadn't even occurred to me to call her.

'I forgive you,' Cass tells me solemnly. 'Here's something to help you on your way.' From her pocket, she pulls a brown envelope that rustles. I rip open the paper. For a moment, I can't speak.

'Fifty pounds,' Cass nudges. 'Thank your fella here for calling me. He said it was an emergency. Luckily the banks were still open.'

Alex is flushing. 'It'll get you across the Channel, at least.'

'I can't take this,' I tell the pair of them, swallowing emotion.

'Think of it as a business loan, interest free,' Cass says, taking the envelope and shoving it into my bag. 'Also, your birthday and Christmas presents. Now, you two better get moving. You're going to have a long night.'

The ancient stone walls and narrow bridges of the city give way to suburbs, wide roads where the traffic moves at a faster pace. We hurtle past the sign that marks the edge of town and I feel a thrill, as if we are sneaking out of school.

The sun sinks behind us, trailing orange and pink through the sky. I can't help but glance in the wing mirror to see Alex's face. It's difficult to tell, but I think he smiles back. Resettling my hands around his waist, I lean against his back to wait out the journey.

With a jolt, I feel the bike slowing. My hands

are almost frozen solid.

'I fell asleep!' I yelp as we pull into a dingy service station.

'Try not to do that,' he warns.

I clamber off with some difficulty and very little co-ordination. My legs have locked into position as well.

'We need a break,' Alex murmurs, eyes on the fuel pump as he fills the tank. 'And directions from here.'

We perch on plastic stools in the window of the service station, nursing cups of weak coffee and perusing a fold-out map. Alex adds yet another sugar to his.

'We've still got a way to go,' he says, 'but I reckon we'll be at the port by midnight. That'll give you time to buy a ticket for the early sailing and wait for boarding.'

'What will you do?' I ask, taking another sip.

'Got an uncle who lives outside Canterbury. I'll drive up to him after you leave and get a few hours' sleep.'

'That's not far from my mum's house.' I smile. 'When this is all over you could come and stay, in the holidays.'

'I would, um . . . ' Alex hurriedly drains his cup, nearly choking on the sludge of sugar at the bottom. 'What will *you* do, once you've made it to France?'

I take a deep breath. The same question has been going through my mind.

'Get a train to Paris,' I tell him, 'wait for the library to open. Search the papers for Mademoiselle Clermont's wedding announcement. Then hopefully I'll be able to say conclusively what happened to her, whether Grandpa Jim was right or not.'

'What if you don't find anything?'

I don't answer. There are too many 'what ifs' to consider, too many fears, and any one of them could send me scurrying home.

The rest of the journey passes without event. The night is clear and still, which bodes well for a smooth crossing in the morning. Finally, signs begin to read 'Dover' in the motorbike's feeble headlight. The cold is the only thing keeping me awake. If Alex is as tired as me, he doesn't let on. By the time we arrive at the ferry port it is nearly one in the morning, the place deserted.

'Do you think it's open?' I hiss into the silence.

Huge freight trucks loom like monoliths across the tarmac. Behind them is a low, square building, yellow light illuminating an entrance sign.

'Come on,' Alex says.

There's a seedy feeling to arriving somewhere this late and I'm immensely glad that Alex is with me. Inside, the terminal is sickly bright and empty. One or two people lie across benches, coats over their heads. At the counter we stand uncertainly. Alex spots a plastic buzzer and rings it.

After an eternity, a large man shuffles out of a back room. He is wearing a shirt with 'Hoverspeed' emblazoned across it, almost hidden by a hairy brown cardigan.

Grimly, he tells me the price of a return ticket. It is more expensive than I thought. The cash in the envelope covers it with a little to spare.

Without it, I would have been stuck.

'Boarding is at three,' he grunts, 'through the immigration gate.'

There is nothing to do but wait, and eventually I drift into a doze. Dimly, I feel the weight of Alex's leather jacket settle over me. The terminal grows louder around us, until finally, there is a great rattling clank. Across the way, the cafeteria is raising its grill.

Alex smiles down, pale and tired.

'They've opened boarding,' he tells me, handing over my rucksack. 'Will you be OK? I feel like I should come with you.'

'I'll be fine.' I yawn. 'And you've done so much already. I can't drag you any further.'

'I would do it, though,' he tells me, eyes on the linoleum floor. 'If you asked.'

'I know. Thanks, Al.'

We pause at the entrance to immigration control, passengers stepping past us.

'Bon voyage,' Alex offers with a mock salute.

'I'll call you later,' I promise.

'You'd better.'

Unexpectedly, he pulls me into a hug. I grip the shoulder of his jacket, feel his breath, warm on my neck. My heart is thudding beneath my shirt, so much so, that I'm sure he can feel it. I lean away an inch, and look up, breathless.

His mouth meets mine. The last call for passengers to board echoes around us and I have to tear myself away. I don't risk another glance back from the gate, but hand over my ticket and walk out of sight, the pressure of his lips imprinted across mine like a word.

38

May 1910

Gui spent the next twenty-four hours in a state of high anxiety. He had not been able to see Jeanne since the disastrous confrontation with Jim. Every time he thought about how his friend had assumed the worst, his stomach contracted with nausea.

He almost tried to send a message to him at La Rotonde, but Jeanne was on his mind, first and foremost. Their entire future seemed poised on a knife-edge.

When they were finally able to steal a moment together, during morning service in a dark corner of the pâtisserie corridor, he held her tightly, as though she would turn to water in his arms. She gripped him back, head buried against his chest.

'Gui, I'm so sorry.'

He loosened his arms around her, kissed her once, twice.

'You have nothing to be sorry for,' he told her.

'But the way Leonard treated you — '

'It was nothing. Jim, though, I am worried about what he thinks.'

'Does it matter so much?' She reached up to smooth a lock of hair from his forehead. 'In a few days we will be leaving Paris behind.'

'I know,' he sighed, 'but he was there for me,

when I needed a friend. I . . . don't have many people who care, Jeanne. I must try to explain to him, somehow. I hate that he thinks badly of me.'

'You have me to care now.' She cupped her hands around his face. 'Five days, Gui.'

'We should leave tomorrow,' he whispered impulsively. 'Or tonight. The longer we wait . . . '

She shook her head, stepped back.

'It is complicated,' she said quietly. 'The Burnetts are major shareholders in the pâtisserie. Leonard's father administrates my trust fund. I need to make sure that if I renege on the engagement, it won't affect my father's business.'

'It is your choice, Jeanne, not theirs.'

'I know, Gui. And I choose a life with you. But I am going to break my father's heart. I must try to make things right for him, if I can.'

Her face was pale in the gloom, begging him to understand.

He took a deep breath, expelling the hurt that came with her words. 'Of course,' he managed to say. 'I know you care about him.'

She left him with a kiss then. Gui watched her go. He was jumpy. Every time the kitchen door swung open, he expected to see her. He lingered at the far end of the room, just to be near the corridor in case she wanted to speak to him.

In the end, she arrived during the afternoon break. No one noticed that Gui only picked at his food, that his coffee was left untouched. His distraction over the past few weeks had been blamed on a liaison with a demanding Belleville girl, a mistake that he was grateful for. Now, he stared at his shoes, caught between joy and the conviction that the world was against him. When the door squeaked and the men fell silent, he knew instantly who it would be.

'Is there a du Frère in here?' said Jeanne. She was acting bored, but there was a high colour to her face. Something was wrong.

'Over there, Mam'selle,' one of the chefs gestured with his bread. Luckily, they were accustomed enough to seeing her around. Only Maurice eyed her closely.

'Josef wants to see you,' she directed over to Gui, already turning away. 'He's in the office.'

'Now you're for it, Gui,' nudged one of the apprentices. 'Must be serious, if herself came to fetch you.'

'Careful, lad,' Maurice muttered, catching his arm.

Gui shook him off, hurrying for the door.

At first the poky office looked deserted, but then he made out Jeanne's shape, standing in the shadow of the bookcase. The lamps were unlit, but even in the semi-darkness he could tell that she was crying.

'What's the matter?' He hurried over to embrace her but she stepped away. In her hand was a sheaf of papers.

'I was right,' she whispered. 'About the engagement. If it is broken off, then my father will lose his share of the pâtisserie. Burnett has lent him money, and my dowry will pay off the debt, Gui. They made me part of the business, and I never even knew.'

Clermont's words came back to him, the day of the flood. *A daughter is a precious thing.*

'I'm sorry. If it wasn't for me — '

'Don't say that!' Her voice was fierce. 'If it wasn't for you I would be trapped . . . ' Her voice disappeared into sobs.

'We promised each other, Jeanne.' He pulled her close, wiped away her tears with his fingers. 'I will never go back on that promise.'

'Neither will I.'

'Then we need to leave. We must leave right now.'

For a moment he thought she would refuse, but then she was nodding, blotting her face with her sleeve. One arm around her, he reached for the door handle. Too late, he saw the shadows outside.

Monsieur Clermont was standing in the doorway, flanked by Josef and Maurice. His eyes took in Jeanne's tear-stained face, Gui's arm about her shoulder.

Before they could speak, Monsieur Clermont's lip curled in rage. He lashed out, breaking Gui's hold on Jeanne and sending him staggering backwards.

'What have you done to my daughter?' he snarled.

Gui caught himself upon a bookshelf. Temporarily stunned, he looked towards Maurice.

The chef would not meet his eyes.

'I'm sorry, lad,' he muttered. 'I couldn't let it go on.'

Clermont was white, shaking with fury. 'If you've touched her, du Frère, I swear I will — '

'Will what?' The force in Gui's voice took him

by surprise. 'Send me packing? Call on your oily friend to threaten me?'

Monsieur Clermont raised his arm to strike, but Jeanne was faster.

'Father, please!' She lunged in front of Gui. 'He has done nothing!'

'Be quiet, Jeanne.'

Her face hardened. 'We are to be married.'

The slap sent a shock wave through the room, breaking even Josef's impassive mask. Jeanne fell against the edge of the desk, clasping her cheek. Anger surged in Gui, and he shoved the older man hard, before reaching out a hand to Jeanne.

There was a sickening silence. Clermont was breathing heavily, looking from one of them to the other.

'This is absurd,' he said, his voice unsteady. 'Jeanne, stop this, now.'

She pulled herself up from the desk and took Gui's hand. Her eyes were cold as she surveyed her father.

'No,' she told him clearly. 'We are engaged.'

'You are engaged to Leonard Burnett. The banns have been read — '

'A business deal,' she interrupted. 'One that I never had a chance to refuse. Guillaume loves me, Father.'

'Jeanne,' Clermont said slowly, and Gui could tell that he was struggling to keep the fury out of his voice, 'if you break the engagement it will hurt me, my darling.'

'You should have considered that . . . ' Her voice faltered. 'You should have considered *me*.'

'But this boy is not considering you. All he

wants is money. He tried, to bribe me, do you know that?'

'No,' Gui tried to interrupt, but Josef had come from nowhere to seize his arm.

'After you fell in the flood,' Clermont continued remorselessly, 'he sought to blackmail us, threatened to go to the papers with some sordid tale that would ruin your name, unless I gave him a job.'

'Stop it!' Gui struck out. He caught the man across the face with his nails and Jeanne began to cry, but Clermont ploughed on, despite the beads of blood that sprang from his skin.

'If only I could have known that he would try to use you. When I think about what he might have done . . .'

Jeanne was sobbing now, torn between her father's outstretched hand and Gui's rage.

'I don't care,' she gasped. 'We're promised. I've given him everything.'

'Of course you — ' Clermont's voice ground to a halt. Jeanne hid her face, unable to look up.

The blow caught Gui across the head like a sledge-hammer. Josef let go as Clermont's fist crashed again, sending him tumbling against the wall. Heavy books rained down around him. Someone was shouting, but one of his ears flooded with liquid. Finally, the assault stopped. He looked up, winded. Jeanne's pale fingers restrained her father's arm.

'Get upstairs.' Clermont threw off her grip. 'Josef, take her and lock her door. Call the doctor. I want her examined.'

Jeanne struggled as she was pulled into the

corridor. With a burst of effort she twisted, reaching for Gui, but then she was gone.

'Jeanne!' he managed to rasp. 'I'll — '

A fist crunched the air from his stomach, followed by a knee, driving into his groin. He retched powerlessly to the floorboards. He felt Clermont's hand seize the back of his jacket, drag him bodily through the door. A crowd had gathered; boots scattered hurriedly from their path. Someone spat on him as he slithered by, but he didn't care, he could only feel pain, and the desperate need to follow Jeanne.

The cold stones of the alleyway bruised his side as he was thrown down the steps. He sucked in air, his face pressed to the muck until he was able to raise his head. Someone sniggered.

'You two, watch him while I telephone for the gendarmes,' Clermont commanded. 'The rest of you, get back to the kitchen before I have you all dismissed.'

After an age, the voices died into a whispered conference. Gui blinked up at the two apprentices who had been left to guard him.

'Hey,' he coughed, hauling himself onto an elbow and spitting out bloody foam. 'Help me up, please.'

One of them came forward, steadied him against the wall.

'What did you do?' the other boy whispered, wide-eyed.

Gui fought the urge to retch again. He felt thin and empty. He explored the skin of his head. Blood dripped from his nose and ear but nothing seemed broken.

'What are you lads doing?' questioned a familiar voice.

'Sorry, sir, but Monsieur Clermont asked us to watch, whilst he calls for the gendarmes,' said one of the boys.

A waft of tobacco reached Gui's throbbing nose, an unusual blend he remembered from a midnight kitchen, as he lay drowsing between clean sheets.

'Patrice?' he croaked. 'Patrice, please.'

'It's 'sir' to you,' the valet said coldly, descending the steps. 'I'm astounded that this is how you choose to repay Monsieur's generosity, Gui.'

'You don't understand,' he protested, shuffling to face the man. 'Clermont is lying.'

Patrice strode over like thunder and grasped Gui's collar.

'Listen,' he whispered rapidly, his face hidden from the others. 'Mam'selle sent me. She'll be in the Place de la Republique at midnight. You must go now. Push me over and run.'

Gui didn't move, the words scudding across his brain.

'Do it!'

He pushed at Patrice. The valet fell back dramatically, dragging one of the apprentices down with him.

'Stop!' he cried, voice muffled. 'Stop him!'

Gui lurched onto the boulevard. The pavements were crowded, afternoon workers swarming back to offices and shops from lunchtime errands. Reaching the other side of

288

the road, he saw an omnibus and staggered aboard. The vehicle honked, trundling on its route, just as a gendarmerie motor car shuddered to a halt outside Pâtisserie Clermont.

39

May 1988

It is early morning when the train slides into the Gare du Nord, but the station is already crowded. Travellers haul suitcases, business-people watch for their trains, suited and stiff, even on a Saturday. I crane my neck; the huge glass roof slopes above me, a sky held together by bolts. It too is alive, grey girders furred with a skin of pigeons.

For a second, I can only stand, my sleep-starved brain disorientated by the language of the city. Then there is a nudge at my back, poking me forwards into the fray. I mumble an apology and try to think straight as I search for signs towards the exit. Instead I find a coffee stall, where the smell of fresh pastry and dark roasted beans is drawing tired travellers like moths. Some of my dwindling money is spent on coffee and a warm croissant.

I haven't been to Paris for years. I can't afford a taxi, so I grab a free tourist map and set off for the Rue de Richelieu, hefting my rucksack a little higher. The walk takes me through the grand boulevards, but I am too tired to notice much, too focused on the task at hand. The library is still closed when I arrive, so I sit on the steps to wait in the warm morning sun.

'Mademoiselle? Excuse me?'

A woman in wire-rimmed glasses is bending over me, concerned.

Blearily, I pull myself upright, mortified to have fallen asleep while waiting.

'I'm so sorry,' I stammer, collecting my bag. 'I've had a long night. I telephoned about seeing some records, yesterday.'

The librarian smiles. 'The young lady from Cambridge,' she says in perfect, accented English. 'You *have* had a long night. We are just opening, but if you wait, I will find the one you want.'

It doesn't take her long to locate the reel of microfilm I'm after. Thanking her again, I follow through the wooden swing barrier that leads deeper into the library.

The main hall is enormous. Desks march down the centre, row upon row of green glass lamps casting their light. I gawp at the ceiling, punctured by star-shaped light wells. Six feet ahead, the librarian raises her eyebrow. I hurry to catch up.

She shows me to a bank of microfilm scanners at the far end, hidden in the shadow of a balcony.

'You load it, so,' she demonstrates.

I assure her that the scanners are similar to those at my own university library. She makes a dubious noise in her throat but wishes me good day, instructing me to return the reel to the main desk when I am finished.

I crank the film to its starting place. It contains copies of *Le Petit Parisien*, the newspaper in which society weddings were announced, every issue that was published in 1910. If she married well, this is where I will find Mademoiselle Clermont.

The library is quiet, a beautiful spring morning outside the windows. I bring out the photograph of the group outside Pâtisserie Clermont. The girl stares back at me, eyes unreadable.

Newsprint slides into focus. I crank the handle until I reach May, scrolling slowly. Wedding announcements were popular at the time. There are whole pages filled with descriptions, portraits of brides inset between the columns.

Then, a few issues in, a face catches my eye.

There she is, alongside three others, Jeanne, née Clermont. She has been photographed wearing a wreath of flowers; they bloom around her dark hair, her pale face, yet she looks sad, somehow blank, on what should have been a joyful wedding day. I see the name linked to hers and realize why.

40

May 1910

How he came to be on the Left Bank he had no idea. The day was bright and breezy, yet it mocked him, the sunlight like needles in his pounding head. He should have jumped off the omnibus when it began to trundle south, but he remained, clinging weakly to the rail as the roads swept by beneath his gaze, blurring into a mess of grey.

How could everything have fallen apart so quickly? He thought of Jeanne. Was she crying even now, cursing him for condemning her to a life of poverty as she packed her bags? Gui rested his head against the rattling vehicle and tried to pull his thoughts together.

No, she had asked him to meet her. They would leave, just as they had planned, and soon all of this would be a memory.

By the time he came to his senses, the omnibus was halfway through Saint-Germain. He leaped off the vehicle as it slowed. He would have a long walk home. Unintentionally, he found himself turning onto the Boulevard Raspail. Once he had walked these streets with Jeanne, with Jim, on that night when his world had changed for ever.

They had been sheltered by the dark, then, by the voices and the music of strangers. He caught his reflection in a glass window: white and bloodied. He looked up in a daze. The electric sign of La Rotonde was unlit, paintwork faded and shabby in the daylight. A familiar silhouette was seated at a table within.

The place was near empty, smelled of damp cloth and stale tobacco. Jim was scribbling furiously on a loose sheet of paper, a glass upended near his elbow. Gui swayed, head spinning from the change in light.

'Stevenson,' he croaked, squinting.

Jim looked up in annoyance only to blanch, his mouth drooping open an inch as he gazed.

'What the hell happened to you?' he managed eventually. Gui couldn't help but notice the frostiness in the young man's voice. He grimaced in pain.

'Clermont,' he told the writer with as much emotion as he could muster. 'He found out . . . '

His vision swayed violently, and he found himself clutching at the table. He shook his head to clear it.

'For God's sake, sit down,' the other man insisted, pressing him into a chair. 'You've had the sense knocked out of you.'

He called for a waiter, and a minute later Gui felt a cool glass being nudged against his hand.

'Drink this,' Jim said.

Gui took a sip. Cheap brandy. It reminded him of Pigalle. He drank the rest, only to find another at his fingertips.

'Sip that one,' the writer advised, and for the first time, Gui was able to look at the young man properly.

Jim was leaning back in his chair, face twisted somewhere between confusion and resentment.

'You look a state. I'm guessing your fortune-fishing at Pâtisserie Clermont did not end well?'

Gui made to push his chair away in anger, but missed his grip and reeled.

'You know nothing of it,' he said, 'Jeanne and I are in love, we — ' Abruptly, his nose began to bleed again. He swiped at it. 'We are eloping.'

'Du Frère,' Jim sighed, 'I shook hands with her fiancé.'

Gui stared miserably at the table before he sat again.

'I have to explain,' he said.

'Then explain.'

Gui lowered his forehead to his hands. 'Jeanne is engaged to marry Leonard Burnett,' he told Jim heavily. 'Her dowry is part of a business arrangement at the pâtisserie.'

'And you've muscled into the middle of that,' finished Jim. 'Was that your plan? Disrupt it all by seducing Mademoiselle, then promise to disappear and let the marriage continue as planned — for a price.'

'No!' Gui insisted, but his head pounded so much that he was forced to close his eyes. 'No,' he said again, trying to breathe calmly. 'I love her. I told you, we're getting out of here, tonight.'

'Tonight?' asked Jim, turning a box of matches in his fingers. 'How?'

'I don't know.' Gui sniffed, dabbing at his nose with his sleeve. 'The train, perhaps. We're to meet at the Place de la République at midnight. At least that's what Patrice said. But I can't see how she will get away. She was locked in her room when they threw me out, and they were calling for a doctor.'

Jim's fingers faltered. The matchbox lay still in his hand.

'A doctor?'

The heat flared to Gui's face. 'We consider ourselves married. It is no one's business but ours.'

Jim laughed bitterly, shaking his head.

'You fool,' he said. 'You truly don't realize you have ruined that girl's life with your grubby plan.'

'Jim, please,' Gui begged, 'there is no plan — '

'Enough, du Frère.' Jim lit a cigarette. He didn't offer one to Gui. 'I helped you before and you lied to me. Why should I believe you a second time?' He sat back in his chair, face hard.

Resentment stirred in Gui's gut, an ugly feeling, laced with hurt.

'To hell with you,' he spat. He knew it was his pride speaking, but he was too angry, too worn down, to care. 'You're just like them.'

Jim's voice followed him out into the fading afternoon.

'I told you, Gui. Never lie to a reporter.'

41

May 1988

I stare at the photograph of Mademoiselle Clermont for a long time, as though that would allow me to speak to her, to reach through time and ask her what had happened that May, over seventy years ago.

Finally, I find a pen and make a note of the announcement and its contents, wondering why I feel so saddened. I can't shake the feeling that there is something I don't know, but, as I feared, I have reached another dead end. Perhaps this was why Grandpa Jim never spoke of what had passed: he knew that he would not find the resolution he wanted, no matter how desperately he searched. Slowly, I gather my things.

The woman at the information desk smiles as she makes me a copy of the article, asks after my research, but I can only nod. Shrugging, she goes back to her conversation with a co-worker. They are talking about an argument with her brother, who lives in Bordeaux.

Bordeaux. I stop in my tracks, thoughts tumbling.

There is a payphone near the doors. Hurriedly I scrabble through my notes, and there it is, the number for the G. du Frère I got from Directory Inquiries. I stare at it. The thought of calling the number again terrifies me, but I have exhausted all other possible leads. I try to be rational, to swallow the fear and guilt that arises when I think of the young man on the other end of the phone. It is my grandfather's guilt, I realize. I have resurrected it, from where it lay hidden. I have pursued it, and now, I have one last chance to lay it to rest. I owe it to him to try.

It takes me three attempts to punch in the numbers correctly. The plastic receiver grows warm under my sweating palm as the phone rings, again and again.

After a minute of waiting and praying, a breathless voice answers.

'*Oui?*'

It is a woman. She sounds young. My carefully prepared words stick in my throat, and I begin the conversation by coughing.

'Hello,' I get out at last. 'I . . . I'm looking for Monsieur du Frère.'

'You mean Gui du Frère?'

I swallow drily.

'Yes.'

'He's away on business at the moment,' she says. 'Can I take a message for you?'

'Oh. When will he be back?'

'Not sure, next week probably.'

All my tension, my excitement, plummets to the floor. The woman on the other end must hear it.

'Who's calling?' she asks with more interest. 'Is it urgent?'

'I . . . know his family, sort of. I did really hope to speak with him today, that's all.'

'Wait a minute . . . ' There is a rustling of

298

papers from the other end of the phone. 'As long as you're not trying to sell something, I can give you the number of his hotel,' she tells me. 'Have you got a pen? It's Paris, 48 34 506.'

My pen blotches to a halt.

'Paris?'

42

May 1910

'Gui, don't squirm so,' Isabelle commanded.

He jerked away from the cloth she was using to clean the wound to his head. He was exhausted, from the fight and the confrontation with Jim and the long walk back to Belleville, but even so, he couldn't settle.

'It stings,' he mumbled, although in truth he didn't care about the pain.

'You are lucky it only stings.' Isabelle went to the stove for more hot water. 'What did you imagine would happen? That girl is from a wealthy family, their marriages are determined by stocks and shares, not love.'

'Don't lecture me, please.' He squeezed his eyes closed.

'I am not lecturing, Gui. Those kinds of matches keep Madame and me in business. It is the order of things. You are a fool to try to defy it.'

He ignored her, twisting his head to see the clock on the mantel.

'For goodness' sake!' She threw down the cloth. 'It has not changed in the last minute. Here, you had better see to yourself. I must get ready for work.'

She sat at a small table and began to remove the rags from her hair. Gui was too uneasy to wait in his own room. He fixed his gaze on the sky. It was resolutely blue. He swiped half-heartedly at the cut above his eyebrow and drank a tumbler of gin to numb the pain. Eventually, he fell into a doze.

Isabelle woke him to say goodbye when she left for work downstairs. She was worried, made him promise to write as soon as he could, to tell her that he and Jeanne were safe. She had sent for Puce to come and escort him to the meeting point at the Place de la République.

'If I cannot convince you to use some caution,' she said resignedly, 'then at least you will have a pair of eyes to watch your back.'

When she had gone, Gui returned to his contemplation of the evening sky. His case stood packed at the foot of the bed. He picked at a crust of bread, stared at the clock. The sky outside welled into a deep indigo.

He should send word to his mother, he realized. Using the cheap paper and pencil on Isabelle's desk, he scrawled a note.

Coming home. Have news. Am bringing a guest. Do not tell anyone of my arrival. Do not worry.
Love Gui

It would have to do. He was loath to write anything of Jeanne in case the letter was intercepted, and he would not know where to start, anyway. The sky retreated another shade. He opened his case, counting out a few centimes. There, lying on top was his treasured

301

book. Its words had bewitched him in the grimy dormitory, spun sketches of wonder in his mind. To be a *pâtissier* — an architect, like Monsieur Carême — had seemed the purest, grandest vocation. Now Gui knew better. The creations were hollow, confections of money and power. He took up the book and fed it to the stove a page at a time.

After an eternity came a knock at the door.

'You look terrible,' Puce declared, puffing his cheeks at the sight of Gui's swollen eyebrow.

'Bourg bastard gave me a duffing,' he replied with as much of a smile as he could manage, imitating Puce's accent.

'Certainly did.' The boy dug his hands in his pockets. 'I am to spy for Mam'selle Isabelle and report back on you.'

'She's too suspicious, but I'll be glad of the company,' Gui told him. 'Will you post this letter for me, after I'm gone? There's no money inside, before you take a knife to the seam.'

The letter to his mother disappeared inside Puce's coat. Gui followed it up with a handful of coins.

'Anything for a friend.' The boy grinned. 'One for the road, before we leave?' He had spotted the bottle of gin that stood by the stove.

'I don't suppose she'd mind,' Gui agreed. 'A small one for you, though.'

He poured two measures into a couple of teacups. Puce dispatched his eagerly. Gui sipped, coughed, then followed suit. It was rough stuff and burned his chest, but it gave him the kick of warmth he needed.

Rue de Belleville was heaving, as was usual at this late hour. They wove through the crowds on the pavements, amongst women like Balourde and the sort of men who were her customers. It was the best place to hide, advised Puce, kicking hopefully at a discarded cigar. Only newcomers and gendarmes walked in the centre of the road. The way sloped downhill towards the canal, and they began to leave the brash noise behind them.

Fewer lights shone in these streets. Gui missed their comfort, the safety that came with a pack of eyes. Buildings grew taller, more respectable. Families here were in bed. Young men with the ink-stained cuffs and yellowed eyes of clerks edged past them from time to time like spiders, alone and ubiquitous in the vast city.

Gui ached to see fields, to feel the cool night air flowing past his skin, as he travelled by train with Jeanne at his side, south and further south.

'You can visit us, you know,' he told Puce. 'I have a friend who works for the railway, over at the depot near Austerlitz. Nicolas, he'd get you on a train, all right.'

Puce just smiled up at him in the darkness.

'Nearly there,' he said.

Place de la République was vast and empty. A light drizzle began to fall, wetting the pavement like fevered perspiration. Gaslights illuminated the base of the monument, jarring in the darkness. The noise of a motorcar door being shut drifted out from behind the stone edifice. Someone was waiting there.

'Puce,' he whispered, 'can you sneak around, see who it is?'

The boy gave a brief nod and melted away into the damp night as though he had never existed.

Gui expelled a long breath, trying to peer closer without wanting to move. Was it Jeanne waiting, or someone else? Fear rose too easily from the surface of his skin and spread into the night like an infection. Footsteps were circling the base of the statue, booted feet, too heavy to belong to a woman.

Tripping in haste, he backed into the shadows of an adjacent alleyway, where he could observe the square unnoticed.

Whoever it is, they will have to pass under those lights, he thought to himself, wishing that Puce would return, *and then we shall see.* He did not hear the movement behind him until it was too late.

The first blow was the worst. It floored him from the darkness, slamming into his skull. It struck again and he felt his flesh split, blood running hot over his scalp. His suitcase was lost as pain burst a dam behind his eyes. He brought his arms up in time to deflect a third blow, tried to call out, but a rag was stuffed into his mouth. It was soiled with tar and he gagged.

All around him were men, four, five, impossible to tell how many. He managed one look upward. Metal flashed: the sinews of his nose crunched as a cane drove into his face and retreated, slick with blood.

His arms were wrenched back, bound behind him with something heavy and leather. He twisted violently and was kicked in the stomach.

It made him retch and he fought the nausea, terrified of choking on vomit behind the rag. Another foot was swinging towards him. Instinctively, he kicked out with both legs. Someone crashed to the ground and he felt a spike of victory.

He should try to get up, he knew, try to spit out the rag and yell, but the cane swung again at his skull; this time he rolled away, slamming into the shins of an attacker.

He expected a reprisal, for a boot to drive into his back, but there was nothing.

'What the hell?' barked a man under his breath, from further up the alley. 'What are you doing?'

'Found this gutter-rat in the shadows,' another voice answered. 'He was watching.'

'So?' The first voice sounded impatient. 'We ain't been paid for no kid. Just smack him and he'll be off soon enough.'

Gui heard muffled cries, small boots kicking at the pavement. *Puce*, the thought emerged through the pain. *No, please.*

'Jesus, he's strong for a starved rat,' someone mumbled. Then came the sound of a heavy backhand connecting with skin. Puce fell into view, crying, his hands clapped to his face. *Stop*, Gui tried to choke, but all that came out was a whimper. As if that was his signal, Puce looked up under his lashes and nodded. His eyes were dry and calculating.

'Help!' he bawled, with more volume than Gui knew a small body could hold. 'Over here, help — '

The cry was cut off abruptly as hands seized the boy's throat and began to squeeze. He saw Puce's legs kicking. Words gone, Gui yelled, rolling back and forth in an attempt to reach the attacker. There was a cry of pain; small feet hit the ground already running, vanishing into the darkness in a blink.

'Little rat bit me on the face!' a man swore. 'Went for my eye, like an animal!'

'Quiet!' the leader snarled again.

'Hello?' A woman's voice rang out across the square, clear and fearless. 'Gui? Are you there?'

Jeanne. He twisted his head to an impossible angle, despite the agony in his skull, until he could see. Far beyond the end of the alleyway, Gui saw her run out from behind the monument, Patrice beside her.

She was dressed in a pale green travelling coat, her hair loose. The streetlight caught upon her face and in that moment she was so beautiful that he forgot everything else.

Then all around him men were swearing. He was being dragged away, the square receding, Jeanne and her light being swallowed by the dark. He fought with everything he possessed, until pain exploded at the back of his neck and he sank into blackness.

43

May 1988

The streets pass in a blur as I run towards the Opéra district. Twice I cause traffic to screech to a halt, but I don't care. The taxis flying past me could be horse-drawn carriages; the whirr of a moped could be a motor car, rattling its way towards Pâtisserie Clermont.

These are the roads my grandfather walked, with du Frère and Mademoiselle Clermont. If I run fast enough, it feels as though I could push through time and emerge into the troubled splendour of those years, to find the young man who would become J. G. Stevenson.

Gasping for breath, I slow to a halt in the middle of the thoroughfare. Stores selling cheap handbags and pharmacies with green neon crosses stretch down the street. The painted advertisements and grand façades of the *belle époque* have vanished. That world is long gone, and so is he.

Then, on a corner of the grand boulevard, I see it: familiar ornate stonework over arched windows that once held a world of luxury. All that remains of Pâtisserie Clermont. Slowly, I approach. It is now a shop, selling stationery. My reflection hovers above the shelves of pens as I stare in. I imagine my grandfather's eyes staring back.

An alleyway runs next to the shop. I am drawn down it, despite the waft of rubbish. On the wall halfway along is what looks like a brass plaque, scratched and damaged by men and time. It says something about deliveries, the letters faded against the pitted metal. There are stone steps leading to a back door, the ground littered with cigarette butts. Without knowing why, I sit and stare out onto the busy street.

A flash of colour attracts my attention. Opposite, beyond the trees that line the boulevard, is an illuminated sign. It advertises a hotel, the one the woman on the phone told me about.

The stairs to the reception are steep. I climb them cautiously, a hundred possible introductions running through my head. A strange sorrow mingles with anxiety and anticipation. The receptionist tells me that they do indeed have a Monsieur du Frère checked in for the night and rings up to his room, but gets no answer. There is nothing I can do but wait.

The hotel lounge is empty, a clock ticking into the carpet. Large windows overlook the boulevard. For a long while I stare at the building that was Pâtisserie Clermont, my imagination turning the shadows of the alleyway into lurking figures, making the trees younger, the streets emptier. Shoppers and tourists come and go. I write in my journal to pass the time. Afternoon breaks free, sliding towards the early-evening wasteland.

Then a taxi pulls up to the kerb. Two suited men are climbing out, laughing. One of them has dark, curling hair. I press myself to the window to watch as they walk into the hotel. Their voices drift towards me from the stairs.

I can't look around. Instead, I fix my gaze upon the table, hands clenched in my lap to hide their shaking. Footsteps cross the carpet. I hear the whisper of fabric and catch a breath of aftershave. I look up, into ice-blue eyes.

'You are looking for me?' the man says in polite confusion, extending a hand. 'I'm Guillaume du Frère.'

44

May 1910

It was the cold that woke him. Not biting and instant, but a deep, aching chill. Something was wrong. The memory of panic lingered in his mind, but all he could think of was the cold. It was insidious, crept into his clothes and skin. He twitched. Water sloshed; he was submerged to the waist.

Must get out. The thought surfaced and he clung to it. *Must get out of the water.* He tried to open his eyes. One obeyed, dried stuff cracking on his lashes. The other didn't. Light entered, grey and damp, but light all the same. Earth rose above his head on either side. He was in a ditch.

Must get out. The first turn of his head was like a split-second bellow and nearly sent him under again. Fraction by fraction he shifted himself onto his side. He paused for breath. Embedded in the mud was what looked like a tooth. He felt around his mouth with his tongue. There were gaps and the taste of blood.

Must get out. A handful of earth crumbled under his fingers. The second was firmer and held his weight. Another handful, another inch.

He worked his way up onto flat ground, his wet trousers clinging like huge, dead eels. Dry earth was a blessing. It was morning, he realized.

Somewhere, the sun was rising on the fortunate. He must have blacked out then, for when he woke again there were noises, scurryings in the dirt.

He saw children, menacing beings in ragged clothes. They bared gap teeth when they saw him looking and gathered at his feet, making fast work of his laces. He tried to shout as they pulled the sodden boots from his feet, but all that came out was a strangled noise. The ratchets of pain came again and he rolled on his side to vomit, thin bile running free. The monstrous children ran off, jabbering like crows.

Hands were resting on his head, cool and steady. A woman's face, a scarf wrapped tight to her forehead. Her eyes were pale blue, like much-washed cotton. *Jeanne*, he thought and tried to speak, but the words were buried in pain. More hands lifted him; carried him to a wooden box lined with rags. It looked like a coffin. He struggled, to show them that he was alive. *A marriage, not a funeral*, he tried to tell the people surrounding him, but they clacked in strange voices that he didn't understand.

'What do they want?' he eventually heard someone ask from nearby.

'Blown if I know, they're speaking in slum talk,' a second voice answered.

'Don't you know any?'

'*I* am from Belleville, thank you very much.' It sounded like Puce. 'We'll have to use signs.'

He was trundling next, the broken ground like an anvil to his skull. He groaned.

'Sorry, Gui, only way,' Puce's voice told him.

311

'You'll have to hold on.'

A pinprick on his arm, a wave of relief.

'Shouldn't move for at least a week,' a stranger was saying. 'The head must heal itself. I can see to the rest easy enough, but not that. Give him food when he wakes, whatever he'll take, and dose him up on this, morning and night.'

His nose came to life again before his eyes did. He smelled familiar perfume, felt a touch on his forehead.

'Isabelle?'

A hand was holding a cup to his lips; water mixed with something else, bitter and cloying. He coughed into it, like a horse at a trough, but it went down his throat. Nothingness arrived in the form of a leaden pillow.

Sometimes a hand covered his own. If he remembered, or could tear himself away from sleep, he squeezed it. He did not know to whom it belonged, for the skin was rough and callused.

The moment his bad eye opened along with the other took him by surprise. For a long minute, he concentrated on blinking it clear, looking at a beam of sunlight that painted the wall.

He was in bed, in his room in Belleville. It was hot. He kicked at the blankets, but all his leg did was jerk. He tried again and managed to flip a corner back. The effort exhausted him. Nearby, someone was sitting on a stool, thumbing through a newspaper.

'Nicolas?' he croaked incredulously.

His friend looked up sharply, almost fell over in his haste to kneel beside the bed.

'Gui! You're awake, how do you feel?'

Gui made to sit up, but his friend pressed him down. The face from the previous winter was broader than he remembered, crisped and browned by the sun. Not a boy any more.

'You mustn't move yet,' Nicolas told him, settling on the edge of the bed. 'Doctor's orders.'

The words took a while to process in Gui's brain. He was weak and trembling, head in a fog.

'Where's Jeanne?'

'She's fine,' Nicolas soothed. 'Here, you have to drink this, the doctor said it would help you get better.'

'I have to tell Jeanne about — ' Gui frowned. He could recall walking to the square with Puce, but not what came after. 'I have to see her.'

'I know. Now drink this and stop grousing.'

His friend's southern accent was so comforting he could cry. The bitter liquid stuck in his throat again, but he swallowed, and slept.

The next time he woke up, Puce was there. Gui was propped up in bed, given a bowl of broth. As he ate shakily, Puce helped to fill in the missing pieces of his memory.

'That attack was arranged,' the boy said, accepting a biscuit from Isabelle. 'Those bastards were hired thugs, and they had their orders, clear 'nough.'

'But who from?' Gui laid down the spoon. He had barely managed two mouthfuls. 'No one else knew about it, save for you and Jeanne and Patrice.'

Abruptly, a memory returned, of trying to

explain, of hopelessness and hurt and the taste of brandy.

'Jim,' he whispered, resting his head against the wall. 'I told Jim.'

'Who?'

'A writer I met, at La Rotonde . . . ' Words were still a struggle. 'I tried to tell him the truth, but he didn't believe me.'

'Well, someone told tales to Papa Clermont,' the boy sniffed. 'I'll bet it was him what hired those men. They knew they had to drag you off smartish when Mademoiselle appeared.'

'Jeanne was there?' Gui shoved the food away. 'What did she do? Where is she?'

'Puce tailed the men who took you, he followed them all the way,' said Isabelle quickly. 'Then he came and got me. We never would have found you otherwise. They dumped you miles away, in the middle of the slums — '

'I asked about Jeanne.'

'You should rest now.' Isabelle unstopped a blue glass bottle, poured a measure into a glass with some water. 'The doctor said very clearly, you are to do nothing strenuous. He will be here later to check on you.'

She gave him the glass.

'What is this?' he asked.

'It's medicine, to help you rest.'

Silently, Puce took the bottle from Isabelle and handed it over.

'Morphine,' Gui read. The bottle was almost empty. 'How long have you been giving me this?'

Isabelle looked uncomfortable. 'The doctor said — '

'How long?'

A newspaper lay on the floor. Slithering awkwardly from the blankets, Gui made a grab for it.

'Ten days?' he whispered in horror, staring at the date on the top line. 'You've kept me here for ten days and didn't tell me? What about Jeanne? Where is she?' There came no answer. He tried to get up, but only succeeded in knocking the bottle to the floor, where it smashed. 'Where is she?' he yelled, half sobbing.

Pain assailed him out of nowhere, blue and yellow snow fizzing over his vision. By the time he looked up again, the room was empty. Milky liquid pooled on the floor, dripping into the cracks between the boards.

He pushed aside the covers and rose to his feet, only for his knees to give way. He dragged himself back onto the bed, horrified by his own frailty. For the first time in many days, he didn't sleep, but stared instead at the roof-tops outside the rotting window frame. When it grew dark he heard someone tramping up the stairs.

'Gui?'

It was Nicolas, still in his work clothes, coal dust clinging to his hair. He closed the door carefully behind him. From his pocket he drew out a dark bottle of beer and opened it.

'Isabelle told me what you said earlier.' Moving slowly, he poured half into a cup for Gui. 'You shouldn't be angry with her, or the boy, whoever you want to blame. They're good people.'

Gui took the cup, staring down into the amber

liquid. 'You know them so well?'

Nicolas gave a half-smile. 'Had the chance to get acquainted, while you were out. The kid, Puce, he's a smart one. He came to the depot, kept asking for Nicolas until he found me. He said you'd been hurt, brought me here. Isabelle explained what was what.'

Gui took a sip of beer and was powerfully reminded of nights in the dormitory, of oil lamps and cards and the bodies of others. He and Nicolas had promised to stick together.

His eyes prickled, he rubbed at them. 'Nicolas, I'm sorry,' he started awkwardly.

His friend held up a hand, halting, accepting.

'*I'm* sorry.' He traced his thumb over the letters on the beer bottle. 'I always hoped that you were doing well, even if it meant you didn't have time for your friends on the tracks.'

Gui closed his eyes at the reminder of his selfishness, but Nicolas ploughed on, taking a deep swig, down to the lees.

'I never wanted to be right,' he murmured. He was unfolding something from his pocket. 'There was this English guy, kept coming around here.'

'Jim?' asked Gui. 'What did he want?'

Nicolas's face darkened.

'Reckon he was the one gave you away,' he said disgustedly. 'Reckon he thought you were only out to cause trouble, so he ran to the girl's father. He came poking about, while you were out cold. Bold as brass, saying someone at Clermont's had told him about the blackmail and that he knew you'd pull a vanishing act on Mademoiselle as soon as things got tough. He'd

316

written about you in the paper, came here to see if anyone had news of you.

'He told me what he wrote. Load of filth and lies. Soon as he finished, I broke his nose for him. Then Puce and I brought him up here to look at you.'

Nicolas's laugh was hollow. 'You think you're a mess now, should've seen what you looked like then. We didn't know whether you were even going to wake up.'

For the first time, Gui realized the fear and uncertainty his friends must have been through, while he slept. He reached for Nicolas's hand, but was waved off.

'Anyway, this Jim guy went white all over when he saw you, beaten almost to death. He thought you'd run off, see, but we set him straight, showed him what he'd done by ratting on you. He tried to come back a couple of times. Isabelle sent him away, said he'd done more than enough to hurt you.'

'Nicolas,' Gui said seriously. A terrible fear had been uncoiling in his stomach while he listened. 'I have to see Jeanne. I have to explain to her.'

His friend straightened out the piece of newspaper from his pocket. Carefully, he laid it on the blanket.

'He brought this along, that Jim fellow. Kept saying he knew you wouldn't forgive him, but that you deserved to know.'

The newspaper was a cutting, with dense columns and oval pictures. Gui picked it up limply, looking for the date. It was three days old, printed a week after his attack. He was about to throw it down, when one of the photographs caught his eye. A slim, pale face, dark hair hidden, in a mass of flowers; wide, blue eyes that even monochrome print could not subdue.

Mademoiselle Jeanne Clermont, the announcement read, today married Mr Leonard E. Burnett in a small ceremony at Église de la Sainte-Trinité. The new Monsieur and Madame Burnett depart for their honeymoon this evening from Boulogne-Sur-Mer on the TSS Ryndam. They will spend a month touring the east coast of the United States of America, before Monsieur Burnett takes up a post as Managing Director of the new Burnett & Sons office in Montreal, Canada.

45

May 1988

The man opposite me pours a glass of wine from the bottle he ordered, presses me to drink.

'You look so pale I'm scared you will fall over,' he says in English.

'I'm sorry.' I laugh nervously, taking a sip. 'It's strange to be talking to you, that's all.'

'Well, you certainly have me intrigued.'

We are sitting in a brasserie around the corner from the hotel. After I explained my reasons for being there, Guillaume suggested it was best discussed over dinner. I think he guessed I hadn't eaten since the morning.

He has changed out of his suit and looks relaxed in trousers and a grey jumper. He peruses the menu, giving me a chance to study his features. He is well built, has the easy charm of a man in his thirties who has grown into himself, but his eyes are blue and shrewd.

He orders the chef's special. I ask for the same, knowing that I won't be able to concentrate on the food, no matter what I eat. The restaurant's doors and windows have been thrown open, letting in the noise of the street and the warm evening.

'So,' Guillaume pours himself a glass. 'Are you going to tell me how you know so much about my family?'

I push a breadcrumb around the tablecloth, trying to find the right words.

'It all started with my grandfather, after he died,' I say slowly. 'I found a photograph of him with two other people I had never seen before. It had a name written on the back: Clermont, Paris.'

The man glances up at me sharply, but does not interrupt.

'My grandfather,' I clear my dry throat, 'was a journalist here, in nineteen ten. He revealed an affair between two people at Pâtisserie Clermont: the daughter of the owner, Jeanne, and an apprentice named Guillaume du Frère. Whether he did it rightly or wrongly, it destroyed them, and haunted him for the rest of his life.'

For a long while Guillaume is silent, digesting my words. I take a large gulp of wine.

'I wonder,' he asks carefully, 'if you could start from the beginning.'

He listens patiently, and soon I forget my apprehension. He only interrupts twice, once to examine the address given to me by the gallery manager, another time to read my grandfather's undelivered letter. He laughs when I tell him about my mad ruse to retrieve the evidence from Hall's apartment, my escape from Cambridge on the back of a motorbike to cross the Channel.

'So that was you,' he says slyly, cutting into his steak when it arrives, 'on the telephone? You hung up.'

My face, already flushed from the wine, reddens further. I focus on my food, grateful for the excuse to look away.

320

'I suppose I should have asked you about all of this then,' I admit, 'but I was scared. It was just too strange. I'd been chasing down Guillaume du Frère for months, and when you answered the phone . . . '

'You thought you had gone back in time?'

I smile wryly. 'Something like that, yes.'

'I am not surprised.' He laughs. 'Guillaume du Frère, *your* Guillaume, is my grandfather.'

'Is?'

My food is forgotten. I never imagined that the young man in the photograph could still be alive. Guillaume chuckles again, devouring a potato.

'Old goat's hanging on still. He's nearly ninety-six. Lives in a nursing home just outside the city. Bordeaux, that is.' He points to the piece of paper from the gallery. 'I bought that painting for his ninetieth birthday. It wasn't easy to track it down. Grandpa Gui told me once that he remembered seeing it being sketched out. He knew that the artist's name started with an 'A', so I did a bit of digging and found the thing. The family clubbed together to buy it. It's hanging in his room.'

'That's what I don't understand. Why buy him something that could only cause him grief?'

'Grief?' Guillaume is thoughtful, playing with his cutlery. 'I suppose we think of the past in different ways as we grow old. I don't think it causes him grief. Rather comfort.'

'But he lost her to another man, where's the comfort in that?'

'Lost who?'

'Jeanne, Mademoiselle Clermont.'

I can feel myself getting emotional and push away the rest of my uneaten food. The photograph of my grandfather with du Frère and Mademoiselle Clermont lies on the table between us. I shove it towards him.

'My Grandpa Jim kept this picture as a reminder. You've seen the letter. He wrote dozens like it, for years. He *never* forgot what he did to them.'

'What did he do?' Guillaume asks, bewildered.

'He revealed their affair to the whole of society,' I say hotly. It's as if he hasn't been listening at all. 'It must have prompted Jeanne's decision to marry Burnett instead of your grandfather.'

The man is looking at me strangely.

'But this woman was my grandmother,' he says. 'Grand-mère Jeanne. I must admit, though, I've never seen a picture of her this young.'

'She married Leonard Burnett,' I splutter.

'Yes, she did,' interrupts Guillaume, 'in nineteen ten, like you said. I don't know many of the details. I only know that in nineteen eighteen, at the end of the war, she came back to France. I'm not sure her and grandfather were ever officially married, you know. They pretended they were, but to be honest, I don't think either of them cared. They started the shop together, and when she died, he passed it on to me. We share a passion, you see.'

He fishes a business card from his wallet: du Frère & Sons, Bordeaux, I read. *Master Pâtissiers, est. 1920.*

By the time we step outside, the effects of the wine, the story and the warm summer air all conspire to make my head spin. The secret that haunted my grandfather, that he lived with for over sixty years, was nothing more than a bad decision, made in the heat of youth. His had not been the last word in the story.

'So,' nudges Guillaume, pulling me out of my reverie, 'you have your answers and I know a little more about my family than when I woke up this morning. What happens next?'

'The first train back to Calais, I suppose. I still have a review to attend.'

We walk along in silence for a while. The city smells of petrol and food, of cigarette smoke and possibility. Outside the hotel, we come to a mutual halt.

'That's where it was.' I point across the road. 'Pâtisserie Clermont. I wish I could have seen it.'

'So do I,' he says, quietly, staring with me from under the trees. 'Why do you think I always stay in this hotel?'

'Come back with me,' he asks after a moment. 'Come to Bordeaux. You can see the shop, and I can take you to meet Grandfather. He'd like that.'

'I'd like that too. Another time, perhaps.'

At home, my own mistakes are waiting, to be faced and seen through. I feel a smile creeping onto my face. 'Besides, I think we Stevensons have meddled with your family quite enough.'

Guillaume offers a wry smile of his own. 'Can I at least persuade you to stay with me tonight?

323

No disrespect, but hotels are expensive at this time of year.'

'Guillaume — '

'Nothing like that! I'm a married man. There's a sofa in the room. I'll sleep there and you can have the bed. You look like you could use the rest.'

Dawn wakes me with a stuffy head, tangled in a duvet. I flail at my watch to stop it beeping and peer around. The hotel room is dark, but a strip of light is sliding under the curtain. Two feet poke out from a blanket over the arm of the sofa and I laugh to myself. Quickly, I haul on yesterday's clothes, cram my bag under my arm and let myself out.

It is not even six o'clock. The morning is chilly and perfect. I feel like an unexpected visitor, surprising the city without its make-up. A road-sweeper trundles past on his machine, brushes revolving in the gutter. Almost everything is closed, but down a side street I find a newsagent that is just rattling open the shutters. I ask if he has a photocopier. He nods vaguely, gestures towards the back.

There, below the packets of rice and tea, I copy everything that I've collected, the photographs, the newspaper articles, the letters and my own journal, the discoveries unfolding sheet by carbon sheet into the plastic tray. Halfway through, the shopkeeper brings me over a tiny cup of coffee, so strong and sweet that it sticks to the roof of my mouth. I nod my thanks. Slowly, he returns the gesture. When I pay at the counter, he digs around and produces a brown paper bag to protect the pages.

The sun is fully up when I emerge, the city awake, though a little bleary still.

'Guillaume?' I call into the warm room when I return to the hotel. The bundle of blankets on the sofa is empty but a shower is hissing in the bathroom, along with the bass timbre of somebody humming. Scrawling a note, I place it carefully on top of the photocopied pages. After that, it's a matter of seconds to stow my remaining things, shoulder my bag.

'Petra?' Guillaume's head sticks out of the bathroom, soapy and dripping. 'You're leaving already?'

'A train to catch. Thank you, for everything.' I point to the coffee table. 'That's a package for your grandfather. All of my research. I don't know what he'll think, but I'd like him to have it.'

'Of course, as soon as I get home.'

I grin and hurry towards the door.

'Wait!' His voice stops me in the corridor. I look back from the stairwell to see him leaning out, a towel wrapped around his waist. 'Where do I find you? If the need should arise?'

'Poste restante to Cambridge University,' I call back. 'Address it to P. Stevenson.'

46

June 1988

'That's the last one.'

Whyke dusts off his hands and slams the boot of the car. It is crammed with boxes of books, listing like a galleon with one wheel on the kerb.

'Sure I can't tempt you with any of the periodicals?' he offers.

I laugh from the pavement, brush a strand of hair from my face.

'No thanks, I've got my own stuff to move in a few days.' I can't help but eye the car appraisingly, wondering how many miles it will manage. 'Where did you decide to go in the end?'

'Belgium.' Whyke brings out a pair of sunglasses with clip-on lenses. He puts them on only for one of the lenses to fall off instantly. 'There's someone there who I liked very much at one time. The University of Leuven has an opening. I might go and surprise him.'

He gives up with the lens, puts it back into his pocket.

'I'm sorry about everything,' he tells me, for the third time. '*I* think it would have made a fascinating thesis. It's certainly the most excited I've been about one in a long while. But then, the examiners were never going to listen to me.'

I shrug calmly. 'It doesn't matter now.'

'Speaking of which,' Whyke continues, pulling a piece of paper from his inside pocket, 'I had a chat with an acquaintance of mine, an editor who works in literary biographies. Told her a bit about your research. She said to give her a call, especially if you can deliver a work to rival that of a certain biographer we know.'

I fold the paper with a smile.

'Thanks. I'll see what I can do.'

'Well, good luck.' He offers a dusty hand and I clasp it warmly. 'I'll be keeping an eye out.' He peers at me, taking in my outfit, my attempt at dressing up. 'You look very nice.'

'I'm going on a date.' I can feel the colour spreading towards my ears.

'Well, I'd better let you get on then, Petra. Cheerio.'

The car wheezes into life behind me. Cutting through a dark archway crammed with bicycles, I emerge out onto King's Parade. The early-evening sun catches in the windows of the chapel, throwing light onto glass and stone, dust and pollution. The frenzy of the previous few weeks is forgotten.

It all seems rather theatrical, especially now that the city is quiet, released from the final goodbyes of another generation. Those who remain are in it for the long run, but my time here is over.

The memory of the review still makes me wince; how I tumbled into the room exhausted and dishevelled. How the panel remained stony-faced as I confessed that I had no thesis, and instead told them the truth.

327

When I finally made it back to my room, I found a dozen angry answerphone messages from Hall, threatening me with legal action. I erased the lot. Let him write what he likes. Even if he blows the scandal out of all proportion to sell his book, I know the truth.

I know that J. G. Stevenson was a man with a past; I know he was a man who made mistakes. And I know that J. G. Stevenson was my grandfather, who I loved, and who loved me. Nothing that Hall writes will be able to change that.

The official university letter — revoking my place to study — brought with it a sense of excitement, of freedom rather than disappointment. I'm departing the city for new streets, for a different chapter.

Somewhere behind me, the chapel bells toll six. Alex is late. The thought of him, panicking about which awful T-shirt to wear, makes me smile. I sit on the wall to wait.

There is a second letter in my pocket. I didn't tell Whyke, but it is the real reason for my calm in the face of what, for most people, would be deemed dismal failure. It was passed on to me this morning, a French stamp on the envelope and a return address for somewhere near Bordeaux.

Dear Miss Stevenson,
We have never spoken, and I do not know
if we shall ever meet, so you must forgive
me for writing to you so informally. My
health is bad and I prefer to put pen to

328

paper in my own time, than struggle with a telephone.

My grandson came to visit recently and brought me a packet of papers, the contents of which surprised me more than I can say. They told a tale I never thought to hear again, since I believed there were only two people who ever knew it in its entirety, and that was my Jeanne and me.

The story you sent brings joy and sorrow in equal measure to my heart, for it gives life to a time I tried very, very hard to forget.

My grandson worries that he proved to be a poor historian, for he only remembered a few details of my early life. I will be happy to fill the remaining gaps for you here, provided that you excuse my occasional brevity; I am no longer young and even writing tires me greatly.

Those days, working at the pâtisserie, falling in love with Jeanne . . . We could not have known, but the age was like a dying creature, one glistening with its last breath. I remember now, we thought the world would open its arms to us, would welcome a pair of fleeing young lovers.

We were to do just that, run away together after we were discovered. I can look at your grandfather's article now with even a little humour, but at the time it was a red cross upon our door.

I was young and naïve, determined that nothing should stop us from being

together. I had reckoned without the inter-
ference of those with higher powers.

Our rendezvous was never made.

Dark days. I hounded myself, trying to
find a reason for Jeanne's betrayal. My
own hurt prevented me from seeing the
truth: she assumed I was the one who had
broken my word, had lost courage and fled
the city. Your grandfather's article compelled matters to be resolved. Ashamed
and abandoned, she agreed to the marriage
in order to salvage her family's reputation
and dismiss the rumours as idle gossip.
She was not to know that the damage was
already done, and so she was wed and left
the country, never knowing that I lay only
a short walk from her doorstep. It causes
me pain to think of it, even now.

I returned to Bordeaux, and when war
was declared, I joined the army at the first
call with nothing to lose. It was by grace
and luck alone that I survived. I lost my
best friend Nicolas at the Western Front in
1916. Wounded, I returned home to my
mother, yet lost her to influenza two years
later.

Jeanne told me in later years that her
time in Montreal, her marriage to
Leonard, was little more than business.
Though it may surprise you to hear me say
so, he was not a cruel man. When the war
ended and the time came for Jeanne to
leave, he did not prevent her.

By the time she found me, I was a shell

of my former self. She could have given up on me then, but she stayed, brought me back to the world. Eventually, I recovered, and this time, there was no one to interfere.

She had enough money to rent a little shop, and we did what we knew best: we started a pâtisserie. It was hard, but we — who had known true sadness — were never unhappy. After many years of hoping, we had a son, Patrice, and in time, he gave us three grandchildren — young Guillaume among them. I am thankful that Jeanne lived to meet them all, if not to see them grow.

I read your grandfather's letter again, after all these years. I have to admit, I knew that he wrote, but ignored the letters in my anger. I read too of your concern for how he may have hurt us. I ask you to put it out of your mind. Jeanne and I had nearly fifty years together to make up for the eight we lost. I am sad he died with such a burden of guilt upon him.

For a time, it is true, I cursed him more than anyone, but if I met him now I would shake his hand and say, 'Jim, your granddaughter has given me more than anyone else could; she has given an old man back his memories and reminded him of the people he loved, at the end of his days.'

Yours, for as long as I remain,
Guillaume du Frère

Acknowledgements

Any thanks I have to give must go first and foremost to my family: for the earliest bedtime stories, the most recent words of encouragement, and vitally, for helping me find the freedom to write. To my agent, Ed, for giving me that elusive first chance, and for sticking with me through many (many) drafts. To Harriet, editor extraordinaire, into whose hands I was happy to place the fates of Gui, Jeanne and Petra. To Gallica, for keeping knowledge free. To Emma, who offered advice at a pivotal moment. To the Truslers, who kept me afloat. To the Newnham Englings, to Jenny and to Beth: for help unquantifiable. And to Nick, for the present and the future.

We do hope that you have enjoyed reading this large print book.

Did you know that all of our titles are available for purchase?

We publish a wide range of high quality large print books including:
Romances, Mysteries, Classics
General Fiction
Non Fiction and Westerns

Special interest titles available in large print are:
The Little Oxford Dictionary
Music Book
Song Book
Hymn Book
Service Book

Also available from us courtesy of Oxford University Press:
Young Readers' Dictionary
(large print edition)
Young Readers' Thesaurus
(large print edition)

For further information or a free brochure, please contact us at:
Ulverscroft Large Print Books Ltd.,
The Green, Bradgate Road, Anstey,
Leicester, LE7 7FU, England.
Tel: (00 44) 0116 236 4325
Fax: (00 44) 0116 234 0205

Other titles published by Ulverscroft:

THE STALL OF SECOND CHANCES

Dana Bate

Sydney Strauss is obsessed with food. Not just with eating it, but with writing about it as an aspiring cookery reporter. Food journalism jobs are more coveted than cupcakes, however, and so she is stuck working for one of TV's biggest egomaniacs — until she's left scrambling for shifts at the local farmers' market. Selling muffins at the Wild Yeast Bakery is hardly going to make her the next Nigella. But soon Sydney is writing the market's weekly newsletter, and her quirky stories gain attention from a prominent food columnist. After years of being left on the shelf, she's even dating again. And then Sydney gets a shot at the story, one that could either make her career or burn it to a cinder — along with her relationship and her reputation . . .